Drift
&
Dagger

Drift & Dagger

KENDALL KULPER

Little, Brown and Company

New York Boston

Little, Brown and Company

Hachette Book Group
1290 Avenue of the Americas, New York, NY 10104
Visit us at lb-teens.com

Little, Brown and Company is a division of Hachette Book Group, Inc.
The Little, Brown name and logo are trademarks of Hachette Book Group, Inc.

The publisher is not responsible for websites (or their content) that are not owned by the publisher.

First Edition: September 2015

Library of Congress Cataloging-in-Publication Data

Kulper, Kendall.
    Drift & dagger / Kendall Kulper.
        pages cm
    Companion to: Salt & Storm.
    Summary: As a boy in the late nineteenth century, Mal's only friend was Essie, daughter of the Roe witch, and it was she who discovered that he is a "blank," not affected by magic, setting him on a career as a con artist, traveling the globe in search of a legendary magical dagger that can steal a witch's power.
    ISBN 978-0-316-40453-2 (hardback) — ISBN 978-0-316-40455-6 (ebook) — ISBN 978-0-316-40457-0 (library edition ebook) [1. Stealing—Fiction. 2. Swindlers and swindling—Fiction. 3. Conduct of life—Fiction. 4. Magic—Fiction. 5. Witches—Fiction.] I. Title. II. Title: Drift and dagger.
    PZ7.K9490164Dri 2015
    [Fic]—dc23

                                                                                                                2014045507

10 9 8 7 6 5 4 3 2 1

RRD-C

Printed in the United States of America

For my brother, the world traveler

One

PRINCE ISLAND

THE FIELDS BELONGED TO US. ME AND ESSIE. The sailors had the docks, with their ships, their ropes, their barrels of whale oil sweating in the sun. The islanders had the town, the wood-shingled houses and the gossip. The Roe witch had the cottage out on the rocks, and she kept it for her own. But the grassy fields in the center of the island, wide and wild and swaying like a second ocean of pale green—they were only ours.

Most days I'd leave behind the town and she'd leave behind the cottage and we'd meet in the grass, standing up on tiptoes to look over the tall stalks that blocked our path and tickled our cheeks and ears and foreheads. But that day, the day we found out what I am, she met me at the border of the fields, the place where the grass just started to poke out, strangled and scraggly, from the sandy soil. She had something she wanted to show me, she'd said, and she held out her hand for mine.

We were little back then, Essie just eight and me barely older, nine, maybe, although I didn't really know and no one knew for certain. We took the little trails I'd shown her before, made by birds and rabbits and foxes and all kinds of small animals, and we walked carefully, our fingers twisted together, because the grasses were the place for those small animals to keep their homes and nests and eggs and secrets and we didn't want to disturb anyone. This was our home, too, and we understood.

She led me through the grass all the way to the center of the island, so far from the ring of ocean surrounding us that it was nothing but a line of blue in the distance, and when she'd looked around to make sure there was no one watching, she nodded at me and I grinned at her and we stomped down on the grass, pressed it down and cleared it out of our way and made it soft for sitting. Essie lifted her hands above her face and spun around, twirling so fast her braids streamed out behind her, her eyes closed and her face tipped to the sun. It looked like fun, so I spun right along with her with my arms tucked close to my chest and my eyes open so that everything tilted and whirled and blended all together—sea and sky and grass and clouds and sun—and when I finally stopped and collapsed on the ground, breathing hard, laughing, the world kept turning like a pot of stirred water.

"Sit down," I said to Essie, but she didn't stop, her skirt puffed out like a bell around her, her face screwed up, determined, like this wasn't a game at all. Her little feet danced quick and nimble on the grass and then she stumbled, lost her balance and almost crashed into me but just managed to catch herself, heaving for air, on the ground.

"There!" She let out a big breath. "Fifty spins and we're safe."

"That's a spell?" I asked, and Essie plucked a stray bit of grass from out of her braid and nodded.

"'Course it is," she said, and she would know. For a few minutes, we just sat together, catching our breath, the stalks of grass bowed over our heads, the sky a circle of blue above us. It was quiet here—or, no, it wasn't quiet, really, with the little scurries of insects and animals and the scratch-crackle of the grass, but it was quiet the way our island rarely was: no wind. No ocean. Like we'd wrapped woolen mufflers around our heads and blocked out the noise.

"You could almost pretend we're someplace else," Essie whispered to me once. "Like this grass goes on forever. Like there's no water at all."

Essie propped herself up on her palms and tilted her head at me.

"What did you bring, Mal?" she asked, and Mal—that's me.

I pulled something out of my pocket: the fragile skull of some small creature. I'd found it by the shore of the slough, sticking out of the mud like a pale lump of wood, and I brought it to Essie because that's what we did when we met in the grass: We brought something to share with each other, a secret or a story or a song, a bit of cheese nicked from the dairy or a broken toy plucked out of the trash bins behind the grand houses at the northern end of the island.

Essie held out her hand and I tipped the little skull onto her palm.

"It's so delicate," she said, running the tip of her finger over the skull, and she handed it back to me.

The things I brought tended to be stolen or picked up out of the gutter or won in fights with other children, because how else was an orphan on an island in the middle of the ocean supposed to get his hands on anything? Not even my clothing belonged to me, not really, because it came first from other boys, boys with mothers who wanted to do a good deed and stopped by the priory with clothing tattered and patched and musty from sitting too long in cabinets and chests. "It's for the poor orphan," those women would say. "Surely he must be needing something."

And then I'd walk out in pants too short for my long limbs and shirts meant for the chubby bodies of the island boys, and I'd hear their taunts.

"Look who's wearing my shirt," they'd say. "Look who's stolen my cap."

Maybe they'd stop there or maybe they'd try to take their things back, but it didn't matter either way. Nothing on this island belonged to me.

Except Essie.

"What've you got?" I asked her, that day in the grass, but I didn't expect much. She didn't live in town, like I did, but instead in the cottage way out on a tail of rocks at the very end of the island with her mother. And she was always only Essie's mother to me, even though to the rest of the island and the rest of the world, she was the Roe witch, the famous witch, the storm-raiser, the water-tamer, the wind-binder.

Essie usually brought stories, which she made up herself or heard from the sailors who came to the cottage every night, without fail, to visit her mother and buy from her the charms and spells and potions and powders meant to keep them safe at sea. So I was surprised when, instead, she reached into the tiny pocket sewn into her dress and pulled out a bit of rope, a cord no thicker than her pinkie.

"Here," Essie said, and she threw her braids back over her shoulders and put out her hand.

"Here what?"

"Give me your hand."

"What for?" I asked, but I held my palm out all the same. Even back then, my fingers were long, and I can remember my nails were broken where they weren't black with dirt. Essie, who liked things clean and neat and proper, frowned at them a little.

"What are you doing?" I asked. Essie had taken the cord and held it between her hands and whispered something under her breath and it looked like magic. That was what her mother, the Roe witch, was famous for: her magic. Even though Essie wasn't anywhere near as good as her mother—"*Yet*," she'd say, determined—she'd sometimes play with magic. All the children on the island did, from time to time, singing spell songs at each other and carrying around good-luck trinkets. It was a game to us but to the sailors and the whale men, the magic was the only thing they could count on to keep them safe at sea. Every ship had spells burned into her masts. Every sailor had charms knotted around his wrists and neck. If Prince Island had a reputation for relying too much on magic, it also had a reputation for never losing its ships, for holds stuffed full of whale oil and a graveyard with real graves—not tiny stones set in rows and inscribed with the words LOST AT SEA.

"I'm practicing," Essie said, running the rope in between her fingers, and then she looked up at me. "But don't tell anyone—it's a secret."

"Don't tell anyone—it's a secret." That was Essie's favorite thing to say and I heard it from her dozens of times, hundreds, maybe. It's a secret, it's a secret, and Essie was full of secrets, made up of them, breathed them and held them close. It didn't matter if her secret was that she sneaked an extra roll at breakfast or that she hated her mother—they mattered to her and she tended them, kept them locked up like a cage full of birds. They made her feel full, I think. They made her feel rich.

She looked back down at the rope in her hands without waiting to see if I'd agree to keep her secret, because, of course, we both knew that I would. I kept her secrets and in return, she didn't look at me funny, the way all the other islanders did.

"Where did you get those bright green eyes?" old women would ask me, and I can still remember how they'd grip my chin in their hands and twist my face this way and that, and if they had a friend with them, maybe they'd call over to her, "Have you ever seen such a pair before?" And maybe the friend would say back, tittering behind a handkerchief, "Perhaps back in the winter of thirty-two, but not in a long while since." Then they'd both laugh, and I knew they meant I was an outsider, even if I'd been born here same as them.

The first time I ever blinked at Essie she tilted her head at me and called my eyes different, and I got all ready to puff up at her, point out to her that it was rare to see a pair like hers, blue like summer sky on this island of grays. But then she laughed in a way that I understood "different" was a good thing. Different was what she was, too, and when we were together, alone, like we were that day, we were the same.

Essie held the cord between her hands and wrapped it around my wrist, once, twice, not tight enough to dig into my skin but enough to feel it. Gently, she bent over to tuck a knot into the end of the rope, and as she leaned in, strands of her hair fell forward, tickling me.

The string wound around my fingers until my hand looked like a cleat covered in rope tethering a ship to the dock, and where the ship would be, Essie held on to the end of the cord, working slowly, gently. She wrapped the string over, under, around, through, weaving a kind of glove, careful not to pull it too tight. I tried to flex, testing the cord, and she let out a little breath of exasperation.

"Are you trying to do a spell?" I asked.

"I'm *con-cen-trat-ing*," she said, her face bent so low to my hand that her nose nearly brushed my fingers, and I didn't say anything else.

"There." Essie sat back on her heels and watched me. "How do you feel?"

"I feel the same. My hand feels funny."

"Funny how?"

"Funny covered in rope. What did you do?"

But Essie just tilted her head at me, studied me like a question, and then rose to her feet. "Can you stand up?"

It was a little awkward, getting my balance with one hand, but I could. Essie frowned.

"Take a few steps."

So I did, leaving our little nest to wade through the grass, the tops of my ears level with the stalks. I could hear the wind again, loud and white and constant.

When I came back to Essie, she had her hand in her mouth and chewed on her finger, her face scrunched in thought.

"Is the rope supposed to be a spell?" I asked, holding out my hand. I didn't feel anything, but that didn't surprise me. "Is it Roe magic?"

"I can't do Roe magic," she said, which was true. The Roe witches tethered the wind. They controlled the waves. It was powerful, rare, and Essie would have to grow into it when she was older.

She looked down at my hand and then took it gently between her fingers, turning it this way and that. "It's rope magic. A common charm. I thought of it last night."

"*You* thought of it?"

"I showed it to two sailors and it worked perfectly on them. I did it just the same now."

"What's it supposed to do?" I asked, examining my hand, and she let out a sharp sigh.

"Don't you feel anything at all?" she asked, and when I shook my head, she stared at me hard, sucking at one of her fingernails. "I did it right." She said it with certainty, her eyes narrowed at me like it was my fault the spell wasn't working.

"Here." She reached into her pocket again and pulled out an iron disk about the size of a coin, with a hole punched out of the center. This one I recognized as a Roe charm, the kind that dangled from belts and necks and mantelpieces all across the island.

"Hold this," she said, but I'd been raised around enough magic to know not to take a charm if I didn't understand what it did—magic could be dangerous, although most everyone agreed it was worth the risk. When Essie saw me hesitate, she picked up my hand—not the one covered in rope—and pressed the disk into my palm.

"It's just a simple charm. It won't hurt you," she said, and I opened my palm and studied it. This was the first time I'd ever held a charm. I'd heard witch's magic made the skin tingle, but it felt like nothing more than a coin to me.

I looked up just in time to see Essie take a little knife from her pocket.

"What are you doing?" I asked, but I wasn't scared, because this was Essie, my friend, and even with a pocketknife bright between her and me, I trusted her.

"I want to see something." She held my rope-covered hand and looked up at me with a question and *Oh*, I thought, *she wants to cut the rope.* After I nodded, she took the point of the knife and dug it right into my palm, so quick and so hard that when I jumped back, red splashed against the white cord and left a cluster of crimson freckles.

"What was that?" I asked, and I dropped the disk and dug into my pocket and pulled out my handkerchief and wrapped it around my bleeding hand. "You didn't say you meant to cut me!"

But Essie looked as though she hadn't heard. She bent down and picked up the charm and stared at it. Stared at me.

Back at the charm. And then the knife, the blade edged wet with my blood.

"It's meant to protect against knives," she said, and she held up the charm and the knife and I took a step backward, but instead she raked the blade across the top of her hand. It glided over her skin as sweet as a ribbon and left not a cut or a mark. She blinked at me, and I stared back at her, and it didn't make sense, any of it, any of what she had done or what had happened, and my hand ached and my head ached and she leaned in and whispered to me, "Magic doesn't affect you."

"Yes it does," I said, the words coming out of me rote, automatic, because of course it did. "Magic affects everyone."

"Not *everyone*," Essie said. She gave me a strange look. It took several long moments before I realized what she was thinking, the word that was dead bad luck even to say aloud.

Blank.

That was what you called a person immune to magic, except they weren't really people at all—they were monsters, inhuman devils who terrorized good, innocent folk and ate babies and destroyed families and spread their affliction like a disease, like all they wanted was to turn the entire world as dead and empty and lifeless as they were.

She stared at me and I could see what she was thinking— *You are a blank*—but I couldn't be one of them, I couldn't. I was just a boy and I lived on this island, this island that near floated on magic. Someday I'd become a rope-maker or a canvas-sewer or a blacksmith, and every one of them relied on magic in their work. None of them would ever apprentice a boy immune to magic, and why would they? Black luck, associating with one of those monsters, one of those *things*.

I couldn't be one of them. I stared at Essie and tried to tell her this but I had no breath in my lungs and my head was swimmy and anyway, she was looking at me like she already knew. She was looking at me like I was a freak, an animal, a sickness that could spread, and I'd never seen a look like that on her face before.

And somehow I was on my knees, and somehow the nest of grass felt like a cage, a black place, because Essie was a little girl made of magic and I was a monster and we weren't the same after all. We were the worst kind of different. A hole opened up inside me, the edges jagged and raw, and within the hole was an emptiness so heavy I actually put my hand to my chest and tried to touch it.

I looked up at Essie and she was still staring at me, and surely she was wondering what would happen if she touched a blank. Surely she was remembering all those days and afternoons we'd spent together and wondering if I'd infected her already, if I'd destroyed her magic somehow, just by being her friend. I wanted to apologize and I wanted to say I didn't mean it and I couldn't help it, and I wanted to tell her, *Don't go, please, please don't go*, but before I even opened my mouth, she was on her knees beside me, her arm around my shoulders, her mouth close to my ear, and she whispered to me, "Mal, it's all right. It's our secret."

She held me in her arms and whispered to me and sang to me and told me she didn't care about what I was. I was Mal. That's what she said. She said she wouldn't tell anyone about it, and she did it with a smile, like she was happy to do it, happy to know something about me only we knew. We still belonged to each other. We kept each other's secrets.

"I'll keep your secret," she said, and she did. She kept my secret for four years exactly, and then, without warning or remorse, she turned on me, exposed me, and drove me from the only home I'd ever known.

She did that with a smile, too.

Two

BOSTON

I REACH INTO MY POCKET AND PULL OUT my watch to check the time, even though I know it can't have been more than a minute or two since I last looked. Eight minutes to nine, and another jolt of nerves ripples through me. I squeeze the little brass watch until my fingers tingle and go white, and then I slide it back into my pocket.

Check the knife sheathed at my hip. Check the rope looped over my shoulder. Bounce a bit on my toes, shake out my hands, take a deep breath. Wait.

It's the waiting that always gets me, makes me feel like I have bees swarming through my veins, and I know I'm not good at it—keeping still, waiting—haven't been able to do it, really, for ages now, for five years, ever since I was thirteen and I lost my only home and my only friend in the space of a few seconds. Ever since then, running, moving, going somewhere or leaving someplace behind has been the only thing that makes sense to me. It's the only thing that calms me, keeps me stable and feeling sane. That's why standing still—even for only a few minutes, even here on this street corner in Boston at night, the stink of mud and grass and animals from the Common drifting toward me like fog—has me nervous enough to want to bolt straight for the docks. I picture it: money in my hand and a smile on my face and my feet anxious for the feeling of rocking, swaying, motion.

But Boone said to wait.

So I wait.

I hold off checking my watch as long as I can bear, long enough that I begin to worry I've missed the moment, but when I rip the watch from out of my pocket and see it's only four minutes to nine, I let out a sigh so loud and sharp that a pair of gentlemen out strolling the streets glance my way, their faces pinched with suspicion.

"You, boy!" one calls, leaning on his cane. "What do you think you're—"

"*Leeet ev'ry old bachelor fill up his glass!*" I sing at the top of my lungs, lurching toward the two men. "*Vive la compagnie! And drink to the health of his favorite lass*—join in!—*Vive la compagnie!*" I try to throw an arm around one of the gentle-men, but when I near them, they scuttle away, throwing dark glances over their shoulders and muttering to each other about the state of drunkenness in this city.

I watch them go, singing the song quietly to myself until they disappear down the street, and then I sigh again and head back to the fence.

From far away, the *bong* of a bell rings through the air, and every inch of me perks up, heats up, tenses like a spring.

It's time.

Nine o'clock, just like Boone said, and I take a moment to glance around me and make sure the street remains deserted before I turn to the fence, slide my boots into the whorls of wrought iron, reach up, and climb.

I catch sight of something etched into the top of the fence as I vault over: a curling design that looks like it's there for more than just aesthetics. I'd bet anything it's a spell to keep out intruders, but it won't do anything to keep me out, and I'm on the other side of the fence in a matter of seconds.

Now I can't help the grin sliding onto my face, because if waiting is torture, then this is pure pleasure. This is what my body is made for, the thing I do best, and as I run across the grass to the handsome two-story building lit up like a lan-tern before me, my muscles and bones and sinews work so smoothly, so effortlessly that I feel like I could fly.

When I reach the building, I pause, tilting my ear up toward the window just above me. Boone said the meeting would likely be held in the library on the southeastern corner of the building—and this is the northwestern. But he also said to be careful, to check every window just in case there's someone watching, something we hadn't foreseen, and what Boone tells me to do, I do.

Quiet in this window, so I run to the next, pause just long enough to hear past the pounding in my veins that the room is silent, and then I keep running, my boots as light and quiet as the pads of a dog.

"Little wolf pup," Boone sometimes calls me, grinning, and I always smile back, because it's a joke, mostly, the kind of joke only Boone could find funny. I'm a wolf pup because I'm quiet, because I can run fast, because I don't scare easily, and because someday I'll grow up and turn into a monster, get claws and teeth and go wild and unpredictable and maybe rip out someone's throat. That's what it means to be a blank, and Boone knows it, but he also knows it can be useful, my blankness, and that's why I'm here tonight.

Another quiet window, and that leaves just one more, bright and shining. I creep up to it, one hand fingering the rope around my shoulder. I can hear the muffled briskness of a man's voice, and I reach into the small pack at my hip and pull out the long, curling ear trumpet Boone gave me two years ago on a job in Prague. It doesn't work quite as well as a spying spell, but when I press the bell against the window and fit the end of the funnel into my ear, the indistinct noises on the other side of the glass grow clear.

"...with the right kind of persuasion, it can be possible to achieve the desired results," a man is saying. "Now, we will see if this mouse will grace us with an example of her singing."

Frowning, I pull away from the building and slowly look over the edge of the windowsill until I can see into the room. At least two dozen men of various examples of Boston elite—doctors and scientists, modern men and medical miracle workers—sit around a small dais occupied by a short, round man with a sand-colored beard; an ornately carved wooden table; and a tiny silver-wire cage, inside of which rests a small brown mound of quivering fur.

The bearded man pulls a thin, evil-looking wand from his vest pocket and sticks it between the bars of the cage. Although the little mouse uncurls, blinking bright black eyes at the audience, she doesn't seem to sing, and the man begins talking quickly about past experiments, mouse physiology. I bite back a groan. Either the tiny thing has stage fright, or it's not really a singing mouse—the kind I see in the hunter markets, the kind that trill out high-pitched versions of sentimental songs and sell for fifty cents—but just a common house mouse, which is to say, a fraud.

For the first time tonight, I wonder if Boone's plan is going to work.

"I've had a stroke of brilliance!" he'd said three days ago, and he pulled out the local society paper and opened it with a flourish. "There!"

"'This Wednesday evening, the Boston Society of Natural History will hold a meeting devoted to the discussion and exhibition of subjects exhibiting natural magical properties,'" I read out loud. "'Any gentleman wishing to attend or present at this meeting is welcome to contact the Society's secretary, Doctor Henry Kneeland.'"

"Easy pickings, my boy!" Boone had said. "*Eas*-y pickings!"

But if the best these distinguished gentlemen have to offer are singing mice—hoax or no—we're wasting our time.

"Yes, *thank* you, Dr. Gould!"

I watch through the window a man with a gold badge pinned to his lapel rise to his feet and begin clapping politely, the noise rousing a few audience members, who startle and blink and clap with dazed looks on their faces.

As a red-cheeked boy about my age helps Dr. Gould and his terrified mouse from off the dais, the man with the badge gestures to someone just out of my view.

"And now, for our final presentation of the evening, I will ask Dr. Dalton to take the floor and discuss the specimen he has brought with him."

Dr. Dalton strides up to the dais, followed closely by two well-heeled footmen, who pull along behind them a strange contraption. It looks a little like an oversized version of the kind of hook on a pole used to display wired skeletons in medical colleges, except the thing that hangs from this hook isn't a skeleton but a monster: a three-foot-long, swollen, yellow-gray sack of meat shaped like a rotten silk balloon, hanging with thick ropes that twitch and sway with the movement of the pole so that it's almost as though the giant thing is still alive.

"Gentlemen!" Dr. Dalton doesn't speak so much as bark, and between that and his specimen, the few audience members who looked like they were threatening to fall back asleep sit up in their seats. "What I have for you is a genuine example of the rarest of ocean creatures: the legendary *kraken*."

Eyes widen, spectacles are removed from or slid onto noses, a murmur of excitement vibrates through the glass, and I grin and pull the rope from my shoulder. A ruddy kraken. Boone knew what he was talking about.

Krakens are powerful, potent—and priceless. A single arm or tentacle can go for twenty dollars, and the blasted things have ten of them. They can be cut open and dissected, their different organs used for a dozen kinds of spells. Kraken gills will give a man the ability to breathe underwater. Eat one of their stomachs, stewed in a broth of seawater, and you can drink from the ocean without going mad. Invulnerability at sea, protection from drowning, strength and speed and luck, sharper vision, keener navigation, and the ability to foresee changes in weather—the kraken can grant them all. It's a bonanza if you can find it, if you can catch it, because the kraken lives in the deepest, coldest, darkest part of the ocean and typically only sees the surface in one of two ways: cut out of the stomachs of sperm whales tough enough to survive a kraken fight, or rising from the ocean to drown ships and pull apart sailors like an old lady snapping open peanuts.

And now there's one hanging from a pole not ten feet away from me, ready to be wheeled away and bundled and boxed and sold for a fortune.

"You'll know it when you see it," Boone had told me this morning, when I asked him what he was after, and I'm looking at it right now.

"Excuse me, Dr. Dalton."

Dalton pauses from where he's lifting up one of the kraken's tentacles with a long hook on a stick and frowns at the speaker, a thin man in a black jacket who looks about as out of place in that room as I do waiting outside this window. He's got a kind of sharp intelligence in his face and features different from the stolid, stately look of the professors and doctors and scientists sitting in the audience, and he's younger than them, too—maybe the youngest person in the room aside from the footmen and the red-cheeked college boy.

"I'll get to questions in a moment, ah, Mister—"

"Doctor," the man corrects, smiling broadly. "My name is Dr. Whitney."

"Yes, Dr. Whitney. As I was saying—"

"I don't have a question."

Dalton blinks at the man, the tentacle quivering at the end of the hook. "Pardon?"

The man smiles again, almost patiently. "I said: I do not have a question."

Creaks and shuffles as the men in the audience all turn to look at him, their faces pinched with confusion. Dalton lowers the hook and puts a hand on a hip, leaning forward with an almost predatory frown.

"Well then, state your business and I shall continue with the presentation."

The man nods and lifts his hands, almost like he's asking the entire audience to join him in song. "All I have to say is this: Everyone in this room must shut their eyes, stuff their hands into their ears, and forget they have ever seen me."

There is a moment when silent surprise hangs in the air, and then, like mechanical dolls, the men spring to life to follow his directions, clapping hands to the sides of their heads, squeezing their eyelids closed, all while the man in the black jacket continues to smile politely.

Watching over the windowsill, I grin.

Time to get to work.

Three

BY THE TIME I HOIST MYSELF ONTO THE windowsill, the man in the black jacket is there, opening the window for me.

"You said nine o'clock sharp," I say. "I had to listen to that man drone on about the bloody mouse for at least ten minutes."

Boone rolls his shoulders in a kind of full-body shrug as he steps aside to let me into the room. "There was a presentation on cursed gully snakes that went long," he says. "Just be grateful you didn't have to sit through the debate over the existence of fanged chickens."

I hand him the rope and examine the room. It looks much like any gentleman's library—dark wood shelves and glass curio cabinets—except instead of a fine stock of books, the shelves display tiny animal skeletons, chips of rocks, vials of violently colored powders.

"Seas, Boone," I say, crossing over to one of the shelves. "They've got a claw from a miniature cloud dragon!"

"Forget it. The market bottomed out on dragon claws six months ago."

I'm about to turn away when I catch a flash of glittering red on a shelf, and I lean in to see an egg-shaped, ruby-colored stone nestled on a pillow, along with a tiny handwritten sign that says FIRE-FLESH ROCK OF BATAVIA. PLEASE DO NOT TOUCH.

Fire-flesh? I lift an eyebrow and pluck the rock from its pillow, and it's as cool as a river stone in my palm.

"Mal—focus, and get over here."

I drop the stone into my pocket and turn back to Boone and the room full of dignified men, their eyes squeezed shut and their fingers pushed into their ears like a group of children playing a parlor game.

"How long will they be like that?" I ask, and Boone gives them a dismissive glance.

"Oh, however long they can stand it. The stronger-willed ones will be out a few minutes, at least, and I'd expect the weaker ones to be here all night."

"A few minutes?" I look up at the monstrous kraken, which emits a strong odor of brine, chemicals, and decay. "Will we have enough time?"

Boone just smiles and walks over to one of the half-dozen curiosity cabinets that line the walls of the room. "I saw this coming in," he says, opening the glass case and pulling out a small bottle filled with what looks like black ash. "Blesti dust."

He hands me the bottle and pulls out a white scarf, which he drapes over his mouth and knots tightly behind his neck, and then nods. I uncork the little bottle and pour some of the black powder on the floor, where it swirls and blossoms into a fist-shaped puff. Boone gives a little intake of breath, and I try to imagine what it is he's seeing: a screen of black, rising like a menace and filling the room with darkness. But to me, it all looks the same. No cloud. No darkness. Just a pile of dust on the floor and a few sputtering wisps of ash.

Boone's eyes widen, his movements jerky and uncertain, and although I know the scarf should prevent the worst of the dust from getting into his lungs and temporarily blinding him, I still put out my hand and lead him over to the kraken, moving slowly and carefully as he navigates through the room.

"How is it?" I ask, and Boone grimaces behind the scarf.

"Ruddy dark. Let's get this over with. Think we can wheel that thing down the hall?"

"Of course," I say, wrapping my rope around the kraken, but I frown up at it, nearly twice my size and easily three times my weight. "What in blazes are we going to *do* with it?"

"This building used to be a medical college," Boone says, groping for the rope and grabbing a tentacle instead. He drops it, shuddering, before I slide the rope into his hand. "There's still a room for dissection in the cellar, and lucky for us, several members of the Society store their tools here at the ready. We'll hack off the best pieces we can carry—no need to take it all. Ready?"

"One moment," I say, and I walk across the room to where Dr. Gould sits, blind and deaf and hunched over the silver-wire cage, where the little mouse races back and forth, squeaking out a pitchy rendition of "Take Your Time Miss Lucy."

"You little scamp," I say. "You *can* sing."

"Mal?"

I take the cage from Dr. Gould's lap and open it before reaching in and picking up the little mouse.

"Fancy yourself a pet?" Boone asks, squinting at me in a resigned way, but I set the mouse down on the floor to scamper away. "It'll probably end up dinner for an alley cat."

"Singing valiantly until the end," I say, watching it disappear under a bookshelf. "All right, let's get this disgusting bag of money down to the dissection room."

Together we wrestle the kraken on its pole past the still-silent, still-blind gentlemen, me leading the way and Boone following behind, cautious and uncertain.

"There," he says, pointing down a short hallway to a door set into a wall. The kraken sloshes and shivers as we pull it to the door, which opens not to another room, as I expected, or even to a set of stairs, but instead to a kind of overlarge dumbwaiter.

"For the cadavers," Boone says cheerfully, and he grabs a

lit lantern from a side table before shutting the door behind us and motioning to a pulley in the corner. "Down we go!"

As I yank the rope, dropping us a few inches with every pull, Boone tugs the scarf off his mouth and blinks like a bat in sunlight.

"That's better!" he says, smiling, and he tilts his head at me. "You really didn't see a thing?"

But he knows I didn't. He knows, more than anyone, maybe even more than me, the reaches of my blankness, just how much magic I can stand—or not. He asked me not long after I met him what I could do, but I was fourteen and scared and didn't know, and so Boone, smiling that smile of his, said it was all right, we would figure it out together, and what it meant was that he would try to kill me with magic and see what I survived.

He learned—and so did I—that I cannot be hexed or cursed or blessed or saved, not by magic. Fire conjured by a spell doesn't burn me, but I can drown in a wave controlled by a witch. A sword imbued with a magical spell can still cut me, because it is a sword, but I can fight off a weak man with a charm for unbeatable strength. And I could stand motionless on a street corner when Boone, running from an angry boardinghouse owner out for rent money and blood, first knocked into me, grinned, and said, "Run back there, boy, and tell that furious man chasing me that you saw me run in the other direction."

I blinked at him and didn't move, and the smile on Boone's face flickered.

"I said: Go back there and tell him I ran somewhere else."

"Do what?"

Boone's eyebrows lifted in surprise. "Interesting," he said, and then he disappeared and left me with the familiar feeling that I'd just been unsuccessfully bewitched.

He found me the next day and told me what I had already guessed: that he was a Silvertongue, someone who can say things to people and get them to do it—most of the time, so long as they aren't too distracted or angry or strong-minded. He told me also that he knew I was immune to magic, and when I'd cringed and tried to dart away, he grabbed me by the coat collar and bought me lunch and explained that immunity to magic was something he'd been looking for in his line of work.

He was a hunter, someone who made a living tracking down special things, magical things, trinkets and charms and fantastical ingredients for spells, the kinds of things that reeked with magic and sold for sacks of money. It's dangerous work, and the biggest problem hunters have—and the one that made Boone the most nervous—is that half the things they're contracted to find and sell are extraordinarily good at killing people: tongues of animals said to sicken whoever touches them, hidden jewels that have cursed centuries of owners, sand from the deepest part of the ocean that bursts into flames the moment it touches air.

It helps, then, to have a partner who isn't affected by magic. It helps to have someone like me (and there are whispers, here and there, of hunters actually buying and selling blanks, passing us along for certain dangerous jobs—although I've never met a hunter who admitted it). There's danger in working with a blank, of course. The stories say blanks destroy magic, and they're not entirely wrong. When I touch a weak charm, it won't work properly, and even strong charms can lose their powers if they touch my skin for a while, so I'm always careful not to handle magical things for too long, slipping them into pockets or bags or handkerchiefs. It's different with Others, who manufacture their magic; "It's like fallin' into a whirlpool!" a palm reader in Aberdeen told me once, taking her hand from off mine and staring at me in wonder. "Like gettin' sucked by a leech!"

But Boone just smiled from a distance. "We'll be careful," he told me.

And then there are the rumors that blanks go mad at a certain age, lose their minds and lose themselves to the monster inside them. I don't know if it's true or not, if I'll get older and feel myself slip away, or if it's another old superstition, like how you can spot a blank by his burning-red eyes or how no horse will ever consent to carry a blank (neither true, at least in my case). But the madness...That I do feel sometimes, itching my skin, whispering to me at night, begging to come out, and the older I get, the stronger the feelings....

But if Boone worries about my growing older, he keeps

his worries to himself, and after all, I was just a boy when Boone took me on. Any danger in the future was worth it to him to be able to say, "Mal, reach into that pool and pull out that amulet," and know that it wasn't his hand that would be sheared off as though by a huge, invisible sword.

He wanted a partner, and I wanted, I don't know, something, anything that would give me a place and a purpose, and I saw it in his good shoes and broad smile and way of talking that made doors and skirts fly open. And when he said to me, "It's hard out there for a man alone, Mal, my lad. Harder still for a boy without a last name or a pa or a friend in the world and I need you, boy, but you need me more," maybe he was lying to me or Silvertonguing out of pure habit, or maybe his words had power even without magic, maybe he just knew what to say to a skinny boy with too-bright eyes and no notion of what to do with himself. But whatever it was, it worked, and I've been stuck with Boone like I'm stuck with my immunity, a part of me I couldn't change even if I wanted.

"There we are!" Boone says as I lower the dumbwaiter to the cellar. He lifts the lantern to reveal a smooth wooden table decorated with a variety of metal saws and files. Once we push the kraken into the dissection room, he looks it over and then counts off the body parts on his fingers. "Right. Two tentacles, the eyes, the gills, the ink sac, the heart, the fin, and as many of those little suckers as we can scrape off.

We'll put everything we can carry in those canvas satchels there. Ready, then?"

I glance at the collection of bright saws and instead unsheathe the knife at my hip, and Boone gives me a look.

"Something about a table full of foot-long bone saws that gets you a bit nervous, boy?" he asks, and I shrug.

"At least I knew the fellows this knife's been inside," I say, and he smiles.

"Can't argue with that. All right now, no worse than cutting in a whale. Let's get to it."

He grabs at a tentacle and hacks, and I slide a stool over from a corner to better get at the kraken's head. It's brutal, messy, smelly work, and in no time the floor is slick with oozy liquid, the air heavy with the scent of rotting fish, but we move quickly, efficiently, my knife slicing through the kraken's tough skin and prying out the delicate organs, which Boone wraps in wet newspaper before sliding them into one of the satchels with all the love and care of a midwife bringing a baby into the world.

"That'll get us thirty dollars," he says, tucking one of the eyes in next to the heart. He milks the ink from the sac into a glass bottle, and when it fills to the brim, he's practically singing: "Eight dollars an ounce, at least!"

By the time the kraken is a shredded mess and our satchels bulge with bits and pieces, Boone has calculated our total take to be close to a thousand dollars—more money than either of us has ever seen, let alone made on a job. It's the kind of success that two independents like us, working as a pair without the support of one of the hunter confederations that span countries and include dozens of specialized hunters, could never bring in. It's enough to make us famous. Enough to ensure that Boone won't be buying drinks at the hunter bars for the next decade. Enough, maybe, to give us the kind of legitimacy to start our *own* confederation, get out of the dregs and the scuttle and organize an operation from the comfort and security of a four-floor mansion in Bowdoin Square.

Boone describes it all to me, his voice full of love, of longing, and I smile less because I care about all that than because I'm happy he's happy. Jobs don't matter to me. Money doesn't matter to me. But Boone picked me as his partner, and I need to prove to him that I'm more than just a blank, more than the bad thing, the dangerous one, but smart and successful and strong. When Boone claps his hands together and laughs and says, "We did it!" all I care about is that one little word: "we."

After we load the satchels onto our backs, Boone takes us through a hallway that leads to a set of narrow stone stairs and a back door. Carefully, he pushes it open, letting in a rush of fresh night air, and after a moment checking to make sure no one's watching, he motions for me to follow him, outside and across the grass and back over the wrought-iron fence. He's laughing before our boots even touch the cobblestones.

"The heart alone could fetch a hundred dollars!" he says, grinning as we jog together down the street. "To never be beaten by an enemy at sea—whether man or beast or force of nature! Can't you imagine a band of pirates killing for something like that?"

"I can," a voice answers from behind, and before I can turn to see who's spoken, a pair of hands has grabbed me, thrown me off balance, and set a knife at my throat.

Four

I SEE A FLASH OF FOREST GREEN LIT UP IN the glow of a streetlamp, and then I see nothing but the black sky as the knife in the hollow of my throat forces me to tip my chin up. There's a noise, a kind of strangled gasp that I realize comes from me, and then I hear Boone let out an exclamation and begin to speak, before the man with the knife barks out, "Quiet!"

Whoever's attacking us isn't from the Society—the voice is harsh, rough, lacking the soft affectation of the Boston elite, and with my back up against his chest, I breathe past the stink of the kraken to smell gunpowder, liquor, sweat, and salt air. He's a hunter.

"Put down the bag," the voice says, and I try to see what Boone's doing without moving my head too much. He sounded caught off guard earlier, but when I glance at him now, he seems cool, in control, his hands lifted as though he's calming a skittish horse.

"All right, now," he says. "Just let him go."

I feel a ripple of something run through the man, a shudder that causes the knife at my throat to tremble and scrape along my skin, and the man sucks in a breath and hisses, "I *told* you to *stay quiet.*"

A weight drops into my stomach as I realize this man has some sort of protection against Boone's Silvertongue— a charm or a spell against magical deception. It's the kind of precaution a skilled hunter would take before going out on a job, and it means one of our greatest weapons is now useless.

Boone looks nervous, adjusting the straps of his satchel over his shoulder, and when he smiles, he does it without his usual smooth cool.

"And what are the Drakes doing in Boston? I thought the pirate confederations headed to the Mediterranean this time of year," he says, and he gives me a look that I recognize, a look that says *Distract him.*

"Drakes, eh?" I say, and I try to sound as confident as possible given the steel tickling my throat. "I suppose you *would* be interested in the kraken. Can't be easy keeping all those ships seaworthy."

"Enough, you," the Drake says, but I just turn my head as much as I dare, trying to catch his eye.

"What were you thinking?" I ask. "Wait for hunters like us to do the dirty work and then steal it?"

The man laughs. "*You're* the thieves. The Drakes have a deal with that scientist what brought the kraken here. I was supposed to wait until their meeting ended and then deliver it to the docks, but then I see you two running through the streets, flapping your gobs about hearts." The knife presses deeper against my throat and my head feels swimmy with panic. "Now shut it, and slip that bag from your shoulders."

"All right," I say, my voice all breath. Carefully, trying hard not to move my head, I reach up to move the straps of my satchel from my shoulders. As I slowly lower the bag to the ground, I slip one hand into my pocket and quickly pull out the red fire-flesh rock that I stole from the Society. Holding it loosely in my palm, I tilt my chin just low enough to catch Boone's eye and give him a slight, slow nod.

"You, too, skinny," the Drake says to Boone, and his eyes flit from my face to the Drake's before he smiles.

"Well, now, let's just hold on a moment," Boone says, although he slides the bag off his shoulder. I can feel the Drake's muscles tense behind me.

"We've got at least a thousand dollars' worth of goods in here." Boone licks his lips, his eyes glittering. "What say we split it? You can't be making more than five hundred dollars for this job!"

The man laughs again, but he sounds less sure of himself now. "It's worth more than five hundred dollars to stay good with the Drakes," he says. "Didn't you hear what they did to that hunter out off the coast of Spain? When they caught him tryin' to steal a bunch of blessed canvas, they tied him between the masts of two of their ships and sailed them off'n opposite directions!"

"That's too bad," Boone says, still dangling the satchel at the end of his hand. "I would have taken our offer, if I was you."

"What—"

But before the Drake can get out another word, Boone shouts, "Now!" and I jerk my hand up and back, pressing the fire-flesh stone against the Drake's face. The sizzle of his skin mingles with his scream, and he drops the knife, backing away from me, one hand to his smoking cheek. At the same time, Boone reaches into his waistcoat and pulls out a small bottle of some lime-green liquid. He throws it onto the street, where it shatters and erupts into a sickly-sweet pale cloud. The Drake, still distracted by his burned cheek, stumbles right into the cloud, and his cries grow suddenly sharp, panicked, his eyes wide and white with fear. Boone, his face tucked into the crook of his arm, bends down and snatches the satchel from the ground before jerking his head toward the street beyond.

"Run!" he shouts, but I'm already moving, racing after him, ignoring the warm wetness on my shirt collar.

"A fire-flesh stone!" he says, laughing, and I grin back at him.

"And when did you get your hands on nip of nightmare?" I ask, but he just laughs again as the Drake's cries of panic follow us. I can't say I have much sympathy for a man who held a knife to my throat, but knowing what he's going through right now, the potion transforming all his worst nightmares to reality, I feel a sudden rushing gladness that I'm immune to magic.

A thought that completely vanishes moments later, when we turn a corner and nearly run into what looks like the rest of the Drakes, standing shoulder to shoulder with more guns, knives, and clubs than I can count, and I wish, not for the first time in my life, that I had a single protection spell on me.

A coughing, sputtering Drake pushes from the back of the crowd and points at us.

"That's them!" he says, and from his slightly green-tinged skin and the egg-shaped red welt on his cheek, I recognize the man who held me at knifepoint—impossibly standing in front of us.

"What in blazes..." Boone mutters. "You're a Traveler!" And he is—one of those Others who can instantly travel from one point in the world to another: in this case, to his fellow Drakes to warn them about us.

"The bags," one of the Drakes says to Boone, tilting his gun toward us, and I tense, balanced on the balls of my feet.

"Wait a moment," Boone says, but he sounds different now, desperate, his hand clenched around the straps of both satchels slung over his shoulder. I see his other hand, the one closer to me, flutter to his pocket and pull out a short glass vial about the size of his pinkie.

"Your spells won't work on us," the Drake with the gun says, and he nods at another Drake, who spreads his hands out wide, sending a ripple of air like a heat shimmer across the group. I recognize the simple shield spell, and I glance at Boone, nervous. He just smiles, crooked and sly, and opens his hand enough to show what's inside the vial: not a potion or a powder but an iridescent blue stone.

"It's called a mercy stone," Boone told me once. "Think of it as a means of escape. Bite into the stone, and it will whisk you away somewhere safe."

Well. Not me. But I knew then what he meant, and the Drakes know it now, too.

"Take another step closer and we'll disappear," Boone says, holding up the vial, and for a moment I see the Drakes look nervous. Then the green-skinned one laughs.

"We're supposed to believe you carry about a mercy stone?" he asks. "When I held your partner at knifepoint! What hunter goes without protection against knives but can afford a mercy stone?" He lets out another peal of laughter. "Most likely just a bit of paint and a pebble. Go ahead, then! Bite the blasted rock!"

I glance at Boone, his smile slipping, the hand that clutches the vial trembling. He could do it. I don't know where the mercy stone would take him, but he could bite it and disappear with a thousand dollars' worth of magical meat and all his dreams and plans intact. But if he goes, he goes alone. The mercy stone won't take me anywhere. He can escape, but he'll leave me standing on the street with a dozen Drakes who will almost certainly kill me.

"Boone," I say, my voice low, and he doesn't look at me. Beads of sweat form across his forehead, above his lip. He holds the mercy stone, he holds the satchels, and he watches the Drakes.

"Boone!" I say his name again, and this time his gaze flickers toward me, just for a moment, and I wonder what he's thinking. I wonder if he's looking at me and realizing I'm eighteen now, I'm growing up, I'm no longer the little boy he picked up on the streets but swiftly changing into something else, something dangerous. He looks at me and looks away, and in that instant I see him weighing the balance: How much is it really worth to keep me on as a partner anymore?

"Last chance," says the one in front, the one with the gun, and I hear the hammer cock back.

"*Boone!*" I tense, flinch, and just make out Boone's hand moving swiftly across his body—*he's biting the stone!*—and then I see the arc of the satchels through the air, see them land on the street with muffled squelches.

A pair of the hunters bend down to pick them up, and the green-skinned Traveler spits into the street.

"I knew it," he says, eyes narrowed at us. "Take your pebble and your games and stay out of confederate business. Blasted *independents*. Blasted nuisance is what they are."

Beside me, I feel Boone bristle, and I know exactly what he's thinking, that he's better than they think, that his "pebble" is real and that he's every bit the hunter these confederate snobs are, but when he opens his mouth to say something, I put a hand on his shoulder and shake my head.

"Get yourself some charms next time!" one of the Drakes calls as we turn and walk back down the street.

"Yes, you'll find they're very useful if you want to hunt!" another says, and they break into laughter that follows us.

The moment we're around a corner, Boone spins and slams his hand into the wall of a building, the noise so loud that I jump.

"We had it!" he says. "*I* had it!"

"Boone?"

He turns and looks over his shoulder at me, his face dark with anger, and for a moment he looks like he's going to shout, explode, curse the bad fortune of having a blank for a partner when otherwise we could have been off and laughing and a thousand dollars richer. But then, like water falling from a glass, all the anger drains out of him, along with a deep sigh that leaves him looking empty.

"Are you all right?" I ask, worried to hear the answer, and he stares at me for a moment before giving me a smile that doesn't quite reach his eyes.

"I saved your life tonight, boy," he says, and gently he reaches out a hand and touches the blood at my throat, the blood from the Drake's knife, and it's such a rare thing, him touching me at all, that I have to fight off a shiver.

"Don't forget that. I saved your life. Now we're even."

Five

EVER SINCE THAT DAY IN THE GRASS WITH
Essie's rope around my hand and her spell floating across my
skin, instead of feeling magic I've felt something like a sliver
of ice between my ribs or a hollowed-out space between my
shoulders or a mark on my face like a blot warning everyone
that *this one is different.*

Stories of blanks didn't often reach Prince Island—island
superstitions forbade even mentioning the possibility that
magic could leave a person—but I heard enough whispers to
learn about them, about me.

Blanks may as well be dead people. Blanks are like dolls.
Blanks have black eyes or red eyes or no eyes at all. Blanks are
demons, unreal, nightmares, frightening. As I traveled around
the world with Boone, asking careful questions at hunter pubs

and back-alley markets, I learned that I eat babies, that I can fly through the air like a bat, that I can spread my affliction through touch, through kisses, through words. I learned that in other countries, in past centuries, babies found to be blanks were thrown into the ocean or burned alive or buried with iron stakes through their bodies. Safer that way.

Every country and community has a name for us. *Vacare* is the old name—"empty," it means—and you still hear it used in the British Isles or on the eastern shores of the United Canadas. Sometimes it's mangled into a different word, *vacar*, pronounced like "vack-arr" or shortened further into "vac." *Dry* is another word for us, or in remote villages you'll hear that a person's all *wooden*. "As dry as a wooden doll," people say, and it means a man who can't be trusted, who's strange, not right, who makes you feel unnerved or scared and you're not quite sure why. The French call us *bonshommes de bois*—"wooden ones"—and *vazio* is the name in Portuguese, *marioneta sin cuerdas* in Spanish. And in jolly ole London, a lad gave me a fifteen-minute lesson in cockney rhyming slang and ended by telling me to avoid anyone I heard described as a "Frank," a "knacker," or a "good'n ball."

Wherever it's used, it's an insult and any man called one of those words over a pint at a bar had better be ready to defend his honor with a knife or fists or be outcast forever. I once saw a British sailor bust open the head of a carpenter from Gloucester after he called the sailor a "rank, thick-skulled, wooden whoreson." And after he'd wiped the blood from his knuckles and returned to his mug, he explained to the pub that he could stand an insult to his intelligence, his hygiene, and even his poor dead mother, bless her soul, but he could not sit idly and hear himself called a blank.

I am the worst thing there is, I remember thinking, and I waited to see if I'd grow all the other trappings: the claws, the teeth, the red eyes, the foul breath, the slathering desire to eat and rend and kill and blot out. But although I didn't turn into a monster on the outside, I can feel it on the inside, ripping me to pieces, tearing through my veins, whispering in my ears as I sleep, as I sail, as I smile: *You are different you are dirty you are dangerous.*

That's what the people of Prince Island whispered to me, in that handful of days between when Essie told my secret and when I disappeared, never to be seen again. I'd long grown used to hearing hissed insults on the street from the island children, but this came from the parents, from the butcher and the rope-maker and the knots of old men who'd sit on street corners with their pipes and their narrowed eyes. They were scared of me: me, a boy they'd known thirteen years, but now I was like a demon, a changeling, something wild and dangerous that had sprung up just where they felt most safe.

"Stay away from the docks," I heard.

"Stay away from my Charlie and Becca."

"Stay away from the girl."

The girl—that meant Essie, and I wouldn't have gone near her anyway, I wanted nothing to do with her, but I knew what they were scared of. Blanks destroy magic, and she was to be their witch, and no one and nothing could threaten that.

"Stay away. *Stay away.*"

They meant their families. They meant the island. "Stay away"—or what? But I could guess what, because the glares turned into whispers turned into hisses turned into fists curled at sides, ropes swung in my direction, knives flashed beneath coats.

Stay away or we'll kill you, and so I left.

Now we're even.

Boone and I walk north through the city, making our way from the wide, well-lit streets around the Common to Dock Square, on the waterfront, temporary home to the sailors and whalers and hunters passing through. It's late, yet the bars and boardinghouses are full of light, noise, singing: celebrations for men just home from a voyage or for men just heading out. But Boone passes them all like he's walking in a haze, his shoulders slumped, his mouth hanging low in a frown.

Boone traded my life for a thousand dollars of kraken pieces and a chance to become a real success, and I don't know what to say to him, if I'm supposed to say anything to him.

Now we're even.

He said that because I saved his life not long after I met him, only a few months into our partnership, and from that day on, when he introduced me to people, he'd say, "And this is Mal. He saved my life once."

"Oh, and how's that?" people would ask, and Boone would grin. He'd tell the story, and when he finished, sometimes people would laugh. If they knew him well enough, they'd ask if he was telling the truth or just trying to Silvertongue a good story.

"It's the truth," Boone'd say. "He saved my life."

What happened was I was fourteen, and Boone had taken me to Baltimore, to a ship on the harbor where he'd heard there'd be a good game of cards with men who didn't know what he was. I went along with him because I had nowhere else to go and because after four months of tagging along behind him like a little lamb, like a puppy he couldn't shake, I started worrying that he'd lost interest in me. To Boone, a blank was like a new toy, something fascinating and curious, but lately he'd been ignoring me, saying nothing when he got up in the morning or went out at night, like he half hoped I'd just go away on my own.

So that night, when he put on his coat and splashed water on his face and strode out of our tiny boardinghouse room, I sprang up from my corner and followed him, worried that if I didn't, he'd never come back.

We took a rowboat to the ship, far out in the harbor, and climbed aboard. Boone got to work, and I found a spot in a corner beside a blessedly empty chamber pot and a bucket half-full of whale oil. While he played his cards, I dozed, looking up every few minutes to watch him win and lie and win some more until I fell asleep and woke up to the sound of one of the sailors calling Boone a cheat.

"Say it!" The man pushed his chair back from the table and took out his knife. "Tell me again my cards are no good!"

I sat up. Boone went white, his mouth opening and closing like a frog's, and I realized that they'd figured out Boone had hoodwinked them out of their money and now the sailor was going to kill him. Boone would die, the sailor would throw his body into the harbor, and I would be left alone, again.

I acted without thinking, jumping to my feet and telling the sailor to let Boone go, and I was tall for my age, but my arms and legs still looked like ropes, my cheeks as smooth as a child's. They laughed at me, and another of the sailors shook his head at me kindly.

"Ah, leave it be, boy," he said. "We'll let you off back at the docks. No need to concern yourself with this cheat—sure an' he's not concerned any about you."

But they didn't understand, and so I pulled a lantern from off the wall and kicked over the bucket of whale oil and told them if they didn't let him go, I would throw the lantern.

The laughter stopped. They each and all might have stopped breathing and wondered to themselves who was this small monster of a boy who'd just suddenly threatened to burn them all alive. Fire, fire on a ship with a hold well stuffed with whale oil, and maybe they could put the fire out before it spread and maybe it would spread to them—I'd splashed their boots, the hems of their pants. There were too many men in this berth, too much smoke already. They didn't move.

In the silence, another laugh rang out, high and joyful, and Boone delicately smoothed the lapels of his jacket, adjusted the cuffs of his sleeves, reached into his pocket, and pulled out his thin knife.

"Well, since none of you wish to be burned alive tonight," he said, and his voice was light and pleasant, "I'll say good evening." Swiftly, he bent over the table and swept something into his hand: his marker, a large button of carved iron. He'd bet something other than money—our clothes, maybe, or our hunting gear—and after he slid the marker into his pocket, he tipped his cap at the sailors, stepped carefully over the puddle of slick oil, and walked out the door.

I followed him out, but just as I reached the door, a sailor jumped at me and the lantern smashed. A blaze like a living thing roared up at us, so hot and fierce that I gasped, unable to move, unable to see anything but the wave of fire or hear anything but the screams of the sailors, and then there was a hard tug on my collar, pulling me to my feet and yanking me through the door, down the companionway, up the ladder to the main deck. Boone, running like a madman, sprinted across the decks and reached the bulwarks without slowing and, like some kind of fairy sprite, leaped into the air and dived into the water. Stunned, I skidded to a stop and listened to the splash, and a moment later his voice rang out at me: "Jump! Jump, you fool, and swim before the whole thing goes off like a rocket!"

I glanced behind me; already a thick plume of black smoke climbed into the air while gasping, soot-stained sailors tumbled to the deck, coughing and wiping the tears from their eyes. One of them fell to his knees, wheezing, and looked up and spotted me. Half shouting and half choking, he pointed at me and said, "There's the boy!" and that was all it took for four lightly singed sailors to rush at me. My feet, acting independent of the rest of me, scrambled to the bulwarks and threw my body over the edge, and I felt myself pinwheel down to the water and land hard enough to knock every breath of air from my lungs.

Gasping, I bobbed for the surface and followed the sound of splashing, which had to be Boone. I swam for the shore as if sharks were nipping at my toes, and Boone and I finally hauled ourselves onto a beach, dripping and panting and half-dead from exhaustion and the other half of us buzzing alive.

"Lor', look at that!" Boone said, his expression huge with amazement, and when I looked back at the ship, I saw she was burning now, lost entirely, and her crew bobbing in whaleboats in the water around her, watching three years of hard work go up in smoke. A splash of water arced up to land on my chest, and I glanced over to see Boone staring at me, his boots still soaking in the harbor.

"You set that whole ship ablaze!" he said, and there was that same look of amazement. My pulse began to tick faster again, not with excitement but fear, because that was a thing blanks were said to do, destroy without a thought, just to see something burn. What would Boone say? Would he cast me out? Little wolf pup, he called me, and I stared at him with wide eyes and wondered if he'd try to skin his little wolf pup now that it had started to show its teeth.

"The whole thing ablaze..." he said again, shaking his head, and then his mouth fell open in a smile. "Boy, you saved my life!"

He grabbed my shoulder, pulled me against him, and even despite the unexpected swim in a cold harbor, he was warm, hot, burning with life.

"You sure you don't have any family, you orphan boy?" he asked, letting me go, and I was so surprised at the question I answered honestly: no. No, of course not. And Boone threw his head back and laughed and said, "Well, now you have a brother."

It was the greatest thing anyone had ever said to me in my entire life.

Six

BOONE AND I PASS THROUGH DOCK SQUARE
and reach the North End, where we've taken out a room in
one of the boardinghouses. Only two years back, in the summer of 1849, a wave of cholera swept through this neighborhood that was so bad I heard they piled up the dead on the
streets like firewood. Even though the blocks are no longer
under quarantine, the area hasn't ever been quite the same.
The rich folk moved out and the newcomers moved in, bringing their languages and colors and crowds, and while knots of
the remaining elite assemble in the neighborhood's last gen-
teel parlors and ask what is to be done about this new *situation*,
I like the changes.

Too much of the same—faces, clothes, attitudes—makes
me nervous and reminds me of Prince Island, where every-

one sees the same things with the same gray eyes and says the same words out of the same wide, flat mouths and different, strange, is a bad thing. They thought of cities as beasts that would swallow up good folk like them, and to be honest, it's how I once thought of cities, too—big and wide and never ending—but I like that feeling, that disappearing into the noise and heat.

Slowly, the buildings around us turn darker, seedier, the streets narrow and poorly lit. We've reached a run-down little corner known as the Black Sea—*sea* because it's a place for sailors and *black* for the character, for the business that occurs there and the looks you'll receive if you mention it in polite company.

This late at night the Black Sea rocks like its namesake, music and laughter and women's shrieks and men's yelling and drunks and fighters and thieves all rolled together on a side street that should have crumpled into the harbor just from the sheer amount of sin its borders contain. It's full of hunters' bars, the tiny hideaway pubs where hunters gather to share stories and make contacts, and as we pass the Crow and Stone, Boone lifts his head and jerks it toward the grubby windows.

"I don't know about you, boy," he says. "But I need a drink."

Together, we push through the doors and are greeted by a warm cloud of liquor, sweat, and women's perfume. Half the men drinking at the bar turn as we walk in, lifting their mugs and grinning welcomes. I can feel Boone relax beside me, the tension and disappointment of the evening melting away as he greets his friends.

"Boone!" one of them says, clapping a hand on his shoulder. "You stink like an old woman on wash day! What've you been up to this evening?"

"Oh, lost time, lost money," he says, and he smiles because that's what he's expected to do here, smile at his misfortune and shrug and count on his friends to buy him a pint of beer to wash away his troubles, which they do.

"One for the boy, too," the man says, sliding a mug at me, and I pick it up and touch it to Boone's.

"Cheers," I say, and what I mean is *I'm sorry, it was my fault, can you forgive me?*

"Cheers," Boone says, and I know we're all right again.

Within minutes, he's laughing, roaring with his friends while I sit watching him from a corner, warm from my drink. There's another hunter in flush from the markets and, as custom commands, he's buying everyone in the bar round after round of drinks, his new money flowing through him like water. It's like this nearly every night in nearly every hunter bar around the world, where it's nigh impossible to pay for your own liquor, because someone came home safe or scored a rare find or cheated out a buyer or lived another day he shouldn't have. That's just how the hunter world works: weeks or months of jobs so difficult and dangerous you wonder if you'll make it out alive, and then a moment of safety, of celebration, like the cork bursting out of a bottle of champagne in one huge, fizzy wave.

"Friend of yours?" asks someone with a light Southern accent.

I look up to see a man leaning over me, his head tilted toward Boone, who stands red-cheeked on a table, conducting a rousing rendition of "Oh, I Can Catch a Dragon, But I Cannot Catch You."

"When he's sober, he's my partner," I say, grinning.

"That man has a voice like a cat caught in a kennel," the man says, eyebrows lifted in something like admiration. He turns to me and lifts his mug. "Name's Joseph Young. I'm a tracker out of Charleston."

"Mal," I say, returning his salute. "The nightingale over there is named Boone."

"Hunters about these parts?" he asks, and I nod.

"All around, mostly. We're just stopped over in Boston for a few days."

Joseph Young shakes his head, smiling. "I tell you—this city's mad for magic. Never seen anything like it! And here I thought Charleston had a good market, what with the fortune-tellers and all," he says, and I smile back—I haven't been to the Charleston hunter market for years, but I remember it: long, skinny covered halls populated with magic folk offering glimpses into the future or chances to change your fortune.

When I was fourteen and newly arrived at the docks, I tried to get my fortune read. I hadn't learned yet just how much my blankness limited me, and card magic seemed harmless enough, and so I took my money to the first teller I could find, sat down in front of her and her cards, and asked her what she could see. I can still remember her face, the way it changed from disinterest to shock to laughter, and how she took my money from out of her pocket and slid it between the upturned cards on the table.

"There's nothing but shadows, boy," she said, and she waved me away.

"How much do you know about this area?" Joseph Young asks me, leaning closer. "I hear there's an island way out a ways, miles off the coast, with a water witch unlike anything else in the world."

My stomach clenches and my hand goes slick around the handle of my mug. "You don't say."

"She's mighty powerful, this witch, and what's more—there's another one. A daughter," he says, his voice dropping low over the roar of the singing crowd. Goose bumps sweeping down my arms. "She doesn't have the water magic—not yet—but she's got somethin' else. Some other kind of magic."

Put down your mug, I tell myself. *Walk away*, but I can't help myself. The hole inside me lurches open just to hear about her, and I find myself twisting closer to Joseph Young.

"What?" I ask, the word coming out of me in a whisper.

"Men say she's a sorceress. They say she can reach inside hearts and minds. They say she's the most beautiful woman in the world." He lifts an eyebrow, a smile pulling at the corner of his lips. "I heard stories of men gone mad just lookin' at her, like one look's enough for a man to forget about his wife and children. Some judge's son out of Boston was engaged to a young lady from the Cabot family, plenty wealthy, a good match for him, but rumor says when he set eyes on the witch girl, he broke his arrangement with Miss Cabot and vowed he'd never leave the island. Caused a right scandal, shamed his father, and didn't even manage to win her favor. That witch girl's got a cold heart and isn't anyone about to claim it anytime soon. When the girl heard about his plans to court her, they say she just laughed."

Playing, she's still playing with people, tearing them apart like a kitten who cares only about sharpening her claws, and my hands start shaking so badly that I have to set my mug, rattling, on the bar.

"I've half a mind to sail out there and see for myself what all the fuss is about," Joseph Young says, and he's still smiling at me, still talking like this is just another hunter's tale to be swapped, but there's a coldness settling inside me, a sickness like dread.

"If I were you," I say, and I have to work to keep the tremble out of my voice, "I'd stay far away from that place."

"What's that?" he asks me, but I've already turned away, my head swimming, my feet carrying me to the door and out into the stale, cool air of the street.

Love magic. It's a game for young girls—say an incantation and drop a bit of candlewax into a bowl of cold water, and it'll form into the first letter of your future husband's name. Or dab a bit of this potion behind the ears like perfume and the boy of your heart will take a fancy to you. It's a joke in the hunter bars, rookies waking up next to clod-faced farmer girls, bewitched into a night of love, and I know enough to laugh at those stories, but it always makes me uneasy. It makes me glad to be a blank.

And now Essie Roe, the most beautiful girl in the world, has this power, and she's using it to break hearts and destroy lives. Of course she is—why would I expect anything else?

There's an old island saying, "Roe women, unlucky in love," and it comes from the fact that no Roe witch has ever married or shared her small cottage with a man or raised her daughter to know a father.

"I'm going to be the first," Essie used to tell me. "I'm going to fall in love. Don't tell anyone—it's a secret."

If I ever pointed out that the people of the island scarcely treated her any better than they treated me, she'd just narrow her eyes and set her hands on her hips.

"It'll be different when I'm older," she'd say. "They'll realize what I am, and then they'll love me."

Did they love her now? The people of my island, who

would sooner see me dead than interfering with her magic? What did they have to say about the beautiful witch girl, who could reach into their hearts and minds and demand anything and everything of them?

It isn't fair. I put my hands to my chest and press them against the bones of my ribs, as though if I push hard enough, I'll be able to stop the ache there. How am I ever supposed to escape her, escape what she's done to me, knowing she's back there on that island, beautiful and magical and invincible? She was my best friend and she betrayed me, but I'm the one who has to hide what I am. I'm the one people call monster, the one driven from his home, the one who has to keep running, *keep running*, so that no one knows what I really am.

I hate her.

The coldness inside me turns to heat, a blaze so fast and sudden that I wish I had a boat so that I could sail right now, right this second, to that blasted island and find her and tell her: *You're the one who should be cast off into the cold.*

The monster inside me is raging, furious, angry, ripping and biting at itself and begging to be let out, *please*, just a little, and so I walk back into the bar and pull out my bag of money and say loud enough for everyone to hear that I don't want the liquor to stop flowing until that bag is empty.

"Good boy!" they cheer, and it's not what the monster really wants, but it's enough to make the sharp edges of the night go soft and blurred, to look around at all the faces smiling at me, all the strangers toasting my good health—"To the boy!" "To Mal!" "To another drink!"—and think of them as friends, family, even though any one of them, if they knew what I really was, wouldn't hesitate to drag me out into the alley and run a knife through my stomach.

"Drink!" Boone slides a glass into my hand and I throw it back and guzzle down the liquor and let it burn me from the inside out, and when someone else gives me another glass, I take that one, too, and the next, and the next, until everything goes warm as honey. There are arms around my neck and bodies pressed against mine—although not Boone's, never Boone's, because he knows what I am and he knows how dangerous that is, but others, laughing others, and between the liquor and the singing, that's enough.

"Haven't you had enough?" a voice asks me. Maybe it's Boone or maybe it's someone else, but I just shout out a laugh like a bark and pull a bottle from behind the bar and lift it above my head. I pour it out like a fountain, the little monster inside me expanding, taking over my arms and my legs and my voice, and it's such a rest, such a relief, to stop fighting it and just let go.

It's working, I tell myself, *I'm happy*, and whenever I begin to feel the slipping edge of blackness inside me, I throw myself back into the celebration and tell myself that this is joy and happiness and belonging that I'm feeling. Every glass, every smile is like a tiny brick filling up the hole in my chest, like a sun shining away at the darkness. For tonight, for this moment, I try to imagine that it's all working, that the hole and blackness are really gone, even though the bricks are made out of sponge and soap bubble and it's a mechanical sun that gives off no heat.

Seven

I WAKE UP WITH A HEAD FULL OF SAND and a stomach full of acid and a feeling like I'm on a ship, rocking and swaying, even though when I raise my head and look out the window behind me, the green branches of trees tremble in the fall breeze.

There's a fumbling at the door, the dented brass knob clattering, and the hunter part of me thinks I should be on my feet with a knife in my hand, and the rest of me thinks to hell with it all—anyone who wants to bash my head in this morning will have found the job already done. I'm just letting my cheek hit the pillow again when the door swings open and in walks Boone, as bright-eyed as ever, two cups and a giant earthenware pot balanced precariously in his arms.

"Good morning, beautiful!" he says, walking over to the

little circular table by the window. He sets down the cups and the pot and begins to pour out rich, dark liquid and the reviving scent of coffee. "The sun is high and we have work to do. Get up!"

I try to swing my legs over the edge of the bed, and everything in the room tilts so sharply sideways that I have to close my eyes until the spinning passes.

"What happened last night?" I ask, and my voice sounds like rocks against sandpaper.

"I believe you got the city of Boston drunk."

I squint at him, rubbing the side of my head, trying to piece together the night before: drinks and dancing and singing and fighting and teary-eyed making up and too much greasy food, and then a panic like a shock of electricity bolts through me, and I snatch my trousers from where they hang on the bedpost and grab my money purse. I can feel it before I even open it, but I open it just to be certain: black and empty of every penny.

Groaning, I throw myself back against the mattress. "I spent all my wages last night. Six months of work."

"For six hours of mad fun."

"Not worth it."

"Well, and what does a young man like yourself need with a lot of money?"

I roll over onto my side to give him a look. "Food. Clothing. A warm bed."

"Then you're in luck, because I've found us our next job."

Gingerly, still feeling like all my bones have been removed from my body, I slide off the bed and pour myself into the chair opposite Boone. "Someplace warm, I hope, for the fall. Portugal, Morocco, the south of France—"

"London," Boone says, and when I groan, he laughs and leans forward. "Tell me: What do you know about the *shar*?"

The word wakes me up even more than the coffee sliding down my throat, and I cough and set down my mug.

"We're talking fairy stories this morning?" I ask, wincing, but Boone just waits for me to answer his question, and I sigh. "It's a knife. Cut a magic person with it, and it steals their Talents. Blacksmith wizards of Iceland created it centuries ago, but it's been lost for generations."

Boone, still smiling, shakes his head. "It's been found."

I raise my eyebrows. "How? Where?"

With a theatrical flourish, Boone pulls a piece of paper out from inside his waistcoat and lays it on the table. "I had to pay five dollars just to get my hands on this."

It's a clipping from a newspaper, one of those small-town leaflets distributed Sunday mornings in church, the paper onionskin-thin and the type blocky and poorly laid out. The article says that on the Friday morning of the previous week, a Mrs. Betty Larson of Surrey Creek, England, had a number of small items stolen from her home, among them a knife of unusual shape and sentimental value. All good citizens were urged to be on the watch for thieves and assailants and to contact Constable Roger Heller with information.

"An old biddy loses a knife and you think it's the *shar*?" I ask, sliding the paper back toward Boone.

"That old biddy, before the poor dear retired to Surrey Creek, worked as private secretary to the late collector Howard LeCouer. Yes, *that* Howard LeCouer, of the Royal Society of Hunters. LeCouer was the leading expert on the *shar*, and rumor has held for years that he discovered it and kept it hidden at His Majesty's special instruction. When LeCouer died, hunters ransacked his home and office looking for it, but although they found plenty of information suggesting LeCouer had found the knife, the knife itself had, well…" Boone lifts his hands and makes a little *poof* gesture with his fingers.

"Then you think for the last twenty years the most coveted magical artifact in the entire world has been rusting at the bottom of some widow's hope chest?" I laugh and shake my head. "It's a treasure hunt, Boone—not a real job. Men spend their lives hunting things like the *shar* and end up with nothing to show for it. It's not worth it."

"I thought you might say something like that." Boone pulls out another piece of paper, and this time I recognize the red ink that signifies a hunter contract. I expect him to hand me the paper, but instead he clears his throat and begins to read. "'Attention: all hunters of durable and intelligent quality. In light of recent news, the American Confederation of Allied Magical Peoples is offering a reward for the discovery and delivery of the magical artifact known as the *shar*. Sum: one thousand dollars.'"

My mouth drops open. It's more money than any contract we've ever worked. "One *thousand*—"

Boone holds up a hand, takes out another paper. " 'On behalf of Mr. Nathaniel Blackstone of New York City, New York, I am writing to offer a reward for the *shar* in the amount of no less than two thousand dollars.' "

"Boone—"

But he already has another paper in his hand. "Viscount Philippe Renoir, four thousand francs for the retrieval of the *shar*." Another paper. "Yata Bapa, famed aerial performer, eight hundred dollars for the *shar* or evidence of its destruction. From the Russian Empire: His Imperial Highness Grand Duke Alexander Alexandrovich of Russia, five thousand dollars and a palace of your choosing." Boone takes out curled-up notices, scratched-out notes, bits and pieces of newspaper, until the table looks like a snowy mountain slashed with trails of crimson.

"Where did you get all this?" I ask, and he raises an eyebrow.

"You'll find you slept in quite late. I've had a productive morning. I went down to the hunters' market at Merchant Row, and there's hardly a wall that isn't papered with these notices." Boone spreads his hands over the pile of contracts. "Others, hunters, collectors—they all want it, Mal. Think about what the *shar* means to them."

I frown, considering it. Collectors want the *shar* because they want anything magically powerful, even if it's just meant to sit in a glass case and give their dinner guests something to feel jealous about. Then there are those who would use the *shar* as a weapon, stealing a magical person's abilities forever. Cut a man who can turn water to ice with a single touch, and if you hold the knife, you have that power, too. Cut another man who can turn invisible, and the *shar* will no longer help you form ice but will grant you invisibility. But the ice man and the invisible man lose their Talents, forever. They become ordinary men, and for most of Them, the idea of becoming ordinary is akin to death.

That's why a group like the American Confederation of Allied Magical Peoples and a famed Other like Yata Bapa want to get their hands on the *shar*—it's too much of a threat to what they are.

"In case you've forgotten," I say, chewing a lip, "you're one of Them, too. Doesn't it make you nervous to be around the *shar*?"

"Not when I know I've got my best friend, Mal the blank, handling it for me. And anytime my nerves act up, I can just count out the stacks of money coming our way and I imagine my fears will float off in the breeze." Boone tilts his head at me, smiles. "Well? What do you say? Should we set off in search of Mrs. Betty Larson's missing knife?"

I think for a moment. This kind of job isn't like those Boone and I usually go after. We tend to specialize in the most dangerous—and valuable—artifacts, which also tend to be jobs where there isn't much competition. Hunters work on a first-come, first-served basis: Competition drives prices down, and besides, only the hunter who meets the buyer first gets paid, so if you just spent six months tracking down the rarest of the rare blue-furred leopard in South America only to arrive in port five minutes behind another hunter, your blue hide's value has just gone from "worth its weight in gold" to "very unusual rug."

Something like the *shar*, a mythical, impossibly rare knife, is sure to draw out hunters from across the globe, and not just independents like me and Boone but also the confederations, like the Drakes and other, even more powerful groups. He should know, today more than ever, that we can't compete with the likes of them, but when I look at him and see the pride burning behind his eyes, I wonder if last night's encounter isn't what's driving him to this. After all, what better way to prove to the confederations that you're anything but an amateur than by snatching the *shar* right from under all their noses?

I sigh and push the pile of contracts away.

"We don't even know where to look."

"I have some ideas."

"We're ages behind everyone else. We've lost too much time."

"Not too much. The burglary was last month. The notices began coming in only a few days ago. And most hunters aren't positioned minutes away from one of the finest and busiest ports in the world."

"Boone—"

"This is our chance, Mal," Boone says, and I want to remind him that last night was supposed to be our chance, too, but I bungled the whole thing. Boone nearly abandoned me as his partner over the kraken pieces. What would he do if he had to choose between me and the *shar*?

"Maybe...the Drakes were right. Maybe we need to know our place," I say, and Boone flinches. "The *shar*...It's too much, Boone. Give me a job I can do, and I'll do it for you. This isn't it."

Boone blinks at me for a moment, and then he nods.

"All right. I thought you might say something like this. All right." He puts out a hand, lays it on top of the pile of papers, looks into my face. "Listen to me. Forget about the money, the competition, the opportunity. Forget about all that. Think about the *shar*. Think about what it means."

I shake my head. "I'm a blank, Boone, not one of Them. I'm not scared of it. It can't hurt me."

"Not you. Think, Mal. Think about your life. Think about what was done to you." He holds my gaze, his voice soft. "One of Them hurt you." He's whispering, whispering, his words like the rustle of leaves. "She took away your home. Your safety. You trusted her and she turned on you and your whole world changed. Think about that. Think about how safe you were, how secure, how happy, and she drove you out. She took it all away, and what's worse, she did it under the guise of friendship. She *betrayed* you, Mal. How can you let her get away with that? Don't you hate her for it? Don't you want to stop her?"

Boone reaches out and his fingertips hover over my sleeve, just barely not touching. "Think about what the *shar* could do. It would be so easy. Once it's in your hands, all you have to do is sail to the island. All you have to do is find her there. She took something away from you. You could do the same to her. It would be fair. It would be right. It's what she deserves." He tilts his head and studies me. "We could still sell the *shar*. A *shar* imbued with the magic of the Roe witch? The whole world would clamor for it. We could sell it for twice its value, and you would get the money, the prestige, but you could also get something else. You could get your revenge."

Leaning forward, he drops his voice even lower, so to hear him properly I have to hold my breath.

"It's what you want, isn't it? Isn't it the only thing you want? Isn't it all you've *ever* wanted?"

And the word that slips from my mouth comes so easily, so simply, it's as though it's been sitting there my whole life, just waiting to come out.

"Yes."

Eight

OCEAN

"THAT'S IT, ISN'T IT?" BOONE SQUINTS AT the island in the distance, a huge, dark mass growing against the horizon like a tumor. We're standing on the deck of the *Chispa*, a passenger ship that will arrive in Southampton, England, two weeks from now, and watching the last bit of land, the tiny period at the end of the shouting sentence of THE UNITED STATES OF AMERICA, drift closer.

"That's it," I say. "Prince Island."

"Funny how I always think it should be bigger." He leans against the bulwarks, rising up on his toes like he's about to lift into the air, and then he drops down to flat feet and smiles at me. "Can't wait to go back there, eh?"

"With a knife," I say, but I say it low enough that the few other passengers mingling on the deck can't hear. We're not the only hunters on this ship; on the opposite side of the deck, huddled together with their backs to us, two Norwegian brothers stand talking to each other in quiet voices. The Erslands are two of the most successful hunters in the world, famed for tracking down and selling magical people, and I'm not surprised to see them going after the *shar*—it's a lot easier to transport magical abilities stored in a knife rather than living, breathing people.

I'm not sure if they notice us, though. We're nowhere near as well known as the Erslands, a fact that rankles Boone more than me. When we boarded the ship, he made a point of saying hello to them, lifting his hat off his head with a smile.

"I'm a great admirer of your work!" he'd said, and they looked through him as though he were a ghost. "Heard the news out of Europe, I wager? Perhaps we should talk! Hunters should work together, after all."

He smiled his broad, Boone smile, but the Erslands only glanced at each other, boredom in their eyes, before one of them turned to Boone with a dismissive wave of his hand, muttering something sharp and hissing just under his breath. Boone's feet stumbled from underneath him and he abruptly turned away, frog-marching in the opposite direction of the brothers—a common deflection spell that I realized too late was also applied to me, because when I stood still, watching Boone walk away, red-cheeked and embarrassed, one of the brothers watched me with confusion. Quickly, I shoved my hands into my pockets and followed Boone down the deck, but as I left, I heard the brothers speaking to each other in rapid Norwegian, and my stomach dropped. Years of experience have made me good enough at detecting the tiny gestures and cues that mean someone's throwing magic at me, and usually I can respond naturally enough not to raise suspicion, but the Erslands are too adept at working with magic folk. And now they know there's something strange about me.

Boone's still talking, chattering away while I throw another glance over my shoulder at the Erslands, and I blink and look over at him.

"What was that?"

"I was saying you'd never expect that bit of rock out here," he says, his smile stretching into a wince, and as I study the approaching island, I'm not surprised to hear it. Ships leaving Boston don't always have to pass by Prince Island on their way to the open ocean, but this ship hooked south to take advantage of fairer weather, hugging Cape Cod before heading east into the deeper waters of the Atlantic. We've been sailing for so long now and we're so far out into the ocean that passengers would be forgiven for thinking land has long been left behind. Prince Island itself is famous, its name synonymous with whaling, and whaling synonymous with wealth, and the witches add plenty to the reputation, but it's so small, so far away, a humble little kingdom at the end of the world.

The ship passes the island's northeastern shore and the

island's only town, New Bishop, the whaling capital of the world. My stomach tightens as I make out the fuzzy shapes of buildings, the black shadows of whalers breaking up the sparkling waters of the harbor, but as uncomfortable as I feel to be standing here, watching my hometown slide past, I'm grateful at least that the ship won't sail any farther south, to the long, rocky tail that's the home of the Roes.

"I wonder what led them out here," Boone says, and I don't have to ask who "them" is to know he's talking about the Roes.

"I don't know," I say, my eyes blurring as they take in the view of the harbor. "A Roe woman was one of the first people to ever come to the island. She had a daughter, who had a daughter, on and on for generations. Now, it's just the mother and the girl."

"Essie."

My insides suddenly twist together, cold prickling along my skin. "Yes."

"Tell me about her," Boone says, his voice light, casual, but he knows it makes me feel anxious and angry to think about her, and when I give him a sharp look, he shrugs. "We're going to be hunting her, aren't we? I should know more about her than that she's a pretty girl who exiled you from your home. What was she like?"

"What was she like…" I know what he means, but all I can think about are the hundred small things I learned about her over the years. She used to dig her fingers into the sand every time we sat on the beach, like she was looking for a way to root herself. She'd go silent if someone teased her, but if she heard anyone say a bad word about me, she'd tell them, her voice quivering with fear or anger or both, to *stop*, because that was *very rude*. She liked pretty things, simple things, all the kinds of things her mother found unreasonably impractical: new dress, delicate shoes, a hair ribbon.

She liked peppermint. I remember that. And books. I can see her: small, sitting by the water with a book in her lap and her fingers sticky with candy. "Sometimes," she once whispered to me, "sometimes the pages glue together an' I've gotta steam them open again."

I remember, too, how she began to change. She stopped putting her hair in two plaits and instead curled it back into an elaborate bun that sat at the base of her neck, "a *sheeng-yon*," she called it, stretching out the word. I stared at her like she was another kind of creature, a grown-up girl who didn't like to go for walks in the grass anymore because it got her shoes muddy. Instead she started suggesting we visit the town candy shop, the florist, the trim little park where the island boys began congregating every afternoon to stop her and smile at her and ask her sweetly why she spent her time walking with an orphan boy and didn't she know she was such a pretty thing?

But I don't think Boone wants to know any of that, and so I just say, "She's not as powerful as the mother. She has her own gift, different from water magic. All the Roes had something special only they could do."

"Like what?"

"Well. One of the Roes could talk to the dead. Another one could erase memories. The mother—she smooths away what people feel, be it grief or joy or anger. She can make anyone feel nothing at all."

"And what is the girl's gift, then?"

I frown. "Love."

"How does it work?"

"I don't know. It hadn't come to her yet by the time I left the island." I drop my head and study the swirl of water curling outward from the ship as I remember Essie at eleven years old, running to me, crying, saying she couldn't stand it anymore, her mother hovering over her every day asking if she felt any different, if there was anything she could do that was special.

"Perhaps I'd pay attention to myself better if the first thing I saw each morning wasn't her face!" Essie had said, and she hiccoughed and pressed her hands to her cheeks, dainty even when upset, using her fingers as the handkerchief she couldn't afford. "She says it's a disgrace that my gift is taking so long. 'A disgrace and a disappointment, Essie Roe!'" She mimicked her mother perfectly, her sweet little face turning stiff and hard before melting back into misery. "But I'm rubbish at magic, Mal, and how can it be my fault my gift hasn't shown itself yet? I can't very well make it come!"

But like the fancy hair and attention to clothes, magic was a world I didn't know anything about. I patted her back and made a joke about it and told her it didn't matter, it would be all right, and she let out a short huff of air. She didn't talk to me about magic anymore after that.

"She'll be their witch someday?" Boone asks, rubbing the stubble on his chin, and I nod. "And when will that be? When will she have the Roe power?"

"Soon enough. It happens to all of them in time." I glance at him. "Is this about the *shar*?"

He lifts an eyebrow, like he's surprised I'm even asking. "Love magic won't be enough, boy. It will fetch a better price with the magic of the Roe witch—the true witch. She needs to have her magic before we cut her."

I shrug and look away. "Makes no difference to me. But I don't know when she'll get her magic. When her mother dies, I suppose. Or maybe when she has a child. By the time I left, she still didn't know what made the magic come. At least, she never told me."

"Hmm…" Boone frowns at the little island, his forehead wrinkling with concern. "Then I suppose we better find that out, eh?"

He claps me on my back and heads belowdecks to find something to eat, and I'm alone on the deck for the first time today, looking out across the water and sky and horizon at Prince Island.

Five years. Five years since I left, and I left like a stranger, like a thief, handing over every small penny I'd saved for a last-minute berth on a departing ship. I can remember the feel of the coins in my shaking, sweaty hands and how quickly I pushed them at the ship's steward, promising him more, promising him anything, if he would just get me on that ship.

I was careful. I picked a foreign ship, crewed by men who did not speak English and did not understand the word *blank*, the word suddenly spat at me from every Prince Islander who dared to come close enough.

For years, I'd put on a show for their benefit. A horse cart would whip past me, narrowly missing me, and I'd pat the charm hanging from my neck and say, "Good thing I have this!" loud enough for everyone to hear. Or I'd come back empty-handed from a fishing trip with all the other boys and toss my hook into the harbor, scowl, and say, "I wasted fifty cents on this and it doesn't even work proper!" But none of that mattered when my secret came out.

We'd gone for a walk, me and Essie, and I was impatient with her because she never wanted to go to the grass anymore, to share stories and tell secrets. She wanted to walk through town, and when I said I didn't, she lied, said her mother had put in an order for cloth at the dressmaker's and asked her to check on it. It was ridiculous, because the Roe witch didn't bother with dress orders and wouldn't ever ask Essie to check on something like that for her. I knew Essie just wanted to go through town because she was looking pretty that day, her cheeks pink and her eyes tilted under dark lashes, and she walked slowly, looking this way and that, hoping to catch someone's eye, I suppose, which she did enough. Even grown men had started to pay attention to her, looking up over their mugs of coffee or newspapers or cigars to watch her as she passed, serene and smiling like a princess.

"Let's go to the docks," she said, and I gave her a look, because the docks weren't any place for a young girl—not any girl, really. The docks belonged to the sailors, the dockworkers, the men of the whaleships and the boys who ran errands for them and dreamed of growing up to hold a harpoon. Although I'd been down there often enough, carrying lunches for a penny or passing along messages from the counting house to the agents' offices back on Main Street, I knew Essie had never been there before. No girl, not even the little daughters of captains about to see off their papas, ever had.

"What for?" I asked, and she lifted her shoulders into a shrug.

"I want to see the ships," she said, which was another lie. She wanted to see the boys, to smile at them and hear them call her pretty.

"Let's go up to Laurie McConnell's farm," I said, reaching for her hand and tugging her away. "I heard his mare had a little colt two days ago and Laurie's letting the boys feed 'im."

"No," she said, and she slipped her hand away. "I'm going to the docks. You can come with me if you want."

I frowned at her, feeling her distraction like a flea bite, just too irritating to ignore.

"The docks are boring," I said, and she gave me a flat look, rolling her eyes at me. She'd just started doing that, and she knew it drove me mad.

"What do you care about ships?" I asked. "You're never going to leave this island."

"So? Neither will you."

"Sure I will," I said, so casual, as though the idea of leaving didn't terrify me.

Essie looked at me like I had slapped her, blinking her wide blue eyes, and then those eyes narrowed. "You said once you'd never leave the island. You promised me."

"So what? If it bothers you so much, why don't you just come with me?" I gave her a look and then smirked. "Can't, then? You're always going to be on this island, and you're always going to be surrounded by an ocean, and your mother isn't ever going to let you leave."

"Shut your mouth, Mal," she said, squeezing her eyes closed, and I knew she was upset, but I didn't care. After weeks of feeling ignored by her, I wanted to touch her, somehow, even if I could only hurt her.

"I'm going to leave you all alone on this island someday, and you're never going to see me again," I said, my cheeks growing hot. "You'll be trapped here forever!"

She shoved me aside, crying, and I felt a little kick of satisfaction to watch her run away. I walked back through town with my hands in my pockets and my face turned up to the sunshine, and I thought about what I had said, what she had said. She deserved it—she deserved to cry and run away and feel bad. But then that little bud of satisfaction bloomed into guilt, and I pulled my hands from my pockets and frowned.

She had to know I didn't mean it. I wouldn't leave her like that, not ever.

I decided to find her, to apologize, to tell her she wasn't really trapped on this island and anyway, she'd never be alone, not when I couldn't ever imagine leaving. I looked for her in all her favorite spots—the park, the promenade, the candy store—before, red-faced and sweaty and tired and irritable again, I finally realized she must have gone to the very spot she had suggested: the docks.

And there she was, sitting pretty as a queen on a pile of crates set up like a throne, a dozen boys and men—islanders and foreigners alike—lounging around her with soppy smiles on their faces, laughing and joking and telling stories and looking for all the world completely enchanted.

I walked up to them all, hands clenched in my pockets, and I could tell she noticed me right away, her eyes passing over my face, her expression twitching. Then she turned to another boy, leaned in toward him with a smile, said something that made him throw back his head in laughter, and when her gaze slid back to my face, smooth and sharp, I knew she had said something about me.

I would have gone right then, but she clapped her hands

and called me over. "Mal!" she said, her high little voice ringing through the air. "I found you a ship to sail! You want to leave, don't you?"

"Essie—" I said, shaking my head, but she ignored me.

"This fellow here says his ship's on its way to the savage wastelands of Mexico. I think you'd fit right in!"

They laughed, but not cruelly—or, at least, not all of them cruelly—and one man, an island-born sailor, put his hand on my shoulder and said, "Ah, but he's a good lad! I'd be proud to have him sail on my crew! How would you like that? I could get you a berth on the *Post Boy* any day you wanted."

I looked at Essie, who glared back at me with narrowed eyes, and I said very clearly, "I just might take you up on that. Nothing and no one to keep me around here, anyway."

The sailor laughed and clapped me on the back. "That's the spirit! What can an island offer that compares to the adventure of the sea?"

"Yes," I said. "That's exactly it."

Essie's cheeks flushed, and she looked very quickly from the sailor to me before throwing her head back in laughter. "Oh, you don't want him!" she said, still laughing. "My mother spent so long on *Post Boy*'s spells, and she'll be furious when Mal ruins them!"

The sailor squinted. "What's that, then?"

"Essie..." I said, my stomach tensing, but she ignored me.

"You don't want someone like *him* on your boat!"

"Like what?" another sailor asked. I looked at Essie and shook my head and her mouth curved into a smile. I felt relief, relief because of course she would keep my secret, of course she was my friend and she cared about me and she wouldn't hurt me, she wouldn't ruin everything for me, and then she laughed again and said it.

He

is

a

blank.

My hands turn white from where I grip the edge of the ship, and I force myself to breathe slowly, in and out, force my heartbeat to plod along in a steady rhythm, but it's difficult to stay calm. I watch the island, thinking, *The next time I come here, I will have the* shar.

Pretty Essie Roe, turning her back on me, betraying me, taunting me up until the last moment before I left the island, when I went to get on the ship and, impossibly, she was there, almost like she was waiting for me. I saw her and I asked her if she was there to tell me she was sorry, but instead her pointed little face twisted in a frown and she said, "You should stay, Mal."

I laughed because I was so angry at her for thinking she could just ask me to stay, erase everything that had happened.

"And how good are you at memory spells?" I asked. "Can you make a whole island forget what I am?"

She blinked those blue-blue-blue eyes, all softness and innocence.

"Remember that day in the grass, Mal?" she said, her voice quiet. "Remember that rope glove? You know, if you weren't a blank—"

But I had finished listening to her and I shouldered my small pack and boarded the ship without looking back, knowing she would still be smiling that sweet little smile of hers. I don't know why she wanted me gone or why she wanted to hurt me like that, but she was smart enough to know what revealing my secret would lead to.

And I can see it, can almost *feel* it, burning away inside me, fire inside the hole she opened up, and the fire is low and dark and red but—for the first time now—it fuels me. For years whenever I thought of Essie Roe, I felt scared. I felt ashamed. I felt her power over me, the power she got simply by being the daughter of the Roe witch, and I know just by virtue of her last name and the blood flowing in her veins and the future waiting for her, she thinks she can do whatever she wants, even destroy a boy's life on a whim, and no one can ever touch her.

But the *shar* can touch her. It can take everything away from her. It can change her, make her see what it's like to feel just like anyone else.

What will she do when she sees me? Will she laugh at me? Will she pretend not to know me? Will she have forgotten me, looking at me like I'm a stranger, like I'm just another sailor swept in with the tide to visit her mother's cottage and buy my charms?

"It's me," I'll tell her, and as I think of this, picture her, grown up and standing in the Roe cottage and just as beautiful as the rumors say, my steady heartbeat jitters and skips. "It's Mal. Did you think you would never see me again? Did you think I'd be too scared to ever come back?"

The island is fading as we sail away, turning back into just another smudge on the horizon, a rapidly shrinking dark spot, and I squeeze my hands over the bulwarks and force my eyes to stay open, even as they water and sting from the salty breeze. I whisper to myself, to *her*, "I'm coming back, Essie. I'm coming back. And I'm going to hurt you just as much as you hurt me."

Nine

A WEEK INTO OUR TRIP ACROSS THE OCEAN and it's eight bells at the end of the first watch—midnight— when there's a knock at the door, and I glance at Boone.

"See who it is," he says, and I rise and cross the cabin. A wave of acrid cigarette smoke oozes out at me as I open the door to a large man with glittering brown-black eyes smoking in the darkness. It takes me a moment to filter through the shadows and my own surprise before I recognize him: It's one of the Ersland brothers, the hunters. Jonah or Jorah or some such.

"*God kveld.* Hee-lo," he says, his accent like heavy square nails pounding into wood. "I am hope I am not disturbing of you. I am request honor of company to, ah—" He mimes lifting a cup to his lips, teeth shining pale yellow. "Hunter fellowship, yes?"

"Yes," Boone says, jumping to his feet and crossing the room in two quick strides. Reaching with both hands, he takes Jorah or Jonah's palm and pumps it. With his usual buoyant smile, he says, "It'd be our honor. Lead the way, friend."

He touches a finger to his brow before gesturing down into the darkness, and in the moment Jorah-Jonah's back turns, Boone glances at me with a raised eyebrow, and I know he doesn't know what's happening but he's pleased about it. It's not every hunter who gets an invitation to drink with the Erslands, and Boone practically floats down the gangway.

I follow them, ignoring the lead in my stomach as I close the door behind me. I don't bother with a key in the lock—which can be picked—but instead take a moment to hang on the inside handle a charm that will bar from entering the room anyone except for me or Boone—Boone because he has a corresponding charm in his pocket, me because, of course, the magic doesn't touch me.

"This way, this way," the man says, and he leads us two doors down to a starboard cabin. *"Velkommen."*

He opens the door of the cabin in one quick motion, so quick that I see Boone's hand twitch reflexively toward the knife at his belt, but inside there's nothing but a cozy domestic scene. The other Ersland brother sits at a table laid out with a shining silver samovar, the source of curls of steam and the rich smell of coffee, and the whole cabin glows golden in the flickering light of half a dozen fat yellow candles.

"Ah," the second brother says, rising to his feet with a smile. "Thank you for joining us. I am Nils. You have met Jorah. We are very pleased to make your acquaintance."

"John Boone." Boone puts out his hand. "And my partner, Mal."

Nils takes Boone's hand, but his eyes glide to me, looking me up and down in one long, careful swoop that gets my heart beating faster. I notice that after he drops Boone's hand, he doesn't reach for mine, but—I realize with amusement—he doesn't mean to offend. Actually, he's paying me a courtesy: Hunters wear so many charms against violence and attack that they can be set off simply by touching someone with an offensive power. He thinks I'm an Other.

"Please," he says, gesturing to a chair. "Sit."

Boone, still smiling that friendly, open smile, takes the seat offered but rakes his eyes over the chair facing the cabin door before glancing at me, and I move quickly to sit there, anxious to get my back to a wall.

I take in the cabin in one easy sweep as I sit: It's neat, carefully laid out, only two small packs and one wooden trunk with handsome iron handles. A journal, closed, sits on the pillow of the lower bunk. I'd make a decent effort to lift it if I thought there was a chance it was written in anything but Norwegian. No charms sit out in the open, but Nils's fingers glitter with two rings—both set with large, square stones—

that are almost certainly charms, and as Jorah takes his own seat, I catch a glimpse of a curved bracelet of bone around his left wrist. It's a charm against deception, and I wonder whether they intend it for me or for Boone.

"Coffee? It is our own brew." Nils lifts the samovar and Boone accepts, complimenting everything from the size of the samovar to the smell of the coffee. I admit, the samovar is a good touch: a communal pot to eliminate suspicion of poison, designed to put me and Boone at ease—which only sets my nerves on edge.

"Two packs and you haul this beauty with you wherever you go?" Boone asks, lifting his small silver cup in a toast. "You're a pair of men who have their priorities straight."

Nils smiles, and when I glance at Jorah, he's watching Boone with a careful, even look.

"We have another trunk in cargo," Nils says, which was exactly the information Boone wanted to know and the reason he asked about the samovar in the first place. "I believe I saw one of your trunks in the hold as well."

"Well, I like to pack light, but the boy refuses to travel anywhere without a full brass band, and really, they *are* so useful when you think about it."

Nils laughs, but Jorah's expression only goes blank. I wonder if his English is so poor he can't follow Boone's wit—Boone's only weapon, if their charms mean the Erslands can't be Silvertongued.

"Smells delicious," Boone says, licking his lips. "But I can't help but think it might be even tastier with something stronger." He reaches into his waistcoat and pulls out a small jade-green flask with a tiny gold top. "Drop of bingo?"

The Erslands nod, after only the slightest hesitation. Maybe they think Boone is planning to poison *them*, but I know that bottle is filled with plain alcohol—albeit alcohol charmed to turn any tampered liquid it touches bright green. Boone pours into every cup, and I tense for a moment before studying the coffee in mine. It remains a steady, muddy brown, and I let out a small breath and drink.

"Well!" Boone says, holding his cup close to his chest. "To what do we owe the pleasure of this invitation?"

"I suppose you could call it...professional curiosity." Nils tilts his head in amusement. "You hunt the *shar*, no?"

"Oh, that little thing?" Boone laughs. "Infinite power and infinite riches and the world's magical population at your mercy? We might be interested. Aren't you?"

"Of course," Nils says, and he says it with a kind of grimace, the white tips of his canine teeth pressing into his bottom lip. A movement to my left causes me to look quickly at Jorah, now running his hands over something small and shiny: a knife? A lighter? A charm? In the candle glow, I can't quite make it out. "We were offered a contract in Albany to track down a young woman who can read minds, but when we heard about the *shar*'s discovery, we abandoned the hunt." He smiles. "This is the first time we are ever failing to collect on a contract."

Jorah's hands move quicker, his fingers flying so fast over the tiny object concealed there that they almost blur. I feel my stomach clench, my feet instinctively roll forward to rest lightly on my toes. If it's magic they're planning, I'm safe, but I see Boone notice Jorah's motions and a tiny muscle tenses just below his eye. Slowly, I slide my hands from the table to my lap and rest one on the hilt of my dagger, jostling it loose and ready.

"Bully for you," Boone says, and he actually manages to make it sound like a genuine compliment. "I suppose we're the competition then, eh? Well." He lifts his teacup in salute. "May the best team win!"

"Yes, indeed." Nils smiles and raises his cup in the air, but both Jorah and I keep our hands below the table. "This is why we are so curious about you. It is only good sense to know other hunters, but we admit we have not heard your names before."

"Oh, no?" The muscle below Boone's eye twitches again. "You're sure about that? I've been hunting for well on a decade. Maybe you heard about a job I did in Guadalajara, about eight years ago. I'd gotten a contract to—"

"No," Nils says, still smiling. "No, I did not hear." He glances at me. "And what have you worked on?"

Boone's expression curdles for a moment, and then he lets out another bark of laughter. "Mal? He's just a boy. My assistant. A good lad, but still learning the ropes."

"Tell me more about yourself," Nils says, ignoring Boone,

and I look around the table, Nils, Boone, Jorah—all of them watching me carefully. "Where are you from?"

"Oh," I say, and I try to keep my voice light. "Here and there. All over, really."

"Forgive me, but I thought I overheard the other day— you come from Prince Island, do you not?" Nils, too, keeps his voice casual, but his eyes burn into me, predatory and possessive, and slowly, I swallow another mouthful from my cup to keep from shaking.

"You've got good ears," I say, and, smiling, he shrugs. "I haven't been back there in years."

"A remarkable place. The Roe witch is...quite impressive." He leans back into his chair. "We've visited the island a number of times in the hopes of better understanding her abilities, but it appears she has safeguards in place."

I bet she does, I think. The Roe witch has been around almost as long as the island, and the Erslands aren't the first— or the last—to try to get close to her.

"We find her magic very curious. There is a...flavor to it. I wonder..."—Nils strokes his chin, watching me—"how much you might know about it."

"What do you mean?"

His eyes glitter, and to my side I feel Jorah tense and see his hands go rigid around whatever he's holding.

"If the Roe witch were to enchant someone," Nils asks, his words so careful, "would you know anything about this?"

Boone's cup rattles as he sets it down roughly on the table. "What is this? What are you asking him?"

"We have noticed something...unique about him and would like to know more. I suppose it is that old *professional curiosity*."

My eyes widen and my hand grips the hilt of my knife so hard I can feel my pulse pound through my fingers, heavy and fast, but Boone looks calm. Careful.

"There is nothing you need to know about him," he says, and Nils frowns.

"This is...what I had thought you would say." Nils nods at Jorah, a nearly imperceptible tilt of the head, and I'm on my feet, my dagger out, my movement knocking over the cups still resting on the table, filling the air with the heavy scent of coffee and Boone's strong liquor, and as I crouch, ready to jump at whoever's going to attack first, Jorah sits still as a post and Nils sweeps out a hand, blinks at it for a moment, frowns, and knocks his knuckles against the table.

"Peace, Mal," he says. "Jorah is only—Jorah, please."

My eyes narrow as Jorah places his hands, still closed around the object, on the table, but when he spreads them open, I see the metallic glint is nothing more than half a dozen solid gold pieces. Money.

"Sit, please, with my apologies for disturbing you," Nils says, and he reaches out a hand to me but gently, like he's coaxing a wild dog. I'm buzzing, practically floating, but I glance at Boone and he nods and I sit.

"Your partner has a nervous disposition," Nils says to Boone, who lifts his shoulders in a jerky kind of shrug.

"He has a talent for sniffing out danger," Boone says, and Nils makes a small noise.

"Hmm. Well. Perhaps his *Talents* fail him now, because we do not offer danger but opportunity. Did you not say that we should work together?"

Boone's mouth actually drops open, his eyes wide and white as saucers, and he glances at me for a moment before looking back at Nils. I don't doubt he meant it when he offered our partnership on the deck last week, but he certainly didn't expect the brothers to take him up on it. The Erslands have always worked alone, even though plenty of other greats have wanted to work with them, from the Penten brothers of the Smoky Mountains of Tennessee to the Amalgamated Thieves' Guild of D'Orsay, and even, rumors say, the New York office of the DeWitts, a band of hunters notorious for their investigative work.

They turn down offers to partner with the great and famous, but they ask to join *us*? I try to read Boone's mind, figure out what he's thinking, but after his moment of initial surprise, his expression's gone smooth and pleasant once again.

"We'd...we'd be honored," he says, and from the glow on his face, I know his ego is beating out his suspicions. This is it, this is what he's always wanted: a chance to get in with the established hunters. I can practically see the cogs spinning in his head, the plans and dreams and goals floating before him, first the partnership and then the *shar* and then his own confederation, with him sitting king-like at the top, his name counting for something in our world.

"Wonderful!" Nils says. "In a show of goodwill, we offer you these gold pieces and our skills. All we ask in return is that you make clear to us your partner's gift."

Gift. I look at Boone, and the smile on his face wilts.

"Mal doesn't have a gift," he says, and for a moment Nils is silent, threading his fingers together before pressing his hands, prayerlike, against his lips.

"Is it that you do not trust us?" he asks, his voice soft. "I will tell you one of our secrets. Jorah is a Percept."

I bite back the swear that climbs my throat. A blasted *Percept*. Of course. They're not quite Others—more like people highly attuned to magic and trained in how to recognize and identify it. Most people, so I've heard, can actually feel magic as a kind of tingle, but Percepts can interpret these feelings and tell not just when a charm or spell has been cast but what specifically that magic does. It's a handy skill to have if you're a hunter and even more so if you're a slaver, searching for a particular kind of Other.

"Jorah is quite skilled at detection," Nils says. "All he requires is a single touch."

Boone lifts an eyebrow and then glances at his hand, remembering, I'm sure, the moment when he crossed our cabin to the open door and took Jorah's hand in his.

"Silvertongue," Jorah grunts, and Nils smiles.

"Yes," he says. "And so, this is our offer: one dozen gold pieces and our partnership, and all this boy has to do is put his hand in Jorah's."

Jorah lifts his hand, stretching it out to me so that it hovers right in front of my chest, his dark eyes unblinking as he waits for me to move. I don't know what would happen if I touched him. I don't know if Percepts can detect blanks or if he'll sense nothing about me or if just by virtue of that, he'll guess what I am.

They can't know I'm a blank. They can't. Maybe for Boone having a blank as a partner is worth the risk, but for slavers like the Erslands, I'm a threat. No slaver would allow a blank near an Other meant for auction—how would they explain to the buyer if the Other's magic didn't work properly? And that's just if they're thinking about business. Because everyone—and certainly any hunter—knows that blanks can't be trusted, that they'll go bad in the end, that they're dangerous and deadly and wild. If the Erslands know what I am, they won't want me to be their partner, and if they don't want me to be their partner, there's no reason for them not to try to kill me.

A drop of sweat slides across my temple and I realize they're all still looking at me, waiting to see what I'll do, if I'll take Jorah's hand.

Instead, I smile.

"Want to know my talents?" I ask, and Jorah's fingers twitch. "Easy to find out. Just ask any bar girl in Boston."

Nils's eyes narrow. "This isn't a joke."

"And Mal isn't one of your targets to be analyzed," Boone says.

"No. But if we are to work with him, we will have to understand him."

"What's to understand? He works well, he gets the job completed. There's nothing more to know."

"Perhaps, as a Silvertongue, you do not value honesty. But for my brother and me, it is essential. If the boy has no gift, then taking my brother's hand will mean nothing. If he has something to hide, we cannot trust him."

"Trust goes both ways," Boone says, but I can hear him wavering. It's the kraken all over again, a chance for him to rise up in the hunter world, and all he has to do is give me up, give up my secret. I stare at him, my heartbeat pounding in my temples, and I'm thirteen years old again, standing on the docks, knowing Essie would never betray me even as the words spill out of her lips. She gave me up for nothing more than to win an argument and try out her blooming, poisonous charm. But for Boone it would be for money and power and everything he wants, everything tied up neat and waiting for him, and I stare at him, I stare at him. Sweat dampens my palms, and he catches his lip with his teeth for a moment—then smiles.

"I'm afraid we'll have to turn down your offer," he says, all pleasance and lightness, and rises from the table.

Relief pours over me like sweet oxygen after a long dive and, stunned, grinning, I stand. Jorah says something in rapid

Norwegian that makes Nils's expression curdle, and for a moment I'm so certain he'll grab me that I put my hand back on my dagger, but his outstretched hand just coils into a fist before slamming down on the table.

"I am disappointed," Nils says, still sitting, watching us. "I am terribly disappointed. If you are not our partners, you are our competition, and we will not give up the chase for the *shar*."

"Well then, what fun is a hunt with only one dog?" Boone touches a hand to his forehead in a small salute. "See you on the trail, brothers. Mal? Let's get back to our cabin."

Without another backward glance, he sweeps to the door, opens it, and disappears, me at his heels, and the Erslands don't wait for us to leave before dropping their heads forward to whisper and hiss at each other.

And even though I can't speak a lick of Norwegian, I'm pretty sure I know exactly what they say.

Ten

LONDON

JUST AS THE PARTICULAR STINK OF BURN-
ing oil transports me to the whaling refineries of Prince
Island, the moment I step off the train and the soot-thick air
of London floods my nostrils, I relax into the familiar patterns of the city.

If the hunting world had a capital, London would be it.
Hunters of every stripe and color know to make their way to
the Fleet Street Market and Hunters' Alley at the western end
of the city, where a person can buy flight-granting feathers
or silver shoes to get one dancing all night. Magic folk visit,
too, to pick up the more exotic supplies for their spell work,
like devil's grit, which comes from the volcanoes of the Pacific

Islands, or hair from the packs of invisible wolves of Russia. There are auction houses, with dozens of sales going on every day, from the tiny lots of broken-down magical artifacts—more curious than useful—to eight-foot-tall cursed idols that have to be carted in under the care of half a dozen specially trained Others.

In London, unlike in the States, it is illegal to buy and sell a person, but magic folk don't seem to count, and so in a darkly lit corner of the market, it's possible to buy trained assassins and little girls gifted with Talents in cooking or childcare. There are offensively skilled folk for armies and plant-charmers to keep your farmlands green and heavy with crops. I've seen water witches, too, and wind wizards for sale—"Never miss a shipping deadline!" the auctioneers bark. "Flabby sails are a thing of the past!"—and they cost a pretty penny, what with ships being so important to trade, to military might and political influence, but none of them were ever of the quality or skill of the Roes. The Roe witch at the hunters' market in London would fetch a high price, but the ability to control Roe magic with the *shar*—that would set off a stampede of buyers.

Usually when Boone and I make our way to Hunters' Alley, it's either to sell off a lot of goods or to pick up a new contract, but today we're here to find out more information on the *shar*. And we're not alone—we parted ways with the Erslands before we boarded the train in Southampton, but otherwise it seems like every hunter in the world has come to the Fleet Street Market, and all of them want to talk about the *shar*. Where is it? Has anyone actually seen it? Who could have stolen it from that old woman, and what did they do with it? We hardly know any more than anyone else, but we have an advantage in Boone's years of contacts and Silvertongue, and we're here to use them both.

"There she is." Boone touches my shoulder and nods at an older woman working a stall near the northern entrance of the market. Unlike most of the other sellers, she's sitting with her feet up, watching the flow of traffic around her stall with all the care and concern of an old dog half-asleep on a sunny front porch, but when she sees Boone, she smiles, her tanned face splitting along ancient lines, and lifts a hand in hello.

"You'd better have brought me something," she says, her feet still propped up on the stall, one toe of her boot making lazy circles in the air.

"Isn't my presence present enough?" Boone asks, but he reaches into his waistcoat and pulls out a golden squash blossom of a bottle filled with sweet-smelling perfume. He hands it over to the woman, who takes it and studies it with the eye of someone used to spotting fakes and forgeries.

When she turns to me, her eyes widen, and she laughs. "Look at this one! Every time I see him he's grown a foot! You'd better be careful, Boone, or all your money will go to bigger hats and longer britches! Come here, boy, and give your auntie Ruth a kiss before you get too tall to see her."

I cross over to the stall and swoop down, pecking her cheek, and she lands a sticky-wet kiss on my jaw that stings and itches and that I can't wait to wipe off. I like Ruth, and I've known her almost as long as I've known Boone, but she has a tendency to look at me the same way she scrutinized Boone's perfume bottle, as though she's expecting to find something she doesn't like. She used to be a hunter herself, and she claims she was part of the fabled Miss Minnie's, the only hunting confederation made up of women—although I don't believe her. Miss Minnie's is full of ladies, gentlewomen with Talents whose families chose not to hide what their daughters were but encourage it, and the membership—secret, of course—is rumored to include duchesses, kings' mistresses, the daughters of bank owners and judges. Ruth might have all the skills of a Miss Minnie's girl, but she's closer to a fishwife than a queen.

"Come in, sit down," she says, waving Boone and me toward a pair of stools stacked at the back of the stall, "and don't tell me you're here to talk about that blasted knife."

"Fine bit of news, isn't it?" Boone asks, and as we sit, he leans in closer with a smile. "The *shar*, discovered at last!"

"Just a load of bother," says Ruth, who isn't one of Them and has nothing to fear from the knife's discovery. "It's all anyone in these parts can talk about, and they all want to know: 'Ruthie, dear, heard anything about the *shar*? Heard anything about who might be working the job?'"

"Well? Heard anything about the *shar*? Heard anything about who's working the job?"

Ruth gives Boone a sour frown. "Then you haven't got

any more sense than the rest?" She nods at me. "You at least I thought would know not to bother with all this."

"What can I say?" I shrug. "He can be very persuasive."

"Not *persuasive*, I hope," Ruth says, raising her eyebrows, and what she means is that it's poor form for a hunter to use his Talents on his partner, and that Boone shouldn't be Silvertonguing me. She doesn't know I'm a blank—Ruth's sweet, and I don't think she'd go as far as kill me if she found out, but she'd at least refuse to work with us again. I just laugh and tell her a half-truth, that Boone couldn't hoodwink me if he tried.

"That's worse, then," Ruth says. "A fool leading a fool."

"Come on, now, Ruth," Boone says, and he's smiling but it looks strained. "Tell us what you've heard."

"What I've heard? All right. I've heard that half the confederations in operation have set their resources on the trail and the other half are getting ready. I've heard that Merritt Basking's scuttled the Lorreys and called them all back to Boston. I've heard the Mountain Men have already stationed agents in cities from San Francisco to Yokohama, and that scoundrel Louis Vitner stormed through here last week, buying up every mind reader and scryer he could get his hands on." Ruth shakes her head. "You're too late, Boone, and this is too big a job for you. Stick to the small fish and let the confederations beat each other bloody over this."

I glance at Boone, wondering if he'll take Ruth's warnings any better than he took mine, but he stares at her, unblinking, his smile stretched and wolfish. "That's not the information I'm after."

"Well, it's what you should be hearing. I mean it—you haven't got the resources to go after the *shar*. And if you do find it—" Ruth's words break off in a bark of cynical laughter. "They'd track you down and kill you before you could say boo."

"I don't have to say boo. I just have to get it to an auction house."

"And what house would take it? What house would risk its relationship with the confederations to trade with an independent like you?"

"A house smart enough to know the money and prestige brought in by handling the *shar* is worth alienating every confederation under the sun, not to mention a house that knows to get good with an independent capable of tracking down something like the *shar*."

"Ah," Ruth says, lifting her eyebrows. "You mean to build your own confederation, don't you?" She smirks. "Boone, the little gray donkey knows he can't charge into war as a king's steed."

"But he can bite and kick and gallop as good as any fancy horse."

Ruth shakes her head. "I'm sorry. I can't help you. Even if I wanted to, everything that comes through here is just rumor and suspicion."

"I've got ears for rumors."

Another head shake, and Boone's smile slips a moment. "Come on, Ruth. There's something you're not telling me." He licks his lips, suddenly serious. "What have you heard? Tell me."

I glance at him, my eyes narrowed. He's using his magic on her, Silvertonguing her to get information out of her, and if it's poor form to try to bewitch a partner, it's the lowest of the low to charm a contact like this, a move so repugnant that Ruth wouldn't be out of line to kick us from her stall and say she never wants to see us again. I tear my eyes from Boone to study her, to see if she can feel Boone's magic. Ruth's no Percept, but the best hunters develop a kind of second sense when detecting charms and spells. Still, not even Ruth would expect an attack while sitting and chatting with two old friends in the comfort of her stall, and when her eyes go droopy, sleepy, her mouth slack, I know she has no idea what's happened.

"The *shar* was stolen by a young man named Graham Childes," Ruth says, her voice flat, stripped of her usual humor and warmth. "Don't bother looking for him; he's already dead. He was a common hunter, just starting out, and I doubt he even knew what he had. Sold the *shar* to a jeweler for the stones in the hilt."

"A common hunter stole the most famous magical artifact in the world?" Boone asks.

"His auntie was Betty Larson's cribbage partner, and for years he'd heard rumors that somewhere locked up in one of her trunks was a fabulous knife. The old woman had spells, of course, against trespassing, but they were effective only against strangers. Graham Childes walked right into her cottage."

"Who killed him?" Boone leans forward. "Who has the *shar* now?"

The Ruth I know would have laughed, teased Boone for his impatience, and maybe stood up to make herself a cup of tea, just to watch him wriggle and wait, but this Ruth just blinks, long and slow, and says, "The jeweler worked with magical artifacts and recognized the *shar*. He bought it from the boy for half a crown and took it here, to London, to sell on the markets, but on the evening he arrived, he was murdered. Throat slit ear to ear and all his belongings stolen."

"Then it's gone?"

Ruth shakes her head. "A woman in the shop across the street told the police she saw three men in red kerchiefs walking away from the alley where the jeweler was killed." Ruth shrugs. "The police haven't a clue where to look. 'Three men in red kerchiefs' means little to them."

But not to us.

Boone and I trade glances, and he nods. "The Luciferidies," he says, his voice soft, as though he's worried he'll be overheard, and a shiver dances down my back. I haven't run into many Luciferidies in my years hunting, but I know enough about them to put them well low on the list of people I'd like to see with the *shar*. They aren't quite a confederation of hunters—at least not anymore. They began as river pirates on the Mississippi, where they steered sleek, small steamboats recognizable by their red devil mastheads and tracked down magical people to sell into slavery.

In the past few years, though, under the leadership of a man named Remy Mickelson, they've grown increasingly hostile toward magic folk. There are a lot of people who are wary of Others, especially the few who use their Talents to attack or steal or manipulate and who prove annoyingly difficult to punish for their crimes. The Luciferidies are among those who think Others should be held accountable for using magic against regular folk, and although they had some support in the States, they managed to squander any goodwill after a particularly nasty incident three years ago. A young girl, an animal charmer, was accused of setting a wolf on a neighbor, and the Luciferidies caught and executed her.

Well, you hear these kinds of stories every now and then, but the girl was four years old and the neighbor bit only once, and after the girl died, taking her magic with her, the wolf came back and attacked another fellow, and most agreed: The Luciferidies had gone too far. As a result, the whole group fled to Europe, where you can still see them on any number of street corners, passing out handbills and proclaiming the evils of magic folk.

"They have it, then," Boone says, sounding nervous. "And what do they intend to do with it? Use it to cut out the magic of every Other they find?"

"That is pure speculation," Ruth says. "But there are whispers that the Luciferidies have plans for the *shar*. They want to . . . do something to it. Change it, somehow."

"Change it? How?"

"I don't know. No one knows."

Boone lets out an angry sigh. "Surely there must be *something* else. Something the Luciferidies have been up to? Tell me."

I shoot him an angry glance. "Boone—" I say, but he cuts me off with a shake of his head, and Ruth closes her eyes a moment, the spell working through her.

"I heard . . . It is just a suspicion . . . A scholar named Romesh Tagore is missing."

"Who is he? Why does he matter?"

"He arrived in London last week to run a stall for the Great Exhibition. He disappeared not long after the Luciferidies were rumored to have taken the *shar*."

"You think they kidnapped him?"

Ruth only shrugs.

"What do they want with this scholar?" Boone asks.

"I don't know," Ruth says. "Something to do with his research, I suppose."

"What is that?"

"I don't know. He disappeared before he could present it."

"You know," Boone says, his face tight with accusation. "Tell me."

She shakes her head again and Boone frowns, leans forward.

"*What is it?*" he asks again, and I glance at him, uncertain.

"Boone..." I say, but he dismisses me with a narrow-eyed glare and turns back to Ruth.

"What was he working on? Tell me!"

Ruth begins shaking, trembling like a rope stretched too tight as Boone's magic works through her. I know what can happen when a person is pushed too hard, when a mind is invaded like this. I can see her quivering, about to snap, and, anxious, I put a hand on Boone's shoulder.

"Stop it," I say. "It's too much!"

Boone's eyes go wide and he sits back heavily as Ruth blinks, shakes her head, smiles, and looks from Boone to me and back again. The color blooms back to her cheeks, and she fans herself with her hand.

"Blast, it's stuffy in here, isn't it? Felt faint for a spell... but as I was saying: I'm sorry, Boone, dear," she says, and she sounds her old self again, snappy and sharp. "I wouldn't be doing you any favors repeating wild speculation. You'll just have to content yourself with lesser quarry than the *shar.*"

"As usual, you are probably right," Boone says, and he leans forward to kiss her cheek before standing up and nodding at me. "Come on, Mal. We've got to get back to our room."

"Take care of yourself," Ruth says to me, and when I bend to give her a kiss, she snatches one of my hands and pulls me close. "And be careful around that one. Too slick for his own good. He'd fool you twice before you knew he opened his mouth."

I don't know what to say. I don't know if I should tell her what he's done; he's my partner, we have to rely on each other, but charming a friend like Ruth just isn't right, and I open my mouth, still not sure what words will come out, but it doesn't matter—Boone laughs and pulls me away.

"Oh, Ruth," he says, his face weary but his smile as charming as ever. "You need to learn to trust your friends! You wouldn't ever think me capable of something like that, would you?"

Her sharp eyes narrow, look him over, and for half a moment I wonder if she sees right through him. But then she smiles. She reaches out and takes his hand and pats it, fond and sweet.

"Not you, Boone," she says. "Never you."

Eleven

"WHAT WAS THAT BACK THERE?" I ASK THE moment Boone and I leave the market. It's a gray day, steel in the sky, the fall wind suddenly sharp and cold.

"I am sure I have no idea what you're talking about," Boone says.

"Ruth. You charmed her."

"I charm a lot of ladies."

"Boone." I stop walking and give him a look, and he pauses before looping an arm around my shoulders and leading me forward. I narrow my eyes at the hand dangling on my shoulder, suspicious. It's a strangely warm gesture for him—he's usually too nervous about my blankness affecting his Talent to touch me—and I wonder if this is his way of trying to make me trust him again, to feel at ease.

"Now, Mal. Where's this burst of morality coming from?" he asks. "I wouldn't have thought you above a bit of trickery to get a job done."

"This isn't a bit of trickery. This is using your magic on a friend who trusts you."

"And what kind of friend lies to another about what she knows? You could tell she was keeping something from us, couldn't you? And she was! As far as I am concerned, she good as invited me to charm her." When Boone catches my frown, he squeezes my shoulder and leans in closer. "Look, boy, I didn't *want* to do it, you know that. But did you hear what she said? The Luciferidies have the *shar*! Ruth was going to keep her mouth shut about it!"

"Maybe she should have," I say, sliding out from under his arm. "Maybe this isn't something we should be chasing after. The Luciferidies...they killed that jeweler. The boy. They kidnapped the scholar. Boone, maybe we should stay out of this. Leave them alone. They got the *shar*—it's over."

He tilts his head to look at me, his expression very cold. "Over, is it?"

"They're going to go after magic folk," I say. "Easier to cut than to kill, right? And in case you've forgotten, *you're* one of Them."

"You're thinking of it all wrong, boy. Once word gets out that the Luciferidies have the *shar*, every Other in the world is going to offer their last penny to get it away from them. The *shar* just tripled in value!" He gives me an open, expectant look, but I just shake my head.

"I don't care about the value."

"No," Boone says, and his eyes go to slits. "But you still want your revenge."

My stomach tightens and I feel the little monster inside me growl. Yes. Yes, I still want my revenge.

"I'm going after the *shar*," he says, and his voice is suddenly soft. "We're going after the *shar*. Together."

I sigh but finally nod my head. And of course I do. I'm Boone's little ragtag, his shadow. Where he goes, I go, always. His smile grows.

"But," I say, miserable, the pit in my stomach deepening. "*Ruth*. That was—you can't do that. Not to her."

Boone just squeezes my shoulder before dropping his hand and starting to walk away, *Conversation over* written in every inch of his body, but I can't let it go. I have to know. I have to ask him.

"Have…have you done this kind of thing before?" I ask, and I glance over at him but he's looking straight ahead, eyes set and steady, hands shoved into his pockets, and I would have thought he never even heard me if not for the muscle along his jaw that jumps and tenses.

"No," he finally says, and he says it cold, as though he's offended I would even ask, as though I'm supposed to trust him, supposed to take everything he says for truth even though

I know, better than anyone else in the world, how good he is at lying.

We don't head back to our boardinghouse right away. As usual, Boone makes a detour for the hunter bars, only we're not here for celebration but to find out information about the Luciferidies: if they're still in London, if anyone knows what they might be planning.

When we reach one of our favorite hunters' pubs, we split up, Boone heading straight for a table of boisterous hunters flush from the auction houses, me for the long, scarred bar and the barkeep. It's a delicate thing, asking for information in a place like this, and I'm not as good at it as Boone. And asking about the Luciferidies only makes this harder—they're vindictive and violent and wouldn't like someone like me or Boone looking into their business. Even though I'm careful, I don't learn much; the barkeep says he saw three men in red kerchiefs come through a few days ago, but they were quiet, bought their drinks and drank them and left and that's the last he saw of them.

I'm thanking the barkeep and looking around for Boone when one of the drunken celebrators, his face red with splotches, launches himself at me, laughing, throwing ale into the air and down the front of my second-best shirt.

"Have a drink, lad!" he says, and the monster inside me

pricks its ears, stretches, paws at the ground, and I take the mug offered to me without another thought.

"Cheers," I say, lifting the mug to my lips, but there's nothing more than a mouthful of beer, and when I set it down with a frown, another man sitting at the bar watching me laughs.

"Een't enough?" he asks, and the smile on my face falters, my hand outstretched to the bar and my stomach somewhere around my feet because I know that accent like I know the sound of my own breathing, and I would bet every drop of blood in my veins that this is a man from Prince Island.

What he's doing in a hunter bar in London is anyone's guess, but I'm not anxious to find out, so I laugh and duck my head and turn without saying anything, turn and look for Boone, for escape. I think I've made it when I feel a hand on my arm and hear the words I've been afraid of since the day five years ago when I sailed away from my home: "Hey there. Don't I know you?"

I swing my cap on my head, yank it low over my ears, smile, and say, "Not likely, friend," but when I try to pull away, the hand tightens.

"I do, I do know you, you're—" He squints at me, waiting for me to say my name, and I'm searching, scrabbling my brain for something to tell this man. No, not "this man"—he's right, I do know him, Percy Blythe, a year or two older than me, and he had an older brother named Charles and a younger sister named Alice, and he was there that day. He was at the docks when Essie told my secret and broke my heart. I need to get away before he says it, before he tells this bar why I left the island, and everyone hears it and someone decides to play at heroism and stamp out the nasty blank.

"Malcolm. Malcolm, een't it?"

"No," I say, and I try to pull my arm free, but again his grip tightens.

"Yes. Mal. I remember. The orphan. The one who always played with the Roe girl. You disappeared. You went away." Percy's eyes are hard as he takes me in, quick as a dog sizing up a rabbit, and when I look back at him, I see he has all the makings of a whale man: the strong arms, the big, callused hands, the cheeks shiny and dark from the sun, and, of course, a Roe charm, dangling from a waxed black string to hang directly over his heart.

"What have you been up to all these years?" he asks, and he asks it as if he's accusing me of something, as if he expects me to tell him I've been eating babies and throwing widows into wells.

"I have to go," I say, because I can't think of anything else to say and because the way he's staring at me—angry, almost, and confused and far too interested—has turned my mind to jelly and ripped open the hole in my chest, and I'm thirteen years old again, odd and cast off and strange, meeting a boy whose life I should have had but who is as different from me as a cow from a castle.

"The witch, the girl, she still talks about you." His grip

tightens, his arm stiff, and now it's clear to both of us that he's holding on to me because he doesn't want me to leave, keeping me close the same way you keep a mad dog close—to stop it from getting away and harming anyone.

"She's pretty as a picture these days," Percy says, his voice hard, "but too good to spend an afternoon with any island boy, and folks say it's your fault. Folks say you turned her off us forever." His eyes narrow. "Hey. Hey, remember just before you left, that day at the docks?"

Knife, get your knife, get it out and put it in his gut his throat his face his chest just stop him silence him keep the secret safe keep yourself safe! The monster inside me screams, but I am like a dead thing, as helpless today in this bar with a knife in my boot and at my hip and a gun in a holster under my jacket as I was that day five years ago with my empty hands and my innocence. And just like on that day, I can only watch and wait for the truth to come out and for the consequences to crush me.

"She called you a—"

"What's this! A new friend?" And it's Boone, it's Boone, and he's got his arm around Percy's shoulders and a smile on his face and eyes like little blades, cutting through me. Percy's hand slackens on my arm. "Lad, I don't know what it is you're doing here in this ragged little pub when the Huntsman serves a better mug and better bowl than anywhere else in London, and it's just a short walk on the other side of the city!"

Percy frowns but lets go of my arm.

"I've a friend here with me," he says, and Boone slaps him on the back.

"Then gather him up and make your way out! The night is young and so are you, and you've got better things to do than talk up with old acquaintances you barely remember. Why, I bet the moment you walk out of here"—Boone's eyes glitter as he nods his head at Percy—"you'll forget ever having run into him in the first place. Isn't that right?"

Another frown from Percy and I think about what I know of Boone's Talent, that his Silvertongue doesn't work well on drunks or when the object of his spell work is too determined or angry or scared. I'm waiting for Percy to call me what I am, and sweat beads along my temples and stars appear along the edges of my vision and I wonder if I should just run, right now, if that's the best that Boone can offer me, and then Percy's frown goes slack, he blinks, he smiles.

"All right," he says. "All right, then."

And he's gone. Just like that. Finds his friend in the crowd and off they go to the Huntsman and out of my life and I am safe.

I let out a breath, my head swimmy and my muscles shaky, and when I look up at Boone, he's got an expression on his face like he wants to remind me of what I was saying to him not an hour ago, accusing him of abusing his magic, when it was his magic that just saved my skin. I'm so relieved that I don't even care. I laugh.

"I know," I say. "I'm sorry. I'll never say a bad word about your magic for as long as I live."

"That's good to hear," Boone says, lifting an eyebrow. "Because it's me and my magic that's going to ensure you live as long a life as possible, and don't you forget it, Mal. Don't you forget it even for a minute."

Twelve

"I'VE ALREADY CHECKED THE HOTEL THE scholar stayed in. The bloke at the front desk told me no one's come by to claim his things, so they were sent back to his home," Boone says, striding down the street with me at his side. "Still no sign of the scholar or any of the Luciferidies."

"Where are we going?" I ask, and Boone says nothing as we make our way down Oxford Street. Then he pauses and sweeps his hand across the view in front of us: Hyde Park, green and mottled with picnickers, the shining waters of the lake known as the Serpentine, and, at the edge of the park, glittering like a child's glass toy, the Crystal Palace, home to London's Great Exhibition.

"The researcher kidnapped by the Luciferidies was in town for this," Boone says, staring down across the park. "I want to know just what Romesh Tagore was working on." He turns to me with a grin. "Besides which, it's supposed to be a good show."

I laugh because he's right. This is the last week the exhibition will be open, and ever since we arrived, we've been hearing breathless accounts of it. Everyone seems to agree: It's an event not to be missed, with the greatest achievements of science, mechanics, agriculture, and artistry on display. Last night in the hunters' bar, I overheard a man tell his friend he had watched as messages traveled through the air, from one side of the room to the other.

"And what's so grand about that?" the friend replied. "Last month I caught a little girl who could send messages from one side of the *ocean* to the other."

The man was already shaking his head, smiling. "No, no, this is *without* magic. Only through the power of science."

"Bah. Who needs science when we've got magic folk?" And as much as the man tried to persuade his friend, his mind was made up.

It seems as though the Great Exhibition was designed with expressly those kinds of skeptics in mind, because as Boone and I weave through a rapidly thickening crowd near the entrance, we catch sight of dozens of signs and brightly illustrated placards describing the exhibits inside: the thresher that runs without animal or magical assistance, the device that fixes an image onto a piece of paper, the machine that allows a blind man to read.

Boone pays our ticket fare and leads us inside the Crystal Palace, where, blinking at the sunlight glinting off the walls and ceiling, we stand nose-to-trunk with a life-sized display of an elephant, its tusks knobbed with huge golden bulbs, its back draped with a velvet canopy studded with rubies. A support lifts its trunk into the air, and I reach out a hand to it, because even though I come from an island that hunts animals even bigger than this, I've never seen anything so massive on four legs. Before I can touch my fingertips to its waxy, rough-looking skin, however, a guard standing nearby clears his throat and lifts his chin, and I let my hand drop back down to my side.

"Stupendous, isn't it?" Boone asks, staring up at all the glitter, the color, the noise, and I have to agree, although Boone and I probably have different definitions about what makes it so amazing. It's a world of art and machinery and industry—all created without magic. I'm so used to seeing Others work their wonders that it's jarring to look up at a full-grown tree enclosed in the glass pavilion, to assume a Grower put it there and then to see a small sign at the tree's base: THIS ELM TREE WAS GROWN AND CULTIVATED WITHOUT MAGIC. I see examples of porcelain finer than tissue, intricately carved golden figures, pressured hoses to put out massive fires, and beside each, that same small note: WITHOUT MAGIC.

Growing up on Prince Island, I had been taught from a young age that a life without magic was dangerous. Sailors relied on the Roe witch out of common sense and safety, and the idea of the witch ever leaving or losing her abilities—it's tantamount to death for all the islanders. But here is a kingdom, a palace of things just as wonderful and awe-inspiring as anything I've ever come across hunting, all built with common hands, ordinary minds. And it's beautiful.

"None of these exhibits are what we want," Boone says, breaking me from my thoughts. I have to tear my eyes away from the graceful glass ceiling of the Crystal Palace, and when I glance at him, he's squinting down and frowning at a stained exhibition catalogue that he retrieved from the floor.

"'Magic as Man's Tool,'" he reads aloud. "'Tagore, Romesh—an example of the application of magic to modern production.'"

"What does that mean?" I ask, and Boone shrugs.

"Let's go find out."

We follow the catalogue's map to the MAGIC AS MAN'S TOOL exhibition, a small, dark pavilion behind the Crystal Palace set up to prove that magic, like the powers of electricity, steam, coal, and fire, is nothing more than something to be harnessed, especially by people who aren't Talented. As we cross inside the pavilion, a large poster hanging at the entrance greets us, declaring magic A GIFT TO ALL MANKIND. Full-scale color drawings depict side-by-side BEFORE and AFTER panels. In one, miles of dusty fields are turning green under a metal canopy. Another shows a desert blooming into an oasis thanks to a curious drill-like device that shoots out yellow rays of light, while in a third set, an image of a ship dead in the water hangs beside a picture of that same ship cruising in the water, sails puffed out with a bell-cheeked blowing contraption. Above each pair reads the same two-inch-tall slogan: THE MARRIAGE OF MAGIC AND MACHINE.

"Good afternoon, gentlemen!" A barker sweeps forward, ushering Boone and me toward his stall, which stands decorated with shining metal cases about the size of a deck of playing cards. "Have you ever been out in the cold, wishing for a light, only to find yourself out of matches? Leave those worries behind with the Reynolds Pocket Firebreather! Simply open the case and press the plunger to release—ah!" The man lifts one of the little cases in the air, snaps it open, and pushes a button to let out a puff of fire.

"I can get the same effect with a tinderbox and a lamp," I say, lifting an eyebrow, and the man shakes his head so quickly it threatens to fall off his neck.

"Oh no, no, no, no, no," he says. "An oil lamp runs on fuel, which will be consumed. A tinderbox relies on a flint, which can fail. The Reynolds Pocket Firebreather, however, uses pure *magical energy*. It will never run dry, never expire, and never grow old or rusted." His eyes shine as he cradles the little silver case in the palm of his hand. "Now this is not an enchanted lighter, my friends. It is the marriage of magic and machine. Why rely on charms or the whims of Others when we have the ability to harness their powers for ourselves?" He holds out the case. "Only five shillings, and that's a bargain."

"We'll pass," Boone says, and he nudges me past the man, who barely waits until we've turned away to draw in the next potential customer.

"Magic and machine?" I ask, frowning. "What do they mean to do—replace all magic folk?"

"Or at least render them obsolete," Boone says. "What these people want most is control. Magical machines…" He shakes his head, a faint smile of disbelief on his face. "Let's find Tagore's stand and get out of here. I've had enough modern miracles for one day."

We ease through the crowd, passing stalls laid out with increasingly elaborate machines: shining silver reapers, a helmet that can supposedly mimic the abilities of a mind reader, a device to breathe underwater. Some of these look like nothing more than enchanted objects of the kind you can find in any market, but there are several, like the lighter, that claim to be powered by something else entirely, a magical force that has somehow been severed from its creator and tethered, put to use like a mule in a yoke.

I don't even realize we've reached Tagore's exhibit until Boone stops walking and I nearly bump into him.

The stall stands wedged between two men demonstrating a tiny portable wind machine and another man dressed in a glossy black tuxedo who is gesturing to a piano that plays itself. It's swept clean, dark and forlorn without any of the usual banners or baubles.

Frowning, Boone leans over the edge of the stall, looking for signs of Tagore's work, and, finding nothing, hops over to look behind it.

"Are you planning on starting your own exhibit?" the man in the tuxedo asks, resting one elbow on top of his piano. "Anything would be better than that nonsense that cluttered up the hall before."

Boone glances up at him, and the smile on his face is like that of a cat spotting a fat gray mouse.

"Didn't like it, did you?" he asks. The man purses his lips.

"It was a late addition and ex-*treme*-ly disorganized," he says. "Only ran for a day, and the whole time the fellow was here, he complained. Too hot in the pavilion, he said, and the British mail system was a disgrace—lost something of his that was supposed to have arrived from Paris, which, *really*, he should have blamed the French. And besides all that, the fellow had an unsavory aspect about him. He drove away visitors."

"Drove them away? How did he do that?"

But the tuxedoed man looks suddenly flustered, like he's just said something he wishes he could take back, and he waves his hand in the air absently, muttering something indistinct before turning back to his piano.

"Out of curiosity," Boone asks, his words taking on that Silvertongue slant, "what did the fellow demonstrate?"

The man pretends to be occupied with his piano for a moment, but I can see Boone's spell working through him, compelling him, and finally he glances back at us, frowning. "It was—hold on, now, you're not one of those City Patrolmen, are you? Because they came about last week, and I'll tell you same as I told them: I did not speak to the man, and I certainly do not know where he might have gone."

"No, I'm not with the police," Boone says, smooth and easy. "I'm just curious, as I said. Surely you must know what it is he was doing, isn't that right? You can tell me."

The man's eyelids flutter over a half-focused gaze, and he says in a dreamy, disconnected voice, "As a matter of fact, I didn't really pay attention to the details. But it had something to do with...Oh, he called it *multiplication*."

"Multiplication?"

He nods, still not quite focused on Boone. "He said it would revolutionize industry. He said no longer would a craftsman have to labor over a single object a thousand times, but instead he could put a thousand times' worth of effort into a single object and simply replicate it however many times he needed. Each copy would come out perfectly alike, perfectly operational."

Boone and I glance at each other. There is, of course, magic that can make copies of things, but it tends to be enormously tricky to pull off convincing imitations in large number, especially if the object in question is complicated, like a machine, or enchanted somehow.

Boone turns back to the man, asking the question on my

mind: "These demonstrations you saw—what kinds of things was he copying?"

Another flippant hand gesture. "Oh, all sorts. Books, ladies' shoes, various small things."

"Magical things?"

The tuxedoed man blinks, and I can tell he's alarmed, he doesn't want to be talking, and I watch as Boone fairly lances the spell into him.

"Were there any magical things?"

"A...yes...yes, once: a magical thing. He waited until the end of the first day. He had a crowd watching and waiting. He pulled out a handkerchief that could render things invisible, put it in his machine, and made...more. A dozen more. He pulled them out of the machine and tossed them into the air and they all...all of them were simply...perfect. He was to perform this trick again on the second day, but before he reached the finale, two men came up to him...two men wearing red scarves around their necks....They took him...they took his machine...and they told me..." His gaze shifts off into the distance and he suddenly shudders, going pale, eyes blinking furiously, and when he looks again at Boone, I can see he's clear-eyed, angry, scared.

"Is there—did I—I didn't—" He glances off into the crowd and startles, eyes wide like he's just recognized something. "Ex-*cuse* me! You'll have to—I'll have to—" And without another word, he disappears, leaving his handsome black piano still plinking out tunes.

"What was—" I say, but Boone, looking through the crowd, cuts me off with a *shh*.

"They're here," he says, his voice low, and I turn, searching the faces behind us, until I see a flash of red: a bandana tucked into the front pocket of a man milling about near the edge of the pavilion. Another man with a red hatband stands a few feet away, one hand closed around something in his pocket. They haven't seen us—or at least they act like they haven't— and carefully, Boone leaps over the stall and beckons me away to the far end of the row of stands. Pulling up the exhibition catalogue, he hides our faces just enough so that we can watch the pair of Luciferidies amble up to Tagore's stall and lean in. They look like Boone did earlier, like they're searching for something, and one of them crosses behind the stall, running his hand along the floorboards, knocking his fist carefully to the floor.

"What are they looking for?" I ask, but Boone just shakes his head, his eyes on the Luciferidies, who appear, at least, unhappy. They stay at the stall for a few minutes, examining every inch of it and the area around it before exchanging a few words with each other, their faces grim and disappointed. And then, as quickly as they appeared, they vanish back into the crowd, and I watch the red hatband disappear behind the other fairgoers.

"I thought the Luciferidies already had Tagore and his machine," I say as Boone crumples up the exhibition cata-logue. "Why are they back searching his stall?"

Boone glances at me. "What did that fellow say about Tagore's complaint of the mail? He was supposed to have gotten a package from Paris only it never arrived."

"A piece of the machine?"

Boone nods. "Maybe the piece he needs to replicate something as powerful as the *shar*. There's quite a wide gap, after all, behind a common invisibility handkerchief and a centuries-old enchanted knife." Boone's smile turns sly. "Well, Mal, my boy: What do you say we take a trip to Paris?"

Thirteen

PARIS

THE CLOSEST I CAME TO DEATH WAS IN Paris, and although it happened on a hunt, it had nothing to do with the normal dangers of hunting.

I was sixteen and we'd stopped the night in the city, searching for a family of magic folk said to weave fabric that renders the wearer invisible. A rich man in Toulouse wanted to buy bolts of this fabric, but the family, unsurprisingly, was proving tricky to find. The rich man had offered a contract to track them down and persuade them to sell through any means necessary, and so I carried money and Boone carried a mouthful of sweet lies and we both carried rope and guns and knives, just in case.

Boone had a list of clubs to visit, green-and-gold-lit underground ballrooms full of women in striped dresses and men in tails and flower-shaped glasses and singing and smoke. He took me with him—which is to say, I followed him. He'd walk up to warehouses and sneak down alleys and lean against boarded doors and scratch with a fingernail and whisper the right word and in we'd go, down into an underground that looked too cavernous to fit beneath such a cramped city. And then it was colors, it was noise, it was Boone kissing women and hugging men and laughing and leaping on top of bars with his fingers choking the necks of four bottles at once and shouting, "*Ce soir, buvons!*"

I'd watch him from my corner, from my table, from under my eyelashes, knowing that this was his world, not mine. Even though I had money stuffed in my pockets, same as him, and the same stories to tell, he belonged and I did not. That was all right, most of the time, because at the end of the night he would find me and he would be warm and sweating and smoky and happy and he'd say, "Home, my boy." I knew home to him meant the closest bed, but to me, in those moments, it meant away from the rest of the world, because he was tired of them and their glittering and their dancing, but he was not tired of me.

So I watched him in the crowd and I had a drink in front of me and I rolled it between my hands and then the girl appeared, just like that, like my glass was Aladdin's lamp

("Not real," Boone said once. "I've looked.") and she was a genie, arriving in a puff of smoke to grant me wishes.

She said something in exhausted French, pushing a cloud of curls off her sweaty forehead, and when I said "What's that?" she laughed and said to no one in particular, "Ah. *Américain*."

She said her name was Giselle, or else she said a string of words I didn't understand and one of them was *Giselle*, and when I told her my name, her eyes widened and then she laughed again and said in an English so accented it thudded to the table, "*Bad*." When she leaned in, the glass beads on her dress tinkled like chandelier crystals. She kept talking, and even if the words hadn't been in French, I'm still not sure I would have understood what she was saying. All I could look at and think about were her brown eyes and the smudged black around them, and the way her lips popped and pillowed her words, and her hands, never stilling for a second but floating around her, forming angles and points and curves around her body.

Her voice lifted up into a question and she paused, eyes wide, eyebrows raised, those magical hands suspended in the air. I blinked like I was coming out of a daze and apologized.

Another laugh, her whole body rolling in a movement so graceful that it almost looked like a choreographed dance, and then she leaned in again, loose strands of her hair tickling my nose, my cheek, and she kissed my neck.

I shivered, even though what I felt more than anything was

a bead of heat slide down from the spot where her lips touched to my stomach and back again. She pulled away and looked into my face, still smiling, head tilted in a question, and when I smiled back, she slid her hand under mine, twined her fingers through mine, and stood up. She looked back at me and asked something, some word that exploded from her mouth so beautifully that the only thing I could say back was "Yes."

I would have followed her anywhere in that moment, but she only wanted to go to the dance floor, where she draped her body around mine as effortlessly as a scarf. I held her close, and she whispered things to me in French; secrets or a song or a charm—I didn't care. I closed my eyes and felt her lips against my neck, my jaw, my mouth, and they were so soft and so careful that they dulled away all the sharp edges of the hole inside me.

The song ended and another one started up and another one, and by the next one I was in love with this girl. I would have given her all the money in my pockets. I would have asked to marry her. I would have offered her my life and my soul as easily as she offered me her hand, and I would have given up everything that I was—Mal the hunter, Boone's partner, Essie's old friend, the blank from Prince Island, magic killer, and killer killer—and started over again, with her, beginning with that moment on the dance floor with her in my arms and her breath in my ear and ending with—I didn't know and I didn't care.

So when she led me by the hand away from the dance floor, I followed, and when we ended up outside, I followed. And when she looked back at me and smiled and blinked her wide eyes and tossed her head down an alley with no lights and black shapes and rough brick, I followed. I followed her into darkness and felt her hand slip from mine, and when I called out to her, two men answered.

Boone found me the next morning. No money, of course. Coat gone, shoes gone, gun—I'd had a gun and never even once thought to use it—gone. I squinted up at him through eyes surrounded by black, blossoming bruises and tried to speak with a tongue so mangled by my newly chipped teeth that it had swelled twice its size. He stared down at me and laughed.

"Honestly," he said, his hands on his hips. "The most powerful spells in the world can't touch you, and you're knocked out by a little French bird working the oldest scheme in the book. Got a weakness for the pretty ones, eh?"

And he bent down and helped me up and took me to a place where my ribs could fit themselves back together and my bruises heal and my tongue get its shape back. Every time he saw me again he would laugh—he'd finally discovered my weakness, he'd say. Eventually, I got to smiling back at him, to joking with him again, because I wanted him to believe that's all it was, that I was like him, chasing after girls and made a fool by a pair of pretty eyes. I didn't want him to know that I thought it was worth it, that pain, that humiliation, it was worth it, and even if I had been killed it would have been worth it, because, if only for a night, I'd fallen in love.

We arrive in Paris by train Tuesday morning, early enough to see the *chiffonniers*, the rag gatherers, picking through the piles of rubbish set out on the streets and filling the baskets on their backs with bits of bone, scraps of paper, soiled odds and ends of cloth to be cleaned, repaired, and sold at the markets later that day.

Our walk to the lodging house takes us through the place de la Madeleine, where already growers and vendors are setting up for the flower market that twice weekly transforms the dense, narrow streets into a green jungle wild with the heavy scents of cut flowers and rich, dark earth. Boone and I wind through the stalls, pausing now and then to lean in and inhale the perfume of the flowers, and after a few minutes Boone turns to me with a raised eyebrow and says, "Smells better than the last time we were here."

I laugh, even though it isn't really funny—last time we were here, Paris was just mopping up from a wave of cholera that left the streets muddy and black with the filth of death. Back then, the stench and misery that clung to the city meant that the most popular things on the market were linen bags filled with lavender and sea froth, a kind of cabbagey magical plant that brings on mild delirium, but on most days, like today, the market has a strict separation of the magical and the mundane.

Boone leads me away from the common plants meant for flowerpots and cooking pots and toward the striped pavilions of the magical plants, and he's smiling like any of the small children who dart from stall to stall to take in the wares. There are the tulips that shift color according to the time of day and vines trained to curl around women's arms and necks like sweet pet snakes and, my favorite, the singing desert plants from the Sahara, which croon out unique melodies in gliding, ethereal tones.

A man tidying up a tray of fire blossoms lifts his chin when he sees Boone and me and calls out, "*Chasseurs, voulez-vous y regarder de plus près?*"

But Boone just smiles and shakes his head. "Another time," he says, waving away the curling plumes of orange-black smoke.

I'm not surprised he's not interested—only common hunters, the hobbyists and the amateurs, specialize in flowers. We bothered with them only once, three years ago, after hearing about a contract from Comte le Corre for a bundle of ever-blooming lilies in honor of his second daughter's wedding. The offer was high enough to warrant our attention because the lilies, grown only in Scotland, are famed for two things: their eternally buoyant snowy-white petals and the poisonous gas they secrete the moment they're cut. You have to breathe the poison for several days for it to take effect, not enough time to kill off the Comte's guests but plenty quick enough to do in anyone trying to transport the lilies over several weeks—unless that person is a blank. Boone took the train, I rented a carriage, and we brought the lilies first to the Comte, where they took a place of honor at what turned out to be the last event he held before he lost his title and his life in the overthrow of the government later that year. Then, when the wedding was over, we sold them to a grubby corner of the flower market where white-gloved and white-faced buyers pick through the more dangerous fare.

The abundance of exotic plants means Paris is also a destination for potion-makers and sellers, and so after getting our fill of flora at the market, Boone and I turn down the *rue des potions magiques* to take a closer look at bottles of every shape and size and color and quality, filled with stuff to heal any affliction or cause any affliction, to transform, to slow, to strengthen, to kill.

Boone frowns as he bends over a row of squat purple bottles labeled, in English, POTION OF STRENGTH.

"*Spécialement pour américains,*" the vendor says, waving a hand at the bottles, but Boone just shakes his head and gives me a look before moving on.

"What a waste of time," Boone says, still shaking his head at the stall. "Everyone knows potions aren't the fashion in America." He gives an injured sniff. It's true different kinds of magic are favored in different regions. Americans tend to rely more on charms—more limited, maybe, in what they can do, but they're tangible and last longer than potions, which, of course, can be drunk only once.

"Remember those crates we brought to Charleston?" Boone says. "Packed with more goose down than in a flock of birds and we *still* lost a third of the bottles, and then not a soul would buy them!"

"Of course I remember," I say. "I walked right into that crate full of busted bottles of invisibility potion. My toes have never been the same."

Boone lets out a bark of laughter. "That's right! And then it got all over the floor and disappeared everyone's feet—except yours, of course—and what did you say? 'Glad I've got on my potion-repelling socks!'" He laughs again and slaps a hand on my shoulder and I smile back at him, but my stomach gives a hard twist. It's easy for him to remember that day as nothing more than another adventure, but my skin goes cold just thinking about it: down in the darkness of the ship, two stevedores cursing at the six inches of nothing dangling from their knees and then going silent, going scared, as their gazes slid to my boots, scuffed and solid and still there. I waited for them to shout, for my secret to get out and for rough hands on my arms and for knives in my belly. Somehow I managed to smile, to say something and save myself and get a laugh out of the stevedores, because of course they'd rather believe the good-natured hunter from the Cape was lucky instead of a demon.

Boone's still going on about that day, the invisibility potion leaking nothingness straight through the belly of the ship, when I lift a hand and ask him if we're going the right way to get to the lodging house. He interrupts himself to think for a moment before leading us away from the *rue des potions magiques*. He doesn't even realize what he's doing, casual with my secret out here where anyone could hear him. Just as we turn down a narrow, sick-smelling alley, I hear a whisper of words snap-crackle through the air: "*bonhomme de bois*"—wooden boy—the French term for what I am, a blank, a monster, a dead-souled creature. My eyes rake across the vendors, searching for whoever might have said this about me, but all I find are faces as still and cool as ever, and I wonder if it is all in my imagination.

Fourteen

"THERE IT IS." BOONE PUSHES HIS HANDS into his pockets and leans against a wall, gazing up at the massive building across the narrow street. It looks like a palace, a fortress, a sheer wall of stone rising up into the air, broken only by grand, tall windows and topped with layers of frothy stonework that, this late at night, are deep and exaggerated with shadows.

A man in a smart uniform stands just inside a gaping black alcove, smoking a cigarette that leaves dim red trails in the air as he brings it from his side to his lips.

Boone studies him, a gleam of excitement in his eyes, and then he glances at me and nods.

"Wait two minutes. That should be enough to get them all," he says, and I nod back as he turns and runs down the street, footsteps echoing between the walls of the buildings, hands waving in the air, his voice raised in panic: *"A l'aide! Il s'est passé un accident! Suivez-moi! Laissez la porte ouverte!"* Without word or question, the guard follows Boone as he races along the street, and I watch, counting the seconds in my head as one, two, three more men peel away from the darkness of the alcove to follow him. He keeps shouting, his voice rising and bouncing through the air, drawing out anyone in earshot, and because Silvertonguing doesn't work if the person you're trying to charm doesn't speak your language, for good measure he switches to English—"There's been an accident! Come with me!"

My hands tingle, my heartbeat quickens, I just want to run forward into the alcove, but I force myself to wait the two minutes, trusting Boone to know how far his charm can spread. When the minutes are up, I slide down the street, keeping to the shadows, and walk to the open gate. Boone told the guards to leave it unlocked—and they did—but I'm still careful to check the hinges and threshold for any charms, any spells etched into the stone meant to detect or deter.

Satisfied, I continue down a narrow tunnel and emerge in a huge stone courtyard, coming out on the other side of the building on the street. To my right, a narrow chapel stands sickly yellow and dark in the light of the streetlamps. It reminds me of the ruins I saw years ago in Italy, a temple of symmetry and balance with its stately triangular frieze, the dome that tops the building like a military cap, the statues and columns and large, gaping windows—black now that it's so near to midnight.

Boone told me earlier that the building I need to go to is directly across from the chapel, so I turn left and continue down the courtyard, passing underneath a row of arches to reach the door.

This time, I see that the wooden door is studded with half a dozen fist-sized metal disks—charms against anyone who shouldn't be allowed inside. I reach into the canvas bag strapped across my back and pull out a stubby stick of red clay. Carefully, I draw a red X on each of the disks before rubbing the clay into the metal. It's not permanent, but it will dampen the magic of the charms long enough for Boone to follow me once he's done leading away the guards.

Next I try the doorknob, and I'm surprised when it opens easily in my hand. Most people don't trust magic alone to keep out intruders, and I always carry my lock-picking tools just in case, but as I open the door and step inside the threshold, I see why they didn't bother with a lock on this door: Just inside, a huge golden grate spans across the hallway, the bars twisty with embedded spells and heavy with bolts and chains.

Frowning, I pull out my kit and spread it on the floor. Boone taught me how to pick a lock years ago, and although I've had plenty of practice, getting through the gate takes longer than I'd like. I have to work carefully, delicately, trusting the sensitivity of my fingertips to know when to rake the pick along the pins and when to put pressure on the tumbler, and only when I hear the quiet, barely-there *click* of everything falling into place do I let myself breathe.

"You're getting slow."

I look up to see Boone leaning against the doorframe behind me, arms crossed over his chest, a bemused expression on his face.

"My tools are all worn down," I say, pushing open the gate with a muffled squeal.

"It's a poor craftsman who blames his tools."

"My tools are all worn down because *you* borrowed them."

Boone shrugs and helps me roll up my kit before handing it back to me. "When we get the *shar*, you'll be able to pay someone else to do your breaking in for you." He sweeps an arm out in front of us. "Blanks first."

I cross the threshold and run a hand along the back of the grate, where several inscriptions have been etched into the metal. Could be spells or could be the motto of the university, and I don't take any chances, rubbing the red clay along every bit of writing I can see.

"The floor," Boone says, and I nod, stepping carefully along the hallway, tapping the stonework with the toe of my boot.

"Keep to the right side," I say, squinting in the darkness at the stones. "I can't be sure, but it looks like the left might have a binding spell."

"Don't want that," Boone says, and after a second's hesitation, he crosses through the golden gate and joins me on the right side of the hallway. He lets me go slightly ahead of him as we walk together, and I run my hand against the walls, check the ceilings for any hidden charms, stopping every now and then to smudge more clay against anything that looks suspicious.

We turn a corner into a stairway, and the sound of footsteps greets us. Without saying a word, Boone and I switch positions. Carefully and quietly, he climbs the stairs to meet the person attached to the footsteps, and I can hear him talking in rapid French, telling whomever he just met that he's a professor here, that he's walking with a student, that as soon as we have disappeared from view, no memory of this interaction will remain, and when I hear a gruff voice reply, "*Oui, monsieur,*" I follow Boone up the stairs, pausing only to glance at the dead-eyed, mustachioed man leaning against the wall.

Out of sight, Boone lets me get ahead again, and we climb three more sets of stairs before reaching a door inscribed with a small sign: ACADÉMIE DES ARTS MAGIQUES.

"There's a repelling charm," Boone says softly. "I can feel it."

I can't, but I trust him to know better than I do, so I run my hands around the edge of the door, searching for it.

"No good. It'll be on the other side of the door," Boone says, and he clutches his stomach, wincing.

"Are you all right?"

"I'll be fine as soon as you get rid of that blasted charm," he says, gritting his teeth. I do another sweep of the entranceway, checking for any other spells, before I try the doorknob—locked, and this time I move my lock pick quickly in place as Boone's breathing grows faster, shorter.

"It's—no—*good*!" he says, and I turn to see him almost doubled over, the repelling charm twisting his insides. "Th-the *lideroot*!"

I hesitate for a moment, about to ask him if he's sure, but when his face goes purple-red and he lets out a grunt of pain, I drop my bag on the ground and reach in a hand, searching for the small, round bottle of powdered lideroot. Carefully, I uncork the bottle, pour a little of the powder into my hands, and blow it into the air, filling the landing with a metallic, bloody scent. Boone gasps, coughs, puts his hand on the stair railing to support himself, and glances up at me.

"This...is why...you need...to pick...those blasted locks...*faster*," he says, wheezing for air, and he walks past me and takes the kit from my hands, safe from the effects of the repelling charm thanks to the lideroot. It works to neutralize any magic in the area, but even though it's incredibly effective, we use it only in emergencies because it destroys *any* magic in the area—including Boone's ability to Silvertongue.

Anyone we meet from here on out we'll have to silence or dissuade without his magic.

Boone's a better picker than me, and he has the door open in seconds, revealing a long, dark hallway studded on one side with closed wooden doors and on the other with small, black-barred windows that let in white squares of moonlight across the floor. We walk carefully, slowly, trusting the effects of the lideroot to linger in the air long enough to cancel out any hidden charms or embedded spells.

"It's down at the end," Boone murmurs, and we move on our toes, silent, Boone just in front of me. We're about halfway down the hall when a noise from behind one of the wooden doors makes me jump, and I grab Boone's shoulder to warn him just as the door swings open and out walks a smartly dressed gray-haired man, carrying a handful of glass tubes filled with brightly colored liquids.

"Mais que faites-vous là?" he says, his voice gruff with surprise and alarm. *"Vous n'êtes pas censés être ici!"*

"Nous venons voir des amis," Boone says, smiling. *"Ne nous prêtez pas attention."*

But the man shakes his head. *"Non, non!"* He reaches for one of the tubes, raising it over his head as though he's planning to throw it against the ground, and Boone leaps forward, tackling him into the wall. The tubes tinkle against the stone floor, and one of them smashes open, releasing a cloud of orange-purple smoke that re-forms into a small, shrieking bird made of fire.

"Get it!" Boone says, grappling with the man, and I race after the bird as it zigzags down the hall, bumping into the walls and doors and leaving round burns that smoke and hiss. I yank the bottle of lideroot from my pocket and quickly pour the powder into my palm before blowing it at the bird. It screams again the second the powder touches its flames, and I reach out with a hand to grab it, but by the time I reach it, my hand closes around nothing but oily, warm feathers, the lideroot having eaten away whatever else of the bird existed.

Breathing hard, I turn to see Boone on top of the still-struggling man, one knee pressed into his chest. The man lets out a cry of surprise as Boone puts a hand to his side and draws out a knife, and without thinking I shout, "No!"

I have to wrench Boone away, and when the man starts to get up, I press him back down to the floor with my boot, reach into my bag with my free hand, and pull out a liquid-soaked rag, which I hold against the man's face. There's nothing magic to the liquid; it's plain ether, and in seconds the man's eyes flutter closed, his hands and legs going still.

When I'm sure he's not getting up, I stand and shove Boone in the chest.

"What was that?" I ask, and I'm quiet, but I can't keep the anger from shaking into my words. "You were going to *kill* him?"

Boone dabs his sleeve at the corner of his mouth, where a trickle of blood stains his lips red. "He would have said something," he says, breathing hard. "He would have screamed."

I look down at the man, unconscious on the floor. "He's not screaming now," I say. "And I can't remember needing to kill anyone before."

For a moment, a grimace transforms Boone's face, turns it from something familiar and friendly into a mask of hunger, rage, desperation.

"Boone?" I mean to say it like a threat, but instead it comes out as a child's confused mew, and he blinks, breathes, slides his knife back into its sheath.

"We have a job to do," he says, and it sounds as though he says it as much to himself as to me. "Let's keep moving." He walks forward, reaching down to pick up the rag from the floor before handing it to me. "Don't ever push me like that again," he says, his voice soft, curling, and my throat goes dry and goose bumps rise across my arms, but I nod, and he smiles.

"Down the hall."

Without another word, he crosses the hall, and even though his movements are light, relaxed once again, I feel like a jangly collection of nerves and bones as I follow him, the bloody scent of lideroot and sweet sharpness of ether perfuming the air.

Boone stops at the last door on the hall, marked with a small brass placard that reads R. TAGORE. It swings forward at his delicate touch, almost as if it were waiting for us, and Boone smiles, begins to walk into the office, and stops.

There's a man standing inside the office, his back to us, his body all but blocking the light from a single candle on the table in front of him. As the door bumps gently open against the wall, the man turns, his face lit up with an expression of bemused expectation.

"Ah," he says, smiling at us like a delighted host. "More hunters, is it? I expect you're here about the *shar*."

Fifteen

BOONE RECOVERS FIRST, TAKING TWO QUICK
steps into the office, his knife ready in his hand.

"Who are you?" he asks, and the man—tall, thin, with a
neatly trimmed mustache and oiled black hair—inclines his
head toward the door.

"Romesh Tagore," he says, his voice light and pleasant, his
accent a mixture of British and Indian. "This is my office, as I
imagine you already know."

"You're supposed to be kidnapped," Boone says, eyes narrowed, and Tagore lets out a soft laugh.

"Kidnapped? By those devil admirers? No, no. It would be
more accurate to say they *hired* me."

"For what?"

But Tagore just blinks before spreading his arms out to

take in his office. "Please. If you are here to talk, let us talk like civilized folk. Perhaps you could introduce yourselves. You know who I am, after all, but I do not know who you are."

"Hunters," I say. "Just as you thought."

"Americans," Tagore adds. "And in search of the *shar*, yes?"

"What did the Luciferidies want with you?" Boone asks, and I hear the edge in his voice, his Silvertongue tone creeping into his words even though the air still reeks with lideroot and he can't have any magic within him anymore. We won't get any answers out of Tagore by magic, and Boone knows it.

Tagore tilts his head, regarding us like two of his students. "You must already know the answer to that, if you came all the way to Paris and my humble laboratory."

"Replication magic," I say, and Tagore gives a curt nod.

"Did you do it?" Boone takes another step forward, and in this small space I can't help but notice he's close enough to grab Tagore by the throat. "Did you manage to replicate the *shar*?"

A moment's pause, and then Tagore shakes his head. "My machine was missing a vital part and failed to work properly. I thought perhaps it had been left behind in London...."

I glance at Boone. "That's what the Luciferidies were looking for in the stall," I say, and Boone nods.

"When I could not replicate the missing piece in their London laboratory, they sent me here to work on it," Tagore says.

"What is it supposed to do?" Boone asks, his eyes narrowed at the machine. "Create an endless collection of *shar*s?"

Tagore tilts his head and considers the machine. "That is the idea," he says, and he gives us both a slight smile. "But I don't think it will work."

"No?"

"No. My machine can replicate simple objects—small charms and minor spells—but the *shar* is too powerful and complex," he says, lifting a hand to the silver-colored box sitting on his worktable, its wire guts raw and exposed under the light of an oil lamp. "It will take many years of experiments until the machine will be ready."

The tension in Boone's face eases slightly, and a hint of a smile appears on his face.

"Then the Luciferidies will have to put their plans on hold for now," he says.

"Well." Tagore lifts his shoulders in a slow shrug. "As with most things, there is more than one method for achieving an objective. I wouldn't count out those resourceful little devils."

"No? They're planning something else?"

Tagore's eyes slide from Boone's face to mine, his gaze lingering on me for so long that my skin starts to itch, and just as I'm about to ask him what he's staring at, he snaps his attention back to Boone. "What is your interest with the *shar*? I wouldn't think an Other would want to get too close to it."

I glance at Boone, surprised that Tagore can recognize him as an Other, but Boone just lifts his chin and stares at the man. "Even I can see a good investment."

"Ah. A capitalist. And what will you do should the

Luciferidies or someone just as nefarious prove the highest bidder? You're not worried that the *shar* could be used against you and your brethren?"

"What they do with it isn't my concern so long as they pay."

"What about you?" Tagore asks, nodding at me. "Do you share your partner's mercenary beliefs?"

"I've got my own reasons to hunt the *shar*," I say. "I don't need to tell you."

"Indeed," he says, smiling a little. He studies Boone, who looks back at him with an expression on his face that seems to say he'd happily trade his arm to get back his Silvertongue, and finally nods. "The Luciferidies have taken the *shar* to their headquarters in Constantinople. On the eighth of November, they will give a party that takes place on the evening of the eleventh full moon of the year, which so happens to be the same moon under which the *shar* was created many centuries ago. They hope to magnify the *shar*'s power and siphon it into one dozen knives—not enough to outfit an army, perhaps, but enough to send to the world's biggest cities."

"To do what?" Boone asks.

"The Luciferidies believe the *shar* can be a powerful tool for controlling Others, and would like to organize a kind of police force dedicated to punishing Others who abuse their Talents. Why worry about how to imprison Them, when you can simply cut the power out of Them forever?"

Boone's already shaking his head. "Who would agree to that?"

Tagore shrugs. "It is a more popular idea than you think."

Boone glances at me, an incredulous look on his face, and I shake my head back at him in disbelief, but there's a part of me that thinks of Boone manipulating Ruth, of Essie and her love magic and lies, and I wonder if the Luciferidies might be onto something.

"And who decides what counts as abusing Talent?" Boone asks, a nervous edge to his voice. "Who reins in the Luciferidies?"

Tagore just spreads his hands out in a look of apology. "Whoever controls the *shar* controls the magical population."

A hardness comes over Boone's face, and he turns to me. "Constantinople. We need to get the *shar*."

"No longer a capitalist, are you?" Tagore asks, and when Boone gives him a sharp look, he laughs. "It is a private party, and the Luciferidies will not make it easy for intruders to find a way in. Every invited guest has been given a totem that he or she must carry to be allowed within the walls of the building. This totem cannot be replicated, and should it be stolen, it will destroy itself. Of course, it can be safely passed along to someone else, and"—something gleams in Tagore's eye—"the Luciferidies have given me a totem. You and your partner intrigue me. You plan on stealing the *shar*, don't you?"

"Of course."

"And selling it?"

Something crosses Boone's face—greed warring with guilt. He's no sentimentalist; I know he doesn't want the Luciferidies creating some kind of international army against Others, but I also suspect he's not worried he'd ever be caught by them himself.

"I'll sell it," Boone finally says. "The Luciferidies don't have deep pockets, and there are plenty of others who want it more."

Tagore nods once, briskly. "Then I will propose a trade. I suspect that if the ritual on November eighth is successful, the Luciferidies will no longer have a use for me or my machine. I was a student of Howard LeCouer, the man who discovered the *shar* in its tomb in Albania, and I have long wanted to complete his research. Working with the *shar*, even if only for a few days, was the pinnacle of my career. I would like the opportunity to handle it again. I will give you my totem on the condition that before you sell the *shar*, you bring it back to Paris and allow me to study it for one day."

"And how do we know you'll give it back?" Boone asks. "How do we know you won't tamper with it somehow?"

"You and your partner are welcome to observe me the entire time. The *shar* needn't ever leave your sight." Tagore puts out a hand. "Do we have a deal?"

Boone watches him for a moment, thinking, and then grins and slides his hand in Tagore's. "Where's this totem?"

"My inner office," Tagore says, motioning toward a closed door at the side of the room. "It is a small, wooden figurine carved in the shape of a devil. You'll find it in the upper drawer of my desk."

Boone nods. "Stay here with him," he says, and he crosses the room, opens the door, steps inside—and freezes.

For a moment, I wonder if he's seen something that's surprised him, but then I realize he's not moving, his weight still slightly forward, his eyes on Tagore's desk. He's been hit by a magical spell.

I turn to stare at Tagore. "What did you—"

"Wait," he says, stepping closer to me. "We only have a moment to talk; I can smell that disgusting powder in the air, and I don't know how long the spell will bind him."

"*Bind* him? What did you do? What are you doing?"

"It's merely a holding spell," Tagore says, waving a hand dismissively in the air. "All the inner offices have them. Designed to trap thieves and spies." He leans in until he's inches away from me, a smile playing at his lips, his eyes bright and glittering in the light, and whispers, "But it would not trap you. *Blank.*"

My throat goes dry and I take a step away from him, my hands tight into fists. "What? What are you—I'm not—"

"You are," he says. "And so am I."

"*What?*"

"Watch." He reaches back to the table behind him and picks up a bottle of gurgling purple-black liquid. I recognize it: edebas, a kind of magical potion that works like a never-stopping acid and can be contained only by certain kinds of magical glass. Delicately, Tagore lifts a finger, and before I know what's happening, he's plunged it into the liquid, swirling it around, and I gasp, expecting bone, blood, tendons, destruction. But when Tagore raises the finger into the air, the skin is smooth and unbroken, even as a drop of edebas slides down to the floor, where it hisses and leaves a perfect teardrop-shaped hole in the stone.

Tagore is a blank.

"How?" I whisper, the word strangling me as it forces its way up my throat, and Tagore just smiles. "You're twice my age.... How are you not—how are you alive?" I stare at him so intently that my eyes water and I blink and rub them, hard, until I see little sparks of light, and then I look back at him, *gape* back at him, my head so full of questions that my ears fill with a kind of rushing white noise.

"It is not the death sentence you think it is," he says, his voice soft. "There is power in what we are, power your partner would never understand."

My heartbeat beats a drum in my veins. "What do you mean?"

Tagore seems about to open his mouth when he pauses, reconsiders. "Tell me: What do you think of the *shar*?"

"The *shar*?" I blink. "I...I..." I shake my head, which still spins with confusion. "I'm helping Boone steal it."

"Then the money—"

"I don't care about the money," I say, the words coming out harsher than intended. "I'd be just as happy seeing it thrown in the ocean. But I have my own reasons for wanting it. There's a girl—a witch.... She...exposed me. I'm going to pay her back."

Tagore gives me a strange look. "She exposed you? She told others what you are?"

I nod, and something comes over him, something like cold rage.

"Despicable," he says, spitting out the word, and something inside me leaps. Anyone else in the world would applaud Essie for exposing me, but he knows what she really did.

"Listen," I say. "You have to tell me: How are you alive? How did you manage to fight off the monster?"

Tagore gives me a strange, surprised look.

"Your *blankness*," I hiss. "I can feel mine inside me all the time, eating me up. It's going to change me if I don't do anything about it, just like it changes every blank, but you, you're perfectly normal. How did you beat it?"

"Beat it? I didn't—"

A noise makes both of us turn, and we watch as Boone's body twitches and shudders.

"There's no time now," Tagore whispers, leaning closer. "Come back later tonight. I'll explain it all to you. The *shar*—"

"I told you, I don't care about that! Tell me how to survive my blankness!"

Another strange, pitying look crosses his face, and he makes a motion almost like he wants to reach out and grab my hand before he stops himself.

"You're thinking about it the wrong way," he says softly. "Your blankness isn't—"

But he breaks off as we hear the sound of Boone's foot hitting the floor, the spell completely weakened by the lingering lideroot, and when I glance back at Tagore, he's moved to his lab table with an air of polite detachment.

I stare at him, willing him to look at me, to talk to me and give me answers or even just some sign that he understands what this all means to me—seeing a blank, a *grown* blank, with a job and a life and no poison running through his veins. How is it possible? How did he beat it? I need to ask him, but he doesn't even look at me, concentrating on a spot on the wall beside him as Boone rummages through the desk, searching for the totem.

"Got it."

We both turn to see Boone standing in the doorway, one hand playing with a small red toy carved in the shape of a devil.

"It's time to go," he says, nodding at me, and when I glance back at Tagore, he's already turned away from us, leaning over his worktable, examining the patchwork of wires poking from his machine.

"Good luck to you," he says, not turning his head, and I want to stay, more than I've wanted anything before in my entire life. I've never even seen another blank in the flesh, and I want to touch him, to assure myself that he's real and I'm not alone.

But then I feel Boone's hand on my shoulder and I close my

mouth. "Power your partner could never understand," Tagore had said, and even though I don't agree with him—I think Boone would understand plenty, would even understand why I might want to spend a few minutes talking to Tagore—if I ask to stay here, I would have to expose him to Boone.

Maybe Boone wouldn't care, but I know Tagore would. He trusted me with his secret, and I'm not going to throw it out into the open without a thought. My throat closes. I can't ever give up another blank.

But I can come back, later, alone.

And without so much as a glance good-bye, I let Boone pull me away, out of the laboratory and back through the dark hallway, and leave behind the closest thing in the world I've ever had to family.

Sixteen

WE HAVE ONLY ONE MOMENT OF PANIC AS
we escape from the university: Coming down a set of narrow stairs minutes after leaving Tagore's office, we see a man,
another guard, standing at a landing below, his eyes half-closed
and drowsy.

I glance at Boone. Under normal circumstances, Boone
would simply say, as loudly as possible, that the man—and
anyone else in earshot—should go somewhere, anywhere else,
but with lideroot residue on our clothing and our skin, there's
a chance Boone still can't Silvertongue.

I throw a nervous look at the knife at Boone's belt, but
before I suggest we find another way to get back to the main
floor, he flies down the stairs, his footsteps soft and precise,
and whispers something in the guard's ear. The guard's eyes

pop open before going glazed and compliant, and I let out a breath of relief as he marches, stiff-legged, up the stairs, his gaze drifting over me as though I'm nothing more than a stick of wood.

When I look back at Boone, he's smiling, a look of deep satisfaction and comfort on his face, like a knight reunited with a favorite sword, and he jerks his head toward the hallway leading to the courtyard.

"Let's go," he says, and we run.

I can't sleep.

I stare up at the dark ceiling of the room Boone and I rented, and breathe in and out and listen to Boone's quiet shifting in the bed beside me and clench and unclench my fists, over and over, digging my nails into the palms of my hands because I don't know how else to keep myself from leaping out of bed and running through the streets, back to the university, back to Tagore and answers and the only other blank I've ever met.

Another blank.

It's as though a light has appeared, as though I've been sailing somewhere in a fog for a very, very long time, the kind of soupy fog where the sky melts into the water, stretches through the boat and through my skin and leaves me chilled and lost from the inside out. And then something cuts through that fog. Light and noise and safety, calling for me, and all I have to do is reach for it.

Rolling over, Boone makes a noise in his sleep, and I glance at him. We walked straight from Tagore's office to the train station to buy a series of train tickets that will take us, eventually, to Constantinople, and the whole time, I could feel it behind my teeth: *I met another blank.* I wanted to say it if only because I tell Boone everything, everything about me, and this is the most amazing thing to happen to me since the moment my secret spilled from Essie's lips and I lost my home forever. Meeting Tagore, hearing someone say we're the same—it's like another kind of home, a different way of belonging. It scares me and thrills me and I wanted to tell Boone, but while I buzzed with Tagore's secret, he could talk only about the Luciferidies, the party, the *shar* so close to our reach, and I told myself: *Soon enough, I'll go back there.*

When we got back to the room, Boone collapsed on his bed, the devil totem placed upright on the table beside him and a smile on his face. He was asleep within minutes, but the longer I stretch out on my own bed, the faster my heart beats, the more my skin itches. It's as though the monster knows how close I am to learning how to kill it for good, and it's decided to throw one last rebellion, twisting my insides into knots.

Finally, I can't wait anymore. I roll from my bed and slide my feet into my boots. I'm dressed in seconds: shirt and coat and knife at my hip and, after a moment's hesitation, I reach into the chest Boone and I hauled from Boston and retrieve my gun, a Colt Dragoon, heavy as a clothes iron and half as reliable. Working by feel and memory, I load the gun, slip an extra box of bullets into my pocket, and buckle the holster and belt around my waist.

With Boone still snoring gently into his pillow, I open the door and slip out into the hallway and a Paris night black as the ocean, the few whale-oil lanterns muzzy from years of soot and smoke.

It takes only minutes to reach the university again, and either the guards never returned from Boone's mysterious accident or they've disappeared to another corner of the block, because I slip through the entranceway, through the courtyard, through the door to Tagore's building and its golden gate without notice. I can still see my red clay, bright as blood where I rubbed it on the doors, the floor, the walls, but I barely give it a second glance—I'm a blank, after all. There's no magic that can keep me out.

When I reach the hallway that leads to Tagore's office, I pause. The man Boone attacked, the one I knocked out— he's no longer stretched out on the floor. I shouldn't really be surprised—the ether I gave him should have knocked him out for only a few minutes—but I can't help the shiver that works through me, and I walk through the rest of the hallway on my toes, shifting my weight soundlessly forward.

The door to Tagore's office stands slightly open, and carefully I reach out a hand and push it wide, my palms sweaty, my heart climbing up my throat.

Nothing.

Empty.

A puddle of wax has formed underneath a single lit candle on Tagore's worktable, and I frown into the flickering shadows.

"Hello?" I ask, my voice soft, but there's no answer. Perhaps he left to take care of his injured colleague. Perhaps he wasn't expecting me back so soon. A reflection of the flickering candlelight dances along the brass doorknob of the door that leads to his inner office, and I cross the laboratory, take a steady breath, and open the door.

"No..." I whisper. Papers, pots of ink, bits of metal, and the smashed-up pieces of a wooden chair litter the floor of the office. I run to the laboratory and fetch the candle, which hisses and spits hot wax at me as I carry it back into the office to look closer. There's no mistaking that a fight occurred here, and as I bend down to examine a torn piece of paper, something bright, something wet catches my eye. I already know what it is before I dip a finger into it, before I bring it to my nose and breathe in iron, before I wipe it against my pants and leave a crimson streak across my clothes. Blood.

For a moment, all I can do is stay crouched low to the floor, rocking on my ankles, my head too empty and too full all at once as the smell of blood reaches through my nostrils to settle at the back of my throat.

Someone attacked him. Someone came after him. I don't know who it could have been—the Luciferidies? Other hunters?—but finally the panic building up inside me forces me to stand, to turn from Tagore's office and leave the candle on the table and walk—no, *run*—as fast as I can, as quietly as I can, down the hallway and down the stairs and out through the gate, through the door, the courtyard, the entrance-way, not thinking, not feeling, not aware of anything except an overwhelming urge to keep moving, which is why I'm thrown completely off guard when a figure peels away from the shadows, knocks into my side, and slips a rope around my neck.

Cold, dumb, numb stupidity throws me off balance and the rope tightens and all I am aware of is that there should be air coming into my lungs and now there is not. Every part of my body is screaming protests, feet kicking and arms scrabbling and eyes bulging, a mass riot that I can't control.

A body behind me, a chest, a man's grunts, and a sound like wheezing, whistling, gagging, and that's *me*, I realize. That's me making those noises, noises of something dying, weak, and no longer in control of its own life, and I have to fight back, I have to. I wrench one of my hands from where it's scratching at the skin of my neck and check my hip for the gun, but it's gone. That's what that bump was a few seconds ago that threw me off—that was my gun being lifted from my waistband and out of my life forever. I have a knife in my boot that might as well be at the bottom of the ocean and I have stars in my eyes and blackness creeping up on me, and just when I'm positive I'm going to die, a voice from another person, someone in front of me, says, "Alive! Alive! Don't kill him!"

The rope loosens, my world stops shrinking, my brain and lungs flood with air, and I don't even realize I'm on my knees on the ground, coughing and choking and the pipe of my throat dented and raw. *Get up get up you idiot get up*, this voice screaming in my head, screaming at me to move or I die. Even though all I want is to spread my arms out on the cobblestones and inhale, over and over, until the wild, desperate, frightened thing inside me stills, I take advantage of being bent over on the ground to reach inside my boot and pull out my knife. I jump to my feet and cough and sputter, and I'm still weak, still scared, but now there's a knife—eight inches of steel just sharpened yesterday—between me and the two men edging closer to me, the two men who aren't strangers: It's the Ersland brothers, Jorah armed with a rope and my gun, and Nils with a smile.

"We meet again," Nils says. "And today, we come prepared." He opens his coat and reveals the butt of a gun sticking up from a holster. It's a small, compact French gun called a Lefaucheux 20-round, notable because it holds twenty cartridges of ammunition instead of six.

"We wanted to continue our conversation from the ship. You will come with us, and we will have a little talk."

"I'm not really interested in talking," I say, and my voice sounds so creaky and raw that I wince.

"We don't want to fight you. We simply have some questions. So you will cooperate, yes? Or we will have to use this." He motions to the gun—still holstered—in a manner that, to someone else, would probably look threatening. But I hear Boone's voice in my ears, reminding me that a gun only beats a knife from twenty yards away. "Any closer than that," Boone told me once, "and in the time it takes to pull out the gun, cock it, and aim, you've been stabbed. So don't get into a knife fight, boy, unless you plan on being shredded to ribbons."

I lift my knife and shift my weight onto my toes.

"I think, no, I won't cooperate," I say, and Nils's head jerks, slightly, to Jorah, still holding the rope and my Dragoon. He leaps forward and I'm ready for him, slashing out with the knife before he can even lift my gun. He lets out a cry and a line of red appears on his face, and his hands go up and my Dragoon clatters to the ground and he falls to his knees. Nils isn't smiling anymore, tugging his own gun from its holster, but before he can move, I'm on him with the knife, slicing at his hands first, then his arms. Then when he takes a step back, I take a step forward, and now he's pinned against a wall with steel between him and me, his eyes wide and blood dripping from his hands to my boots. I touch the point of the knife to the hollow of his throat and say, "Take another step forward."

He makes noises that sound like they want to be words, and when I see his bleeding hands drift to his sides, I press the knife into his skin and say, "Hands up against the wall."

Slowly, they float up and hang suspended, curled into loose claws streaked with blood.

"Even if you kill us," he whispers, "there will be others after you."

My eyes narrow, my pulse hot and fast like I can smell the fight and the blood and the panic. I want him to attack me so I have an excuse to kill him, because I know what he says is true: There are other hunters after the *shar*, and getting rid of the Erslands won't mean Boone and I are safe. But it sure would make me feel better.

All this floods through my head in less than a second, but it's a second too long, because before I can decide what to do there's a groan, a yell, behind me. I just manage to step out of the way before Jorah barrels into me, his hands stretched out in front of him and his mouth open in a scream and his eyes black with anger. I step back, I stumble, I lose my balance for a moment, and he's on top of me, those huge paws of his like bricks pounding into my cheek, my chest, the side of my head. I try to swipe him with the knife, but somewhere in between falling and my nose crunching like a shell, the knife slips from my hand and out of my reach. He lifts me to my feet, turns me around, grabs my arms and twists them behind my back, reaches a hand around to my cheek, struggling, scrabbling at my skin with his nails. Then I remember what Nils told me about him—he's a Percept, he needs to touch to understand a person's power—and I realize that's what they really want: not to kill me, or maybe not yet, but to know what I am.

But even as I feel Jorah's fingers claw at my skin, trying to get a good read on me, I'm not scared. I'm grinning. Sweat drips, stinging, into my eyes, and my arms feel like two rods of hot metal. I can't breathe, and my legs shake underneath me, and I'm grinning. I'm excited, I feel alive, woken up the same way that fear always wakes me up, and I shake myself like a dog. When the hand slides flat against my jaw, all the force and energy and excitement and rage inside me explodes like a firework, and I let out a scream and whip my body into a storm of movement, of power, raw like a machine. I hear Jorah struggle to keep hold of me, and then I hear nothing but white rushing and the sound of my breathing. From very far away I think I know what's happening: He's letting go of me, he's backing away. I'm attacking him with fists and elbows and toes, but all I see of the world is a red curtain of fury. When I finally manage to pull my mind back to the present moment, there is blood on the knuckles of my fists and I'm on my knees with a body underneath me and a face that looks dented and wet like a piece of old fruit. There's an explosion of noise, of smoke, of bits of brick that hit me from behind, and I look up and realize Nils is shooting at me.

He's got his Lefaucheux out in front of him, and he's

fumbling with it, awkward only in the way a hunter who relies too much on magic would be. I scramble to my feet just as another bullet brushes past me, heat and sound and flame leaping out of the barrel with it. But then the Lefaucheux is aimed at my chest and I'm the one pinned against the wall, and Nils nods at me and says, "*Now*, we talk."

"I don't have anything to say to you," I say, breathing hard. Nils considers this for a moment before he glances at Jorah, still on the ground, his eyes squeezed shut, breathing hard and moaning and bloody but awake, and says something to him in their language.

"*Ja*," Jorah says, lifting up one bloody hand, and he passes Nils a fistful of papers: my train tickets. Nils thumbs through them carefully, reading the names, the routes, before stopping at the last ticket.

"Constantinople," Nils says, and he turns to me with a smile. "Then you've heard the rumors, too. You're off to the Luciferidies' headquarters, aren't you?"

"Give them back," I say, but Nils instead lets the tickets fall from his fingertips like snow and turns back to Jorah, asking him a question.

"*Nei*," Jorah says through gritted teeth, and Nils frowns, asks something else, lifting a hand to motion toward me, but Jorah only shakes his head harder and repeats, "*Nei, nei!*"

When Nils speaks again, his voice sharp, annoyed, Jorah lets out a stream of rapid Norwegian, gesturing to me, to his face, to the gun, before shaking his head. A muscle tenses in Nils's jaw as Jorah speaks, and when he finally falls silent, Nils turns to me, the gun still lifted toward my chest.

"He thinks you cannot possibly be worth the trouble you cause us," Nils says. "He thinks we should simply get rid of you now."

"Maybe he's right."

"American cheek. What is it about you that gives you such confidence, boy?" Nils's voice drifts away, soft, thinking. "What kind of power do you have?"

"Come touch me and find out," I say. "Or kill me, same as you did Tagore."

Nils's eyes widen slightly, the gun wavering for a moment. "What did you say?" he asks in that same soft voice, and Jorah barks something in Norwegian that shakes the dreaminess from Nils's face and leaves him steely, casual once again.

"Yes. Yes, I think you might be right," Nils says, and he lowers the gun to my chest and pulls the trigger.

Everything slows down: I shout, I try to throw my hands up to block the bullet from entering my chest and tearing apart my heart, but nothing happens, and I open my eyes and thank whatever good luck is following me tonight, because that stupid fancy gun, that 20-round beauty, has jammed.

I don't stick around to wonder what happens next. I drop to the ground and scoop up my gun, my knife, my crumpled tickets, and then I run, darting down an alleyway, followed by the sounds of shouts and swearing and footsteps. But this is Paris, a city of narrow, medieval streets, of dead ends and darkness, and it takes me only seconds to lose them. Sure, the Erslands know how to track people, know how to cast stones on the ground that would show which way their quarry's gone, how to scry for someone in a puddle of water or a piece of tin polished mirror-bright, but that'll never work on me. As I run through the streets, my mouth stretches into a grin, and I've never been so happy to be a blank, invisible and invincible and alive.

Seventeen

MY NOSE STARTS BLEEDING AGAIN WHEN I
get to the hotel and kick open the door to my and Boone's
room. In the dark, Boone jumps awake, rolling off his bed
with his hand stretching for his gun, but I'm lit up from the
lamps in the hallway, and when he sees it's only me, he tosses
the gun back to the bed.

"Mal! Careful, boy, I almost shot you. You—great seas!
What in blazes happened to you?"

I grin as I walk into the room, still holding my shirt cuff
up to my bleeding nose. "You should see the other fellows."

"Fellows?" Boone gives me a look and walks over to the
whale-oil lamp set on the table before striking a match.
"What's that? Did you fight Ali Baba and his forty thieves?"

"The Ersland brothers," I say, and Boone gives me such a

long stare of surprise that he doesn't notice his match is running out until the flame singes his fingers with a hiss.

"What did they want?" he asks, blowing on his fingers before lighting the lamp with another match.

"What do you think? Information, of course." I catch the handkerchief that Boone throws me and press it to my nose.

"And how successful were they in this endeavor?" Boone asks, giving me a skeptical look, and I let out a sigh and shrug.

"They found my train tickets. They know where we're going and maybe even what the Luciferidies are planning."

"You *told* them?"

"No, of course not. But they might have found out anyway." I drop the handkerchief from my face, crumpling it into a ball, not looking at him. "I…I went back to Tagore's office. There were signs of a struggle and…he's missing. He's dead." The moment I say the words, I know they're true, and although I expect to be filled with grief, disappointment, instead a wild, reeling feeling of abandon runs through me, as though I'm walking the edge of a cliff and laughing like a lunatic. Tagore's dead. Dead! He survived decades as a blank, and then the night he meets me, he's murdered! I want to start laughing, and I do, and Boone gives me a strange look.

"What were you doing back there?" he asks, his voice icy. A smile still stretched across my lips, I shrug again.

"I went—I went to go make sure that man you attacked was all right."

"You…How *noble* of you."

The humor dies as something flares up inside me, and I throw the handkerchief to the floor. "Maybe I wouldn't have had to check up on him if you had acted like a real hunter and controlled yourself back there."

"And a real hunter thinks it's wise to go back to the place he's just broken into?" Boone asks, tapping his fingertips against the table, quick and impatient. "A real hunter picks fights with the Erslands? Shows them our next move? Do you even realize how much you've jeopardized—Where are you going?"

My nose has finally quit bleeding, and I stand up, brush my hands down my pants, and tuck my shirttail back into my waistband. "Out."

"Out?" Boone's voice is very cold. "You're a bloody mess."

But I ignore him, the buzzing in my heart, my brain, my blood like a million bees, a swarm of barely intact energy that I have to put to use, I have to burn away, or it's going to eat me from the inside out.

"I'm going to get a drink," I say, mopping the blood off my lips and chin.

"It's three in the morning."

"And when has that ever stopped *you*?"

A pause, and when I look back at Boone, his eyes are narrowed at me. "The bars have all closed," he says, speaking very carefully.

"I don't recall *that* having ever stopped you, either," I say, turning to him as I straighten my collar. Even though my nose blooms with pain and my hands already are turning red and puffy and my ribs feel rearranged inside my body, the hole in my chest is filled with fire and I need to let it burn wild.

"Sit down," Boone says, sounding suddenly weary, and I laugh.

"I'm going out. Don't wait up."

"Sit *down*. You're injured. I don't want you wandering about on your own tonight. You shouldn't even have gone out earlier. Go to bed and get some rest."

I look at him, watching me with his hand on his temple and a frown on his lips, appearing for all the world like a father disappointed with his wild son. And why wouldn't he be disappointed? When do I ever disobey him? But he's not my father, I don't want to stay in, and now the fire that burned fearsomely wild has turned suddenly cold.

"What will you do to stop me?" I ask, my voice light, and Boone raises his head from his hand, catches my eye. I can see his jaw quiver, the muscles clenching and jumping, and *Get up*, I think, *Throw a punch*, I think, *Come on, let's do it.*

"Where's this recklessness coming from?" he asks, and he speaks so quietly I can almost see him straining to pull back the reins. "Is this Burma all over again?"

Heat prickles across my cheeks in an uncomfortable wave, and I narrow my eyes. "You're bringing that up, then? That was ages ago. I'm different now. I can control myself."

"Can you? You don't look like you're doing a tremendously brilliant job at the moment," Boone says, and he stands up and crosses to the door, closing and locking it in one fluid gesture. Without looking at me, he pulls the covers back on his bed and climbs in.

"Take your shoes off," he says. "I'll not pay a copper cent for laundry just because you get your sheets mucky with mud."

For a moment, I just watch him, turning his back to me in his bed, and I know he does it because he expects me to obey him. The thought makes me want to drag him from between the sheets out into the alley and show him who's really in charge. But then suddenly it feels so ridiculous to me, this tension between Boone and me, that I laugh.

"Poor Boone," I say, and I bend down and yank off my boots. "Did I make you angry? I thought for a moment there that you'd fetch a switch and rap my knuckles."

He's quiet as I pick up the lamp and take it to the night table between our beds, quiet as I sit down, quiet as I slip my suspenders off my shoulders and slide into bed, and then he says, softly, "Boy, you keep making jokes like that and one day someone will take you seriously."

And the fire flares up, hot and angry, before I laugh again and lean in to blow out the lamp. "Maybe so," I say. "But not today."

Eighteen

BURMA. TEN MONTHS AGO. THE FIRST TIME Boone and I fought and the first time I felt the hole inside me turn into the madness of a blank.

The British East India Company had won the war against the Burmese twenty years prior and moved into the cities a good collection of officers in white pants and their bell-skirted, sausage-curled wives. We came to sell off a slew of charms to nervous British women and their maids, who were far enough from home to worry that every shadow meant their deaths. A few nights before our scheduled departure, Boone heard from an officer at a bar about a monkey that lived in western Assam, in a forest bordered by three rivers and a mountain.

"Easy enough to find," the officer had said. "And worth a king's ransom if you can capture it. Fur of gold, like, and turns anything it bites into gold. A fellow found one after the war and made a gift of it to Queen Victoria on her wedding day. Heard he's been knighted and is living rich as a thief in a manor in Wales. The monkey was supposed to go to the London Zoo, but some fool scientist from the Zoological Society went and vivisected the poor bugger. Broke the queen's heart, like, and I bet she'd pay dearly for a replacement. I'd go after it myself, but I've got my duties and a wife besides. But if I were a younger man..."

I gave Boone a look behind the man's back, the kind of look that said I didn't believe this man or the promise of fabulous riches, a knighthood, the favor of a queen. Hunting's thick with such stories, tales more fantastic than their subjects, and Boone well knew it. But when I caught his eye, I could see he was already far gone, his mouth open in a rapturous smile, his eyes glazed over even though it had been ages since he touched the weak ale sitting in a dented metal cup before him.

"And where did you say this little monkey could be found?" he asked, leaning forward, and I frowned. We'd planned on spending the winter in the French Riviera, and now it seemed we would spend it in the jungle.

The problem, as always, was money.

Boone could make it and he could spend it and he always wanted more of it. Like a lot of hunters, he found himself attracted to easy-sounding jobs with big payoffs, but unlike other hunters, he usually had the skills and experience to pull them off. He had me, after all, and that gave him more than enough advantage, and he also had his Silvertongue ability, which made it easy for him to find out any information he needed. But none of it mattered, because he gambled and he drank and he bought lavish clothing and then ruined it by sleeping in the gutter and he liked fine things that didn't last: food and parties and nights in good hotels and women without last names.

Still, this was a job I thought he'd turn down, if not for the dubious knighthood and the fact that we knew nothing about the forests of Assam in Burma, then because the one thing that set us apart from other hunters would do us no good: my blankness. Had this been a fire-breathing monkey or an invisible monkey or a monkey with a poisonous bite, I might have been of some use to Boone, but as it was, a gold-furred, gold-making monkey could run and jump and hide just as well as any other kind, and I couldn't do anything more to help him catch it than run around with a net and a hope.

And yet, four days later, after our stock of charms finally sold out, Boone took me to the British outfitter, loaded our packs with canteens of water and packets of already-stale food, and led us out into the jungle.

"It'll take a month at most, boy," he said as I watched the lights of civilization wink out behind us, but three months later we were wet and cold and hungry and miserable and lost and no closer to finding that blasted monkey than when we left.

"I'm not a tracker," I said to him, huddling over the fire we had made, which hissed and sputtered in the wet air and threw up plumes of smoke that stained our skin sooty brown and made my eyes water. We'd been arguing, again, exhausted, again, and frustrated. We'd just spent two weeks sitting in a makeshift blind in a part of the jungle where a group of villagers had told Boone—or so he said—the monkey would visit. Fourteen hours a day, fourteen days, sitting in a tent just big enough to fit both of us if we crammed our legs to our chests and wrapped our arms around ourselves, and neither of us able to talk or move or make any sort of noise. Fourteen hours a day, every day, for two weeks, enough to drive any man mad. And then in the afternoon, another day wasted, Boone said on second thought, perhaps he hadn't quite understood what the villagers were saying and we were camping in the wrong place.

I'd wanted, for a moment, to kill him. But instead I rose from the blind and dismantled it without a word and stuffed our tarps back into our packs and silently seethed.

Boone tilted his head up at the canopy of trees above us. Beyond the outlines of the leaves, it was possible to make out a dense carpet of stars, brighter on this night with no moon. It was beautiful, but I was tired. I was angry. I didn't want to be in this jungle anymore, chasing something that might not exist, and I blamed Boone.

"We'll find it," he said, his face still pointing skyward, and I took a deep breath and sighed. My skin felt puffy and swollen with heat, my lungs heavy and wet. I hadn't minded the jungle, the raw, earthy smell of it, the warmth like a cloud—at least, I hadn't minded it three months ago. But now when I inhaled, everything stank of rotting trees, rotting animals, and my skin itched from all the moisture dewing on my arms and neck.

"Hey-ho!"

A voice in the distance and Boone and I jumped to our feet, Boone pulling his gun, me reaching for the machete sheathed next to my bag. We hadn't seen too many people out here—tribal folk, mostly, who took our iron trinkets and Western hats and traded us fresh meat, fruits—but this was a British voice, calling for us, and that meant either an army camp, in which case we might see the inside of a bathtub and a bar tent, or another team of hunters after the golden monkey, in which case they'd probably try to cut down on the competition by killing us.

"Steady," Boone whispered, "steady." But hiding wouldn't do us any good; even in this dense jungle at night, our smoke-spewing fire was like a hundred-foot arrow pointing in our direction, and the voice was too close to hide.

The machete grew sweaty under my fingers as I squinted into the shadows, listening for more voices, footsteps.

"Hello?"

The voice came again, closer this time, and we heard footsteps, rustling, twigs breaking, and then, from between two twisted trees, a face popped out, smiling, underneath a trim blue officer's cap.

"Well, hello! I thought I saw a fire," the man said, still smiling, and Boone let out a breath and slid his gun into his holster before introducing us.

Bath, I thought, letting out a breath as I sheathed the machete. *Bath and food and new faces.*

They were a small unit, tasked with escorting a team of royal cartographers around Assam, but they still had enough comforts of home to make their camp feel like paradise. They invited us to supper, a pair of spare cots, and their company as they made their way northward toward the mountains, and we accepted all three.

Being around strangers, new faces, new voices—it was better to me than the fresh food they brought or the change of clothes they offered or the cots they lent us to keep us from sleeping on the ground. I missed being around crowds, telling stories, and I had long grown sick of seeing only Boone and hearing only my own thoughts buzzing like gnats in my ears. I felt more starved for company than for food, and simply being one among them made me feel like a flower after a rainstorm, bright and fresh and full, once again, of life.

The next morning we told them about the monkey, and they laughed and said they'd heard plenty of tales, but they'd marched in these jungles for well on three years and not seen so much as a golden hair.

"You'd do best to give it up," one officer told us. "We've a group going back to the capital in two days, and you're welcome to join them."

My heartbeat picked up. I smiled. Back in the capital, back to the crowds, the noise, the heat and movement of people, back to ships that could take us somewhere new, back to having something to look forward to. I wanted to go. I wanted to go right that second, throw down my pack and run, and even the thought of waiting two days was like ants crawling over my body—I just wanted to kick and scream and *leave now*.

"Thanks, but no," Boone said. "We'll keep hunting."

For a moment, I thought I hadn't heard him proper. What? What had he said? *No?* My pulse seemed to slow, slow, deepen, boom and echo within my body, and then Boone was saying something else, he was laughing with the officer, he wasn't going to leave, we were going to be stuck out here in a wasteland of nothingness chasing a ghost for the rest of our lives. My slowed-down heart suddenly sped to hummingbird speed and I had to turn away. I had to pick up my pack with shaking hands and ignore the machete strapped to the side, the machete that I wanted to unsheathe and slash against the nearest tree until it was reduced to splinters and every ounce of energy within me had been leached away.

I practically vibrated as I walked deeper into the camp, searching for something, anything to take my mind off what I'd just heard. Stay in the jungle for who knows how long. Stay stuck with Boone. I felt like a dead person and I was angry to feel like that. I wanted wind on my cheeks and cities and noise and excitement and energy, and if I didn't get it, I would go off like a powder keg.

Voices, laughter drew me to the edges of camp, where a group of men stood at the river, wet and wearing nothing but their white underdrawers. They were cheering something, someone, looking up into the branches of the tree at the edge of the riverbed, and just as I got close enough to look up, a figure leaped from the branches, arms and legs pinwheeling through the air, and landed with a splash in the water.

More cheering, and the next man hooked a hand over a branch and pulled himself up the tree.

When one of the soldiers saw me, he smiled and gestured toward the river. "Want a go? Smartest way to cool off in this heat!"

I watched the soldier climb, climb, and then push off from the branch, spin midair, and land in the water, screaming with laughter the whole time. Yes. Yes, I wanted a go.

I peeled off my sweat-stiff clothes and my boots, tossed them in a pile at the base of the tree, and took my turn at climbing. The tree itself was of the typical jungle variety—not the smooth-barked trees I saw in America or Europe but more like a thousand slender trunks wound and woven together into one mass, its surface covered with stringy green vines, the fuzz of moss, and slick with moisture. It was easy enough to climb, my bare toes sliding into crevices, my fingers strong and tense, and I grinned as I ascended through the tree. It reminded me of nothing less than climbing a mast, and my muscles relaxed into familiar motions.

"Jump!" one of the men from below shouted, and I realized I had gone high enough, so I settled my feet into the crook of a branch and took a few steps forward. The other men had clutched to tree branches, their knuckles white, but I was used to walking heights like this, usually in a gale with my weight swinging back and forth. When I looked down into the swirling waters, I thought again about the sea, ships I'd sailed on, the many times I'd wished I could have jumped from the mainmast into the ocean on a hot day, and now I closed my eyes and stepped out into nothingness and let myself fall.

Air slapped my bare skin, my face. I was screaming without even realizing it, every inch of me buzzing with fear and happiness and wild, mad joy, and I hit the water and hit the cold and fell into darkness and pushed myself up and broke up through the surface gasping and laughing and more alive than I'd felt in three long months.

Quickly, I waded to the bank and lined up for another turn, my eyes open and bright. I wanted to go again, to jump through the air again, and the next time I climbed, I climbed higher, craving a bigger swoop of fear in the pit of my stomach, a longer fall, a deeper plunge. I jumped two more times, then five more times, even though most of the soldiers were relaxing on the banks now, exhausted. By the time Boone came over to see what I was doing, my skin was pink like a piece of candy and my heart was pounding and I was angry at myself because now when I jumped I didn't get that swoop of fear anymore. I needed to go higher.

"What in blazes are you doing?" Boone asked, frowning up at the tree. I ignored him, reaching for a branch and swinging myself up in a practiced motion. He'd reminded me of what drove me to the tree in the first place, the months wasted, the time wasted, the hours spent crammed and cramped and exhausted and bored, and the hours yet to be spent, which for all I knew would stretch into eternity. And so I climbed, my body like a machine, the branches around me growing thinner, bending deeper under my weight, and somewhere from down below I heard Boone ask, "He's high, then, isn't he?" and another shock of hot anger ran through me and I kept climbing.

"Get down, boy!" Boone called from below, and soon he was joined by other voices, the other soldiers: "You're too high! You can't jump from there!" But I ignored them because I craved air, height. I wanted to look down and feel a jolt of fear, feel *something*. When my hand slipped and I lost a foot of height and grabbed myself at the last moment and heard a wave of gasps below, I grinned, I laughed, I thought *yes*, this is what I wanted, this excitement, this pounding of my heart. And I kept climbing.

I stopped only when I reached the crown of the tree, when the surrounding forest appeared around me fuzzy-headed and green and small, the river below silent and steely. How high was I? Seventy feet? A hundred? I couldn't tell. Not as high as a mast, not as high as I'd ever been, but still well enough into the air that a fall to the water might be enough to kill a man, and I didn't care. Sweat slicked over my palms, and I took a step forward on a branch barely thicker than my arm.

"Mal! *Mal!*" Screaming from below, panicked screaming that only made my grin stretch wider, although I wasn't sure if what I was feeling was happiness anymore but I knew my head spun and all the hairs on my skin stood straight up and I wanted to fly, I wanted to close my eyes and feel the rush of air and movement and falling and—

I jumped.

Everything slowed down, long seconds of screaming, swearing, Boone's voice lifted into a cry of anguish, and I spread my arms above my head and felt wings sprout out of my back and how long did I fall? Three seconds or a lifetime, but for however long it was, I lived in a world of soft, muted colors and kaleidoscope emotions, and then the water grew bigger, wider, blacker, and I hit. My mind went blank, my body went limp, bright lights sparkled before my eyes, and everything hurt and I fell into another world that existed outside of time, only this world was cold and black and I couldn't breathe.

And then I woke up, and Boone was with me, and we were

back in the capital, just like that, like when I'd jumped, I'd made a wish and landed right exactly where I wanted to be. It was my laughing that finally got Boone's attention, him turning on me so quickly and letting loose a stream of information: I'd been unconscious a week and I had a broken arm and he'd thought I was dead and what was I doing, what was I thinking, why had I done that?

But I didn't have an answer. Instead, I asked him where we were going next.

He looked at me for a long time, not answering, and then he took a seat. We were in a room I recognized as one of the Western hotels set up for visiting British and their wives, and it was dark outside, late, Boone's clothes rumpled and dirty and his face lined with exhaustion.

"I've never seen a person act like that before," he said softly. "You lost your mind, Mal. Truly, I thought you had. I thought you were going to kill yourself for no good reason, like you had turned into—never mind that."

He shook his head, and in the pause I sat up a little straighter, my eyes a little wider, and I finished his sentence in my head: *like I had turned into a monster. Like I had turned into a real blank.*

"I didn't know what to think about it," Boone said. "I still don't. I thought I knew you and could trust you, and you go and do a thing like that. We're partners, aren't we?"

"Yes," I said, and he ran a hand over his face.

"We work together, and I need to know I can trust you. I

need to *know* you," he said, and he gave me a funny look, like he wasn't so certain of it himself. "What made you go up in that tree?"

I knew, I knew with every ounce of myself, that he was Silvertonguing me, maybe out of habit, maybe out of foolish hope, because he wanted to know: Was it happening? Was I turning? Was the little wolf pup about to tear and claw and attack, and should he take precautions now, before it got too dangerous? He stared at me, and I knew he wanted me to say something to put his mind at ease, something that would make sense or be funny or at least remind him that I was Mal, his partner, the boy he'd found and not something strange and illogical and unreasonable and dangerous.

"Why did you do it?" he asked, desperate, and I blinked at him.

"I wanted to take a swim."

A muscle just below his eye twitched, but otherwise he didn't move, his eyes still rooted to my face, and I realized I had said the wrong thing.

"Have you gone mad?" he whispered, and the way he asked it made it sound like he was asking himself. Anger flared up inside me; he didn't trust me anymore, he didn't see me anymore, and I sat up in bed so fast that he startled and tensed.

"I'm the mad one? You had me in that blind for two weeks," I said, my eyes narrowed. "You wasted our time chasing a creature that doesn't exist. We had an opportunity to get out and go on to the next job and you passed it up."

But this didn't soothe him, and he lifted his chin, surprise etched into his face. "Was that it?" he asked softly. "Angry at me, were you, for keeping you out on a job too long? Thought you'd throw a tantrum? And here I thought you were near a man, not a little boy."

"And here I thought you were a real hunter," I said, breathing hard, "not a gold-chasing rookie with more greed than sense."

Boone rose slowly to his feet, his hands balled into fists, and instinctively I sat up straighter and glanced around the room for my knife, my gun, any kind of weapon.

"You saved my life once, boy, and I owe you a debt," Boone said, his words careful. "And that debt's so great it's going to keep us partners, and I'm going to leave this room and get us both some dinner, and when I come back, we'll be partners still and we'll forget what's happened and move on.

"But I will tell you one thing: If you ever question me like that again, if you ever take such offense at the work we do that you seek out danger like that again, if you ever needlessly risk your life or mine—I don't care what you did for me. I'll abandon you. I'll leave you forever. And you'll be nothing more than an orphan again, alone and friendless." He leaned in slightly, bending down not quite low enough that we were on the same level but so that I had to tilt my face up to look at him.

"Understand me?" he asked, and my heart pounded and my skin tingled and fear swept through my veins—real fear, not that manufactured stuff I felt up in the tree, part excitement and part madness, but fear that left me cold and shaking and small and thirteen years old again, watching my best friend abandon me. I said the only thing I possibly could.

"Yes. Yes, of course."

Nineteen

THE MORNING AFTER MY RUN-IN WITH THE
Ersland brothers, I wake up with my head a pulse of pain, my
vision blurry and shot through with red, but the thing that
confuses me most is this bleary sense that I did something
wrong. I lie in bed a minute, staring up at the ceiling, before it
all comes back to me in waves of guilt: Tagore's empty office,
my fight with the Ersland brothers, the lightning bolts of anger
that shot through me as I talked with Boone.

I could have killed him last night. Boone, the only person I can trust anymore, and he looked at me like I was a
stranger.

Wincing, I sit up and glance over at Boone's bed—
unmade, as always, and empty. Panic rises from my stomach,
and the first thing I think is *He's finally left me behind*, but

then I blink, take note of the pale sunshine tiptoeing through the window. It's morning, yes, but still early, barely dawn and hours before we have to leave for the train station.

So where is he? Where did he go, and why? To get away from me?

I rub the stubble on my chin and grimace when I find a sore spot on my jaw.

"What did I do?" I whisper, and I look down at my hands until they tremble, and then tuck them quickly back under the sheet. I feel as if I'm losing my mind. I feel as if I'm losing *me*, and with my heart pounding and my head confused, I think, *It's happening.*

Quickly, I slide out of bed to get dressed, reaching first for the clothes I wore yesterday before I catch sight of red-brown bloodstains and, frowning, throw the shirt and pants aside. When I find a clean set of clothing, I dress and am on my way out the door, pausing just long enough to check my face in the small, square mirror hanging by the door.

I look a right mess, bruises blooming across my cheek and jaw, my left eye nearly swollen shut and framed by comma-shaped scratches. There's a basin of water on the floor from Boone's morning shave, and I try to mop up the dried blood as best I can, but it doesn't do much. For once, I look exactly the way I feel.

My hands shake, my chest trembles, my feet itch to move, and so I go—out the door and into the street without any thought of what I'm doing except the assurance that I can't stay in that room, waiting for Boone and worrying about what he thinks of me.

And as I walk, one refrain sifts through my mind, as constant and never-ending as waves: *There is something wrong with me, there is something wrong with me, there is something wrong with me....*

I know. I've always known. I've got something in my blood. Something I can't control. And even though I've expected it for years now, I hoped it would be ages before it actually happened, before the monster took me over. But last night...I felt it. Clawing and free.

Tagore's face floats before my eyes, and I feel a cramp of frustration. How did he do it? How did he survive the monster? He's proof that there's a way I can overcome this madness and stay myself. But I don't even know the first thing to try, and he's not around anymore to ask.

Wheeling madly through the streets, I don't pay attention to where I'm going and nearly knock aside an old woman bent over the empty cart she's hauling behind her. Once she regains her balance, she shoves me and shouts at me in French, something about paying a little mind to where my feet carry me, and asks me what kind of manners I have, and with my heartbeat like hummingbird wings and my mind on the lunacy inside me, her question strikes me as so funny that I stumble away from her as fast as I can before she sees me burst into laughter.

Manners! Oh yes, I'm a monster, but a well-mannered one.

I know how to eat with my fork and how to tip my hat to ladies and how to use my knife to properly cut open a man's throat. And so what if I have a hunger to kill or attack or destroy? I'll be a good boy and wipe my mouth clean of blood as soon as I'm done.

There's a sensation like a million bugs under my skin, and I shove up my shirtsleeves to scratch, raking my nails over my arms, my wrists, my neck, my chest. I know what I must look like, my face a riot of bruises and my nails leaving pink welts all over my body. The people I pass glance away from me, thinking, most likely, that I'm one of those poor opium addicts, freshly stumbled from the den, tossed out addled and penniless to stagger along their streets and frighten their children until I can find enough coin to pay for my next trip, but I don't care. Better an opium addict than a blank. Addicts— they can sit through their misery and eventually come out clean, but this *thing* will live inside me my whole life.

Up ahead, I catch the familiar scent of earth, sweet rot, greenery, and I recognize the flower market. I careen toward it, the wild thing willing me forward, dragging me down the street, through the stalls, and out to what might as well have been my destination all along: *rue des potions magiques*.

It's so quiet, sleepy and shuttered with only a few enterprising vendors and a few mildly curious shoppers milling around, but that doesn't matter: The stall I'm looking for is already open, manned by a dark-skinned woman, her hair wrapped up in a brightly colored scarf and her eyes sharp as she watches me approach.

"*Bonjour*," she says. "*Comment allez-vous?*"

She leans against her stall, tilts her head at me, studying me, and the hunter inside me studies her right back, taking in the peculiar twisted gold charm hanging around her neck— gold, for protection—and the scent of almond oil rising from her skin, mild and bittersweet, meant to sharpen her senses. Necklace and oil aside, though, she wears no charms, no rings or bracelets, no marks scratched into her skin, and that, more than anything, tells me she's an Other.

"I'm looking for something," I say, and my voice trembles. Her sharp eyes narrow.

"Per'aps I do not 'ave it," she says, her accent thick as velvet. "Per'aps you would find it in Pigalle."

Pigalle. Great seas—it's a neighborhood crowded with brothels, with opium dens—and I let out a bark of high-pitched laughter that does nothing to dispel the wariness in the woman's face.

"No, that's not it," I say, my words still shaky.

"I do not 'ave bandages, either," she says, eyeing the cuts and scrapes across my face.

"No. I'm not here for that."

Frowning at me, she crosses her arms over her chest. "Then what?"

I open my mouth to try to speak and find it dry, brittle,

scratchy like old leaves, and I swallow, try again. "I need…
I need…" My words come out in a whisper, and she tilts her
head to hear better. "A…a *cure*."

"Cure?" Her eyes sweep over me, top to bottom. "For *un
sort*? A…ah…a curse?"

"No," I say, and, still shaking, I realize what madness this
is, to come here, to come looking for—what?—and to admit
to this stranger what I am. "It's…it's not for me."

"It never ees." She sighs. "*Alors*, it ees a lovers' spat? What
deed she do to you? *Ne vous inquiétez pas*, there ees a way to
grow eet back."

"No. No, no. I'm looking for…I said it's not for me, but
I need, I know someone and he's a…I need a cure for being a
blank."

A tiny explosion seems to occur behind the woman's eyes,
and she pulls back, breathing hard through her nose, her whole
body stiff with surprise, with fear, and after several seconds
of stunned silence, she's all movement, dipping below her stall
for bundles of herbs, for bottles, her movements so precise and
practiced that for a moment my heart rises in my chest and
I think, *She has it!* before I realize she's setting a warding-off
spell, protection magic, boundary magic—against *me*.

"Wait," I say, and she shakes her head, striking a match
and setting it to the bundled herbs so that they give off a dense,
clean-smelling smoke.

"There ees nothing like that 'ere," she says. "Or anywhere."

"You have to help me," I say, leaning forward, right into

her smoke, and when her eyes widen again, I realize I've made another mistake, confirming for her what I truly am. She reels backward, hands raised.

"*Mais, c'est vous!*" she says. "*Bonhomme de bois!* In the market yesterday! It was you!"

"Quiet!" I say, and I reach through the stall, grab her arms, try to keep her from running or shouting or calling out, and if the market were open, full of customers as usual, someone surely would have tried to stop me by now, help the woman. But it's early yet and the corridors are empty and we are alone and I shake her, shake her until her eyes roll in her head, and I hiss, "*Stop it.*"

"Let me go!" she says, eyes darting from my face to my hands, to where they touch her skin. "*Laissez-moi!* Let me go!"

"I need a cure!"

"*Non, non!*" She shakes her head. "Does not exist! *Bonshommes de bois*—wooden ones—blanks—there is no cure! Please, please..."

"There *has* to be a way," I say. "You sell cures for every kind of magical malady."

"*Bonshommes de bois* are not magic! They are untouchable. There ees no kind of magic to save them. I can't—*non*, I can't, there ees nothing, nothing I or anyone, no one can help you."

I grip her arms so tight she lets out a small yelp of pain, and I can feel the monster inside me relish it, her fear and her pain and her panic, and the rest of me, the other part of me, the good part, the normal part, cringes.

"You don't understand," I whisper, "I'm going mad. It's *changing* me. I have to stop it before I hurt someone. Before I *kill* someone."

"Stop it? Stop it—*oui*." She takes a deep breath, shaky but steadying. "*Oui*, stop it, there is something. . . . Take it."

"What is it? Where?" I let her go, and, wincing, rubbing her arms, she ducks below the stall. I hear the sound of clinking glass, small things being shifted around, and then she rises, slowly, her right hand a fist around something, her whole body drawn tight and shaking.

"'Ere," she whispers, holding out her hand. A tiny red bottle, barely the length of my pinkie finger, sits shining in her palm. "Take it and go."

"What will it do?" I whisper, and she stares at me for a long second.

"Stop it."

I don't think. I yank out the cork, my fingers sweaty against the crimson-colored glass, bring the bottle to my lips, and I'm about to throw it back when I see something on the woman's face, a look of disgust, of anticipation of something unpleasant but necessary, the kind of look you might see on the face of a butcher just before he cuts the throat of a pig, or a whale man as he raises his lance to deliver a killing stab, and carefully I inhale. I breathe in such acrid sweetness that, coughing, I yank the bottle away, throw it to the ground, where it smashes and the liquid hisses, releasing coils of smoke.

Poison.

She tried to kill me, and when I look at her with shock, she stares back as even as a judge.

"That ees the only way you can stop it," she says, her voice very low and very calm. "Eef you want to keep people safe from yourself, you will find ano'her bottle and have courage to drink."

"There has to be another way," I say, and she shakes her head.

"The only safe blank ees a dead blank."

I run before she can raise the alarm.

Twenty

I'M LUCKY. BY THE TIME I MAKE IT BACK
to the room, Boone still hasn't come back, and I can wash my
face and put some food in my stomach and breathe, in and out,
deep and slow, until my heart stops shivering and my hands
stop shaking and I can forget, for a moment, the look on the
vendor's face, her words, her judgment: *The only safe blank is a
dead blank.*

The door opens, and even though I'm expecting Boone,
I still startle to see him. His expression is drawn, tense, and I
can feel my heartbeat pick up again.

I'm sorry, I want to say to him.

That wasn't me, I want to say to him.

And another, very small, very thin voice shouts up from

the hole inside me, *Tell him if he tries to stop you again, you'll kill him.*

"You look a mess," he says.

"Boone—"

"I'm sorry I was out for so long." He reaches into his vest pocket. "I was looking for this."

He reveals a small glass pot of something thick and yellowish and opens it up as he sits across from me at the table. "Do you have any idea how difficult it is to find a healing salve with no magic in it? The apothecaries hardly even knew what I was asking for. Five shops, and then finally someone sent me to an old midwife who makes her own balms. She swears she didn't use anything magical to make it, just comfrey and goldenseal and 'a bit of this and that.' I'm not going to lie—she smacked her gums when she said that, and I took it to mean she added a little old midwife spittle. But it can't hurt, can it?"

He slides the pot over to me, and even though I'm trying to stay calm, my hands shake as I dip two fingers into the ointment. Despite the possibility of old midwife spittle, it smells like nothing more than grass, sweet and earthy, and it reminds me of the grasslands on Prince Island, wrapped up and tucked in and safe.

I rub a little on my cheek, trying not to watch Boone watching me, and when he frowns, I freeze, but he just reaches out to take the pot.

"Let me," he says, and before I can say anything, he puts a finger in the pot and reaches out to touch my face.

I'm a blank, I'm a monster. After the events of last night I wouldn't be surprised if Boone never wanted to touch me again. Every second Boone has his skin on mine, he should be wondering what I'm doing to his Talents, but instead he's firm, gentle, confident, and finally I lean in, close my eyes, inhale the scent of comfrey and goldenseal and feel the double relief of the balm and Boone's forgiveness.

I feel like a small boy, like when I was fourteen, skinny and scared and in need of my first shave, and Boone stood behind me with his straight-edge razor, spread lather on my cheeks, guided the razor over my skin, talking and laughing to keep me from feeling too twitchy, and I was able to relax, let the steel glide over my face, the pulse at my throat.

"There," he says, and I open my eyes and he's smiling at me. "I can't say you look any less a mess, but you're at least on the mend." He screws the lid back on the little pot, wipes his fingers off on his trousers, and stands. "Come on, now. We have a train to catch."

And just like that, we're partners again.

It will take us two weeks of travel, a dozen trains, a ferry, and a suspiciously cheap carriage ride to journey from Paris to Constantinople.

"Someday," Boone says, settling in on our ninth day and eighth stifling-hot train, "someone will make a lot of money by building a route that will take travelers from one place to another on *a single train*."

But it's hard to complain—a decade ago, the hills we're gliding down and punching through saw nothing but herds of cows and gentle rains.

Boone passes his time on the trains doing what he does best: talking with anyone who might be within earshot, especially if that anyone is rich, young, beautiful, or all three. We've booked second and even third cabin compartments on all the trains, but a whispered word or two opens all doors to Boone, and so when the train rolls from whatever rotted-wood, barely-there station, always with the same old woman selling the same too-dry, too-expensive sandwiches, Boone tips his cap, tells me to mind the luggage, and sets off down the train cars.

Sometimes I go with him, and I sit in the corner of the compartment and try to stay out of his way, but most of the time I sit, I look out the window, I tell myself I'm moving forward even when sitting still.

I don't like trains.

Give me a ship, where I can put myself to work or climb the mast or at least feel wind on my face. Give me a carriage with the smell of horse and reins in my hand. My own two feet, my own two hands, sweat on my skin and a feeling that I'm doing something.

But whenever I sit on a train, my breath fogging up the window and blurring the ever-changing, ever-the-same land-scape outside, I feel the walls of the compartment box me in and leave me trapped with nothing to do and no company but my own thoughts.

Alone, I think about London, the magical machines, the Crystal Palace. I think about Paris and finding Tagore's blood and the Erslands, still out there, still hunting me and Boone as surely as they hunt the *shar*. I think about my fight with Boone and the poison in the market and the sickness that's inside me, still, and then I put my head against the window and close my eyes and feel the rumble of the train run through my bones.

"Are you all right?" Boone asks me one morning. It's our last full day of train travel, and I'm as nervous as a cat, my skin slippery and gritty with sweat. He's been watching me. He knows that I'm not sleeping, tossing and turning every night for hours in the bunk above him, and there's something more than concern in the way he asks the question. Something like suspicion.

"Fine," I say, giving him a smile. "Tell Miss Faber in first class I say hello."

I expect him to leave, but instead he crosses his arms and leans against the closed door of our compartment, watch-ing me.

"After we get the *shar*," he says, his voice soft and thought-ful, "after we take it to the island and sell it, we'll have to decide where to set up."

"Set up?"

"Our confederation. We'll need a headquarters. A flat, maybe, to start, and then a building. Where do you want to live?"

I shrug. "Does it matter? We won't be spending much time there anyway, will we?"

"Of course we will. We'll be assigning jobs and recruiting members. We won't have to go out hunting anymore." Boone tilts his head at me, thinking. "Where should we go? London's the safest bet right now, although New York has some good auction houses. Or we could move out past the Appalachians. Less competition there."

"Oh no, nothing but mountain lions and man-eating bears. The perfect place to set up shop."

"Think about it," Boone says. "We won't have to spend our lives crossing the globe anymore. We'll be able to build something." He pulls open the door of the compartment and gives me a small smile. "Bit of rest would do you good."

And he's gone, leaving me alone in the compartment again. I hadn't thought about what would happen after the *shar*, should Boone get his thousands of dollars and fame. I suppose he's right: Setting up a confederation somewhere means we won't have to hunt anymore. What did he say? A "bit of rest"? But just the idea sends a flurry of panic through me. I don't want to rest. I don't want to stay put somewhere, not without knowing I'll be safe there, and I won't be safe anywhere with what's inside me. Besides which, my blankness is only an asset out in the field, hunting. How am I supposed to prove to Boone that it's worth it for him to be my partner if I'm twiddling my thumbs at a desk?

I can see it: sitting in an office somewhere out West, wearing the clothes of a young gentleman and folding my hands in my lap and looking straight ahead and the little monster inside me loopy and mad with inactivity, pacing and wild like a tiger in a cage. I'd have to keep it bottled up, chained, and with no more walls to scale or caverns to explore or masts to climb, it'll fume, an anger and wildness building up until finally I lose control....

My chest tightens so suddenly that I can't breathe, and I stand up, my head swimming, my hands clammy, and reach for the clasp at the window. I try tugging it open to get some fresh air against my cheeks, but the lock is broken, the window stuck, and my heart beats faster. I want to put my fist through the blasted glass, and now I'm shaking so hard that I reach up to our luggage balanced so neatly in the corner and yank it into disarray, throw it open and toss out my clothes, shoes, ropes, knives, my whole lock-picking kit, *smash*, right on the floor, because if I have a mess to clean up, that will be twenty minutes of blessed distraction, of peace.

I take my time. I pick up each shirt, each overdarned sock, and spread it out on the seat, press my fingers against the fabric, lift and fold as though it's paper and every crease is permanent. My hands shake and my heart pounds and my head buzzes, but it's a job, it's a thing to do, and when I think about it, I don't have to think about how in only a few months I might be trapped in an office somewhere while Boone builds something.

"Home is a place to build a future," an old salt told me once. But I've traveled the world and I'm still looking and the world has never felt so small.

It wasn't always like that. Back on Prince Island, surrounded by water, I'd go to the cottage and Essie would pull out her atlas and turn the pages and it seemed impossible, the whole world contained in a single book.

How old was I? Twelve? No, thirteen, of course, and Essie twelve, because when she showed me the atlas for the first time, she said it was a gift of goodwill from a captain—a Caleb's gift, that was the nickname for them, although I never knew why. It was the first Caleb's gift Essie ever received, the first gift that wasn't a little ribbon or a tiny wooden dog or a pendant of scrimshaw but a real, thoughtful, expensive gift. She just started receiving them that spring she turned beautiful, that spring she turned twelve.

"I have something to show you," she said to me one day, one of the rare days when we were in the cottage alone, her mother off on some errand that Essie was not trusted enough to join her for. I followed her over to her little trundle bed tucked into a corner of the cottage. I knew she kept her trinkets under there: all the little things her mother disapproved of, like the stones and butterfly wings and bird eggs she kept because they were pretty, not because of their properties in spell work, or the bright candy wrappers she collected from the gutters of New Bishop or the scraps of lace and bone buttons saved from the bin outside the dressmaker's shop or the pair of little heeled shoes she'd stolen and was too terrified to ever wear or her books.

She had so many books. The books her mother tolerated only because she felt it was important that Essie know how to speak multiple languages and do sums and know a bit about the world, but I knew for Essie the knowledge the books gave her was just secondary. They were windows, she'd say. They were doors. They were friends who truly understood her. I didn't read, which annoyed her to no end, and finally a few months before I left the island, she gave me a blank notebook, the handsome, slim kind good for carrying in pockets.

"Write your own story," she said, and when I left her, she said, "Write to me."

But I didn't do either. I used it for idle scrawls and notes on hunting jobs and tried to forget where it had come from. Books belonged to her, not me.

So I wasn't surprised when Essie led me over to the trundle and reached beneath its frame and pulled out a book. It was large, almost too large for a small twelve-year-old girl, and the cover shone with rich red hide, expensive and rare and the kind of thing that belonged in some gentleman's library next to a leather chair and a fireplace.

Carefully, she carried the book to the table, the spine

crackling as she spread its colorful pages and pinned it open like a butterfly's wings.

"It's an atlas," I said, more to myself because, of course, she already knew. She nodded, tucked a stray hair behind her ear, and ran a hand down the center of the page so slowly, so gently, as if she were petting the fur of a beloved but wild animal, that I shivered.

Spread under her fingers was a big, full-color map of the Atlantic Ocean, rich and blue, bordered by the lacy shores of North America and Europe. Hairline black marks denoted waves, ocean currents, the migration patterns of whales—for even though I'd not yet set foot on a ship, I knew this was a whaler captain's atlas. The white spaces at the edge of the page were scratched over with notes and coordinates, splashed with raindrops or rings from leaky mugs and softened from years of fingertips tracing routes and landings and pathways, just as Essie did then, her white hand skating across the page and stopping at what, to her, to me back then, were small green pinpoints amid the blue mass, unimaginable as real places.

"Here we are," Essie said softly, and she glided a fingertip to a misshapen green dot on the left-hand page: Prince Island in all its glory, nothing more than a smudge on the shoreline, such a tiny speck on this huge page. From there, her finger moved in an arc, sweeping left across the ocean and hopping across the cleft between the pages and stopping at the far edge of the atlas at a group of islands clustered like freckles off the shore of Portugal.

"The Azores," Essie said, whispering the words to herself, and she said it with a Portuguese accent, the way the sailors said it, *Ayy-zoars*, murmuring the letters together into something soft and familiar. I knew, because everyone on that island knew, that the Azores were the first stop for most whalers, important because, like Prince Island, the islands are so far from the mainland that they're the first lumps of land ships see, the first opportunity to check stores or take on a few more hands or drop off the letters the crew has spent the last month writing and worrying over.

From there, Essie turned south, just as I knew she would, following the traditional whaling routes, which follow the traditional whaling grounds, marked on the map as dark outlines of the kinds of whale—sperm or bow or right—haloed in a pink cloud.

"Cape Verde," she said, her finger pausing for a moment, and it was just a name to me back then, just a speck on the map, not rich and alive as it is now, the port of Tarrafal and sands bleached like bone and cloud-wreathed mountains and thick air sweet with smoke and papaya, which falls from the trees and rots in the sun.

Essie turned a page, continuing the route south, stopping to whisper to herself the names of places: Rio de Janeiro and Buenos Aires and the Falkland Islands, all the places the sailors went, places I would go someday, and places she would never see. Every now and then she'd pause, stare at the spot on the map, ask me what I thought it was like. I would tell her I didn't know, because I never would have guessed that there, that point, is where I would kill my first whale and there is where Charles Taber would go overboard and there is where my mates would buy me my first pint, fill me up with liquor, and then laugh when I spent three days in the fo'c'sle sleeping it off.

She turned another page, another, her finger tracing outlines of countries, continents, towns, her tongue curling around the names of places, holding them in her mouth as though they were pieces of candy: Tahiti, Auckland, Liverpool, Tennessee, whisper-soft words that sounded like a spell.

She showed me all her favorite pages, too, stopping there to take in the rainbow-colored maps of countries stitched together like quilts, the ones where the blue of the water had been pushed off the border. She stopped at mountains, at deserts, places where no ship could ever reach, and she would ask me if I ever thought I'd go there. She would ask me that, and I knew she was asking because she knew that she could never leave the island, that she had a job and a duty and a responsibility and a destiny, but I was free, alone, untethered, and I could explore this world that she could only contain in a book, in pages that she caressed so gently.

But I'd tell her no. I always told her no, because even though to be a boy on Prince Island meant one day becoming a sailor, I never imagined myself taking up with my neighbors and going to sea. I didn't want landlocked countries, mountains and lakes and forests. I wanted a place where I belonged, and I thought I'd already found it.

But, of course, I did leave. And I have visited those places. My head vibrates against the glass window of the train, and I stare out at Austria or Hungary or wherever we are flashing past. I wish I could go back there and tell her about it all, about the time I visited Zanzibar, the smell of dust and butchered animals, drinking cinnamon-flavored tea from clay cups that we'd smash on the ground after draining, watching half a dozen slaves chained by their necks carry baskets balanced on their freshly shaved heads. Or I'd tell her about when Boone and I took a ship to Hong Kong to see the buildings tucked between mountains and oceans and slender as skeletons with their bamboo frames, their window shades of red, blue, gold-colored cloth. I picture myself telling her, not the Essie of today or even the Essie of when I left, but the Essie in the grass, hungry for stories and secrets.

"It's so big," she said at last, and I remember at first I thought she meant the atlas that she pulled close to her, but then I realized she meant the whole world. "So big and so much of it."

She turned the pages back to the first one, the one of the Atlantic Ocean and the whaling routes and the notes in the margins, and took her thumb and pushed down on the spot where Prince Island sat, so tiny and insignificant the mapmaker had to mark it with a dash—PRINCE IS., it said—and when she lifted her thumb from the page, I almost expected the island to have been rubbed out, pushed into the sea and sunk, and the space where it was nothing but a stretch of blue.

And I remember what she said to me then, something I didn't understand at the time: "We were born into the wrong lives, Mal."

Her voice was so soft, her eyes taking in the small dot that would forever be her home, and I wanted to ask her what she meant, what she was trying to say, when she closed the atlas with such force that I knew the conversation was over.

"Want to go see if those crabs are back on the beach?" I'd asked, because at the time the atlas held my interest in the same way any of Essie's books did: as curiosities and diversions and nothing more. The atlas was just a collection of places I'd never see and had never had any care to see, and I didn't even wonder then what it might have meant to Essie, her hands pressing down on the cover of the book as though she could let it sink into her skin.

She was right.

We were born into the wrong lives, me and Essie. She should have been the world traveler and I should have had a home always waiting for me, but she took that away from me and she didn't have the courage to leave herself, and we're both of us, forever, trapped.

Twenty-One

CONSTANTINOPLE

WHEN THE TRAIN NEARLY COLLIDES WITH the Black Sea, we disembark to take a ferry to Constantinople, and as we board the ship, we pass signs, written in French, English, and Turkish, that remind all passengers that the use and exhibition of magic within the city limits is strictly forbidden.

Other cities in other countries have banished magic, but Constantinople is the most famous for it, with its bloody wars against magic folk going back centuries. For decades, there have been rumors that the city would install a magical census, that all citizens and visitors would have to appear before military Percepts, and anyone discovered to have a gift would be registered and branded for identification, but the plans have never come to pass (some say because the sultan's own family is thick with secret Others). So instead, Constantinople has settled into an uneasy peace with magic folk: Visit and live here unbothered, but keep your magic to yourself.

That's why the Luciferidies chose the city for their headquarters. It's a long way from their beginnings on the banks of the Mississippi, but they've flourished here, building connections with the sultan and his officers and making a name for themselves as the hosts of lavish, cosmopolitan parties.

"There," Boone says, leaning over the ferry railing, his palms pressed so hard against the wood that it looks as though he's trying to keep himself from rising into the air and taking flight. "There's the city."

He's got better eyes than me; all I see as we approach is a dense blanket of fog, lifting off the water in sheets.

"I don't—" I say, and then I pause. Like a gauzy veil, the fog thins out, lifts, drops away, and reveals the city. I've never been here before, and although I've heard plenty about it, it still surprises me.

Needles and domes—that's the first thing I think, taking in the spiky minarets, the egg-shaped mosques, the harbor so densely crowded with warships that it reminds me of nothing so much as Prince Island at the height of summer, when there are enough whalers anchored at New Bishop that you could walk from one end of Main Dock to the other just by leaping from deck to deck.

It's a beautiful city, but when I turn to Boone to say this, he's already gone, down belowdecks to the luggage room to beat the crowd of gawking Londoners and Parisians.

"Arriving in Stamboul!" the ferry captain says, and even though I know I should join Boone, help him with the luggage, I stay leaning against the railing for a few more minutes as the city solidifies before me. Somewhere in there is the Luciferidies' headquarters, and somewhere in there is the *shar*—and soon enough it might be replicated into a dozen versions of itself or it might be in my hands, ready to be taken back to Prince Island and used to cut out the soul of the girl who betrayed me.

For the first time I put myself in the moment, the *shar* at last in my hand, raking the blade across Essie's skin and telling her that she's nothing now, she's normal. I picture the shock and guilt and grief on her face, and the little monster inside me delights in the image with a rush of pleasure so forceful that, for half a second, I catch myself. The Essie of today, the one I picture as so beautiful and so cold, wrapped up in her love spells and selfishness, disappears, fades away to the little girl who held my hand in the grass and told me her secrets and called me her friend.

"Stop it," I whisper to myself. "Stop it. That's not her anymore. You're doing the right thing. You're giving her what she deserves."

Constantinople grows before me, and I say the words over

and over and over, and by the time the ferry rocks against the dock, I'm ready again to move.

"Just because magic is illegal doesn't mean they won't use it to defend themselves."

"I know."

"But no one can spot you trying to disarm them, understand? You'll have to be careful. You can't be seen."

"I *know*."

"It'll have to be you who goes inside first. We've only the one totem, and the Luciferidies are bound to have Percepts working for them, and I can't—"

"Boone! I know!"

He wheels on me, eyes wild. "Oh, you know, do you? Because you've been dreamy as a milkmaid ever since we left Paris, and I'm tired of reminding you how important this all is."

"Of course it's important," I say, but I'm not even sure he hears me.

"We only have a few hours to find it, steal it, and get it out of the country unseen, and it's not going to be easy. I would get in there and do it myself, but they'll detect me immediately, and so I have to rely on you."

"You *can*," I say, an edge to my voice. "You always can."

"Can I?" He gives me a hard look, and I know what he's

thinking about: running back to Tagore. Fighting with the Erslands. The mess with the kraken and the Drakes, all those weeks ago.

"We've spent a week here, and you've been sitting around with your head in the clouds while I've been preparing—"

"Partying, more like," I mutter, and he stiffens, stops walking, the muscles in his neck tense and twitching.

"Partying? Finding out as much as I can about the Luciferidies' guests. About their headquarters. About who might be guarding the *shar* and who might enjoy their wine a little too much and who could stand to have their pockets lined. And might I remind you that every night I came back and filled you in on what I learned, and now I see what a colossal waste of time—"

"Yes, yes—I heard you. The one with the walrus mustache is a drunk, and the one from Charleston favors men instead of women, and they're likely to keep the *shar* in the western library."

"*Southern*," Boone says. "Southern library! *This* is why we're going over it all now! You act as though you're in control of the whole situation, Mal, but you don't even grasp how important this all is. This is your last—this is *our* last chance."

I pause, look at him, and he looks away.

"What did you say?"

"Nothing," he says, so dismissively, in the way of someone well used to having his lies believed, and when he glances back at me, he sighs. "We can't survive without a big haul, Mal.

We can't survive without taking the *shar*. Either we establish ourselves as hunters to be respected, to be feared, or someone, someday, will kill us and that will be it. We are *so close*." He looks at me, face soft with a plea, and sighs again. "I was going to wait until after to tell you.... I took a wire to New York when the train stopped in Budapest. We have a buyer."

"Already?"

Boone nods. "He's offering one hundred thousand dollars."

The breath strangles in my throat, and I can only stare at Boone, mouth open. He smiles, weary. "Understand now? This is really it, Mal. Get the *shar*, sell it, live like kings for the rest of our lives. This is it, and it's not going to happen again. Do you see?"

I still can't speak, but I can nod, and Boone's expression softens. He reaches out, puts a hand on my shoulder, and squeezes it. "I'm trusting you," he says. "I'm trusting you to do this for me. For us."

"I will," I say, and I mean it, because it's hit me suddenly, what the *shar* can do for us now. One hundred *thousand* dollars. I never imagined it could have been so much. There's never been a haul like that before. Never. It's more money than I can even fathom, and even though I've always said I never cared about the money before... one hundred thousand dollars can buy a lot. Maybe even—a spark of hope lights up inside me—maybe even a cure.

"I can't believe it," I say, smiling, and Boone grins back at me. "I can't believe all that money."

"It's pennies to the buyer," Boone says. "As soon as I told him what I was offering, he knew how quickly he could make back that money. A ship owner with the power of the Roe witch? That *shar* will earn him more money than he'll know what to do with."

"The Roe witch?"

"He would have offered me every cent he had, especially once I told him that after she's cut, she won't have her power anymore." Boone puts his arm around my shoulders, squeezes me, laughs. "That girl is going to make us a fortune!"

"But surely just the *shar*—"

"Oh, he had a good price for the *shar*," Boone says. "Ten thousand dollars, and I'm sure I could have bargained him up higher, but it's the magic he's really buying. Imagine if word gets out! Mal, there might be a bidding war! Do you realize how many people rely on the Roe witch's magic? We could see *twice* as much!" And he's off, laying out his plans, building his kingdom, describing everything he can do with that money, everything he'll *be*, while I watch him, dazed, thinking about a world where the people of Prince Island have to survive without magic and where the Roe witch's power lives inside a knife inside a rich man's desk drawer.

"It's amazing," Boone says, laughing, and he reaches over to give me one of his rare hugs. "I've never been so happy that that girl broke your heart."

Twenty-Two

I WALK TO THE LUCIFERIDIES' HEADQUAR-
ters with a mask swinging from my wrist. The party tonight is
to be a masquerade ball—"And good thing, too," Boone said,
"because you've still got enough bruises to frighten off every
decent person there"—and so earlier this week Boone took me
to the Grand Bazaar to pick out something to wear.

He ended up buying me robes several inches too long, so
I have to hold a bunch of the fabric—thicker than whale skin
and dense with the spicy, dusty smell of the bazaar—in one
hand to keep it from dragging on the ground. He'd told the
man at the stall where we shopped to dress me like a native,
but either the man misheard him or Boone should have speci-
fied just what country I was to be a native of, because no one
on the street wears robes as garish as mine: embroidered blue

and gold and slashed with a sash of silk exactly the same shade as marigolds. I catch stares as I navigate the mazelike streets of Constantinople, although whether that has to do with the color of my robes or my skin, I'm not certain.

Boone wanted to buy me the whole outfit: pants big enough to fit three men and a close-fitting shirt and narrow little vest and shoes that made me trip just to look at them. But I reminded him that I might have to do a lot of running—not to mention fighting—tonight, and I didn't want to have to worry about finding my knife amid eight yards of slippery fabric, so he went with just the robe; the mask, beaten-looking and black and covering only my eyes and nose; and a high, rounded hat that already hurts my neck.

Underneath the robe, I wear my usual pants and shirt and boots, knives at my hips and strapped to my ankle, gun concealed under the waistband of my belt.

"Maybe we should get you a sword," Boone said after I'd put on the costume in our dusty little room. "You'd better look the part."

But a sword might as well be a battle-ax for all I know how to use it, and I feel better with the weight of steel and the Dragoon against my skin.

As I near the headquarters—a huge, ornate building studded with intricate tile work that sparkles with color, even now that the sun has gone down—I rub my thumb over the little wooden devil totem from Tagore and go over in my head what I'm to do.

Get into the party.

Find the library.

Search the library for the *shar*.

Steal it without being seen.

Disappear without being remembered.

Meet Boone at the docks and board a ship and sail away.

And I know there are bound to be guards, people watching, charms and locks and all sorts of safeguards in place, but this is also a private party; the Luciferidies won't be expecting outsiders, and especially not other hunters. They will feel safe and comfortable and close to achieving what they always wanted, and so they'll let their guard down.

I hope.

There's a small crowd of people waiting at the door of the Luciferidies' building, most of them dressed in costumes even more outlandish than mine, a handful with red scarves around their necks or tucked into their shirts or wrapped around their hats. Carefully, I tie my mask around my face, and although I don't like the way it blocks the edges of my vision, as soon as it's in place, I feel better, safer, my nerves disappearing in a rush of tingling, hot blood.

"Jolly good of you to bring me along," a man says as I join the crowd waiting to enter, and his companion answers in an accent as broad as the Mississippi, "Just wait—you'll see a real eye-opener in a minute."

"A show?" a voice asks, and I'm surprised to see it's a woman, European, clad in a flower-patterned yellow dress under a green waistcoat tied shut with a white sash.

"Something like that," the American answers, smiling, and then the woman switches topics to chatter about a little tea set she saw that afternoon in the bazaar and I quit paying attention.

"Excuse me." A thickly accented man dressed like a Turkish cavalryman passes by me on his way to the door, and I can't tell from the mask that hides most of his face, but I think he might actually be a resident of this city. At least, the large woman at his side wears the most authentic costume I've seen so far: a plain black robe underneath a thick white veil that covers all her head and face except for a tiny slit for her eyes. She's clutching the arm of the cavalryman as he pulls her to the door, her movements jerky and nervous.

"We cannot wait any longer. My mother needs to sit," the man says, and the slender, exasperated-looking servant at the door looks for a moment as though he might ask him to get back in line, before sighing sharply and asking to see his totem.

A moment later, the cavalryman and his mother are swept inside, and the line moves quickly, the doors thrown open to let out a din of music, glasses, footsteps, a mix of French and English and American and Turkish voices clouding the air. I present my charm to one of the servants, and he takes it and examines it long enough that my stomach bubbles again with nerves and I let out a laugh.

"Let me in already," I say, grinning at him and at the man standing, staring, behind me. "This robe is choking me half to death."

The servant frowns but accepts the charm. "Straight ahead to the left, please, sir," he says in a thin voice, waving me on.

"Bloody nuisance, if you ask me," the man behind me in line says as we join the queue of people entering the ballroom. He's clearly one of the Luciferidies, practically glowing in voluminous, head-to-toe red robes. He jerks his head toward three men at the entrance instructing the partygoers to put out their hands. "Examining us like we've got something to hide!"

I watch as one by one, the men place their own hands on the partygoers' palms, touching skin to skin for just a few seconds before nodding and waving them inside the ballroom. They're Percepts, checking for magic, and while most people seem more than willing to prove they aren't magic or carrying any charms or spells, several others, like the man behind me, look outraged at the very suggestion.

As one of the Percepts approaches, the cavalryman puts an arm around his mother and begins shouting at him in a language I can't place, waving him away and shaking his head so hard that his face goes red.

"See that?" the man behind me says, nodding at the pair of them. "In this country it's an offense to touch a married woman like that. I *told* Mickelson not to bother with the bloody Percepts, but he wouldn't listen, and now look!" The man steps forward into the crowd, waving an arm over his head. "See here! Here!"

"Your hands, sir?"

I turn to see one of the Percepts with his own hands out, watching me with wary eyes.

"If you want to take my hand at a fancy costume ball, you're going to have to fetch me a glass of punch first," I say, smiling, and the Percept doesn't move.

"Your hands."

I take them from out of my robes but lift them into a shrug. "I haven't anything to prove," I say. "And if I truly was an Other, I wouldn't be foolish enough to walk through this door."

"*Sir—*"

But a shout makes us both turn to look: The cavalryman has drawn a sword impressive enough to convince us all that it's not just part of his costume, and the man in the red robe is trying to calm him down, his face white and panicked.

"I must insist," the Percept says, stepping forward, and I keep the smile on my face as my heart pounds and I wonder what to do—let him touch me and hope he's not sensitive enough to detect blanks? Show him the gun digging into my hip? Play the spoiled partygoer and wave him away with a laugh and a bribe?—but I don't get the chance for any of that because before I can decide, he's launched himself at me, quick as a snake, and I jump back, startled and shocked and reaching for my knife. Just as his fingers brush against the exposed skin of my wrist, the man in the red robe appears, furious and shouting and shoving his way in between us.

"Now, *really*!" he says. "This is an absurd way to treat our guests! You three are dismissed!" He waves a hand at the Percepts, and when one of them opens his mouth to protest, he says in a high, imperious voice, "And I don't want to hear any more 'Mr. Mickelson told us'! When he complains, you can bloody well send him to me!"

Frowning, he turns to me and the cavalryman. "Gentlemen, my apologies. Please, enjoy the party and think no more of this embarrassment."

The cavalryman straightens himself up in a huff, wrapping an arm around his mother before bundling her off into the ballroom, and I turn to the man in red and smile.

"Cheers," I say, and I mean to tip him my cap but only sort of push the huge hat on my head in what I hope is a pleasant-enough manner. He gives me an exasperated nod and then dashes off to shout instructions at the other servants. I stride into the ballroom, still smiling—and stop.

Well, I think. *I won't have to sneak into the library to find the* shar.

There it is, the knife I've chased around the world, shining in the light of a hundred candles and held aloft by a man in all black silk, his face covered in an embroidered, jeweled black sack that looks like a fancy executioner's hood. It must be the effect he's hoping for, because as guests continue to shuffle into the ballroom amid the strains of a twelve-piece band, he climbs to a dais at the center of the room. A thin teenaged boy stands there shivering, wrists bound to a post, eyes wide and white as globes. The man in black throws up his arms and shouts to the crowd, "Welcome! Come in—please! We've invited you here tonight to witness something quite special!"

He sweeps a hand toward the boy on the dais.

"This boy has been found guilty of freezing water into solid ice!"

A few people—all of them bedecked in red—break into cheers and stamp their feet, and the boy's eyes dart from one face to another.

"He has been sentenced to freedom from magic!" the executioner shouts, and the cheering lifts in volume like a storm wave while the boy gulps for air. "Sentence to be carried out... immediately!"

Two men in red leap to the dais and grab both arms of the boy, who's just seemed to realize what's about to happen and begins shouting, howling, his eyes squeezed tight and leaking tears that dribble down his cheeks and freeze solid, glittering in the candlelight like the gems on the executioner's hood. One of the men twists the boy's head toward the executioner as the crowd titters with excitement, and my stomach lurches—are they going to *kill* him?—but no, the executioner just rakes the *shar* across the boy's cheek, leaving a thin red pencil mark from the corner of his eye to the corner of his lip. Then he turns back to the crowd, the *shar* bloody and almost alive, somehow, and someone passes him a goblet of water that he tosses overhead, and for a second the drops rise like confused rain, arc through the air, hiss against the candles of the chandelier, and the executioner lifts the *shar* with a triumphant laugh. The water freezes into a million perfect diamonds that tinkle, bell-like, to the floor, where they're smashed underfoot or scooped up by the handful or avoided like poison.

I'm shocked, stunned, to see how quickly, how effortlessly the *shar* stole that boy's power, but no one is more astonished than the boy himself, who leans slumped against the two men who still hold him and watches the ice spin and stutter across the floor before his eyes roll into the back of his head and he drops right to the ground.

One of the men hauls the boy up by his armpits as the other loosens the rope from the post, and together they carry him away, off the dais and down a dark hall toward—I don't know where.

The executioner bows and slides the *shar* into a sheath at his belt before turning to a pair of servants standing at a blue door in the back of the ballroom.

"Bring in the next accused!" he calls, and the servants swing the door open and return a moment later with a large mustachioed man carrying an assortment of colored glass balls. He smiles at the guests, who've gone quiet now as they watch him the way a pack of hungry dogs watches a cornered rat. The man climbs to the dais, bows, and tosses the balls into the air, where instead of falling, they float like bubbles in an exquisitely slow juggling act.

It is so beautiful.

The glass balls catch the candlelight and throw shards of color across the partygoers' upturned faces as they dance between the chandeliers and the man's hands, and every time he catches a ball and throws it back into the air with a casual flick of his wrist, I get a hiccough of thrill in the pit of my chest. I want to jump onto the dais, to grab him, to tell him it's a trap, *Run away, they're going to cut you, they're going to take away this marvelous gift and turn you dull and ordinary,* but instead I stand with my boots rooted to the floor and my eyes rooted to the man's face, and I watch it change from peaceful concentration to surprise to confusion to fear to desperation, and when the executioner cuts him, I don't look away.

Twenty-Three

HALF A DOZEN MORE OTHERS ARE MARCHED out to the cheering crowd before the executioner finally declares he needs a break from all this cutting, all this magic-theft and mayhem, and slides the *shar* into the sheath at his belt and leaps down from the dais to join the admiring masses.

Half a dozen Others, harmless entertainers, the kind of magic folk you see at village carnivals or corner pubs, their little shows always the same: disappearing flowers or flying through the air or changing themselves into rabbits or foxes or dogs. All of them were caught off guard, which makes me think the Luciferidies brought them in special for this party, carted them in from remote places where they wouldn't know Constantinople had banned magic, where they've never heard of dangerous men in red sashes or the existence of the *shar*.

The Luciferidies could have found Others who deserved to be cut by the *shar*, not these jesters and clowns. I watched a young girl with dark hair, a girl whose only Talent seems to be the ability to float, angel-like, above the ground, and I pictured Essie Roe in her place, black hair and icy eyes and cruel smile, her love magic winding through weak men's hearts like thorny weeds. *She* should be up on that dais; *she* should have her magic taken away from her—that's what the *shar* should be used for, not torturing harmless performers. No one is safer for one fewer floating girl in the world.

"Lovely show, isn't it?" a woman dressed in pink and blue asks me, lifting up a glass and smiling to reveal wine-stained teeth. "Much better than what they put on last year—although, of course, they didn't have that marvelous knife then."

"Yes, I haven't had so much fun since my last bearbaiting," I say, smiling back at her, and when she blinks at me, confused, I say, "Excuse me, but I want to see that marvelous knife up close."

A small knot of people have already gathered around the executioner, including the man in red and the cavalryman and his mother.

"But how does it work?" the cavalryman asks, his words so thickly accented they sound wrapped in wool, and the executioner lifts the *shar* up by the handle.

"Such are the mysteries of the world! We must only be glad that this tool exists! It's not our place to question its power," the executioner says, and the man in the red robes gives a small, irritated snort.

"The spectacle..." he mutters, rolling his eyes at the executioner, and I take a chance and lean in.

"Mickelson's got a lot to learn about tact, doesn't he?" I say, and the red-robed man glances at me, surprised for a moment before his expression relaxes into exasperation.

"You have no idea. This 'entertainment' was all his idea. Seems to think he can drum up more support for the cause by putting on a performance, and heavens—maybe he's right, just *look* at the way these people are fawning over him—but I still say it's all demeaning to our work. We're noble knights defending our world from the outrage of Others—we don't need all this, this costumery, this pageant of nonsense!"

"I'm with you," I say, and I open my robe just enough for him to get a glimpse of my ordinary clothes. "This was the most I was willing to put on tonight. Any more and I felt like a fool."

"You've got it," he says, nodding vigorously, and I smile, thinking of the number of times Boone's told me the quickest way to get a man to befriend you is to just agree with anything he says.

"You've more sense than Mickelson, for sure," he continues, and he puts out a hand. "Thomas Yardley. It is a true pleasure to meet you."

"Michael Howland." I take his hand, still smiling broadly.

"You're out of our American branch, aren't you? I'm afraid I don't get on much with the Yanks."

"I started as a sailor," I say, because this was the story Boone and I agreed on if I was ever asked. "This is my first time in Constantinople, but you look like you know your way around here."

Yardley nods and begins telling me about his work as an officer in the British consulate, and when a servant comes around with a salver of tiny crystal goblets, Yardley takes two before passing one of them to me.

"To the cause," he says, nodding, and I lift my glass and drink with him. A roar of laughter causes both of us to turn; Mickelson's reenacting the reaction of the last Other on the dais, a large woman whose ability was nothing more than perfectly mimicking voices and sounds.

" 'Heaven help me!' " Mickelson calls out in a high falsetto, before switching into a deep baritone: " 'No, heaven help *me!* ' "

Yardley clucks his tongue, shaking his head, and I lean in slightly. "What I want to know is when the *real* show starts."

He glances at me, a strange look on his face. "Oh?" he says. "And what's that?"

A flutter of panic moves through me, but I keep the smile on my face and say nothing, looking at Yardley with what I hope is a knowing expression. It's another one of Boone's tricks to get someone to talk: Simply say nothing.

After a moment, Yardley sighs. "We have it all ready to go. A dozen knives, perfectly honed to accept the magic of the *shar.* We had to take them back to the blacksmith three times before we were satisfied."

"And it'll truly work?" I ask, my eyes sliding to Mickelson, still acting out the most dramatic moments of the evening.

"Of course it will," Yardley says. "Lunar magic is powerful, and it's at its most powerful just at the stroke of midnight." He glances up at a handsomely ornate clock at the head of the ballroom; it shows the time to be just a few minutes to twelve.

"I'll have to drag Mickelson away from his admirers," he says. "We both agreed I would be the one to hold the *shar* during the ceremony."

I look at him, trying to keep a frown from forming at my lips. I might have been able to distract Mickelson enough to slip the *shar* from its sheath, but Yardley—nervous, focused—is another problem altogether.

"What assistance can I offer?" I ask, smiling at him. "I'm anxious to learn more."

He gives me a kind of pleasantly appraising look. "I bet you are, lad! You seem like an intelligent boy. But I'm afraid it's only senior members taking part in the ceremony. You'll just have to watch with the rest of them." He glances at Mickelson, who's taken out the *shar* again and is now talking about the gems in the handle, pointing them out like an overly excited child describing a new toy.

"That is not jade—it is emerald," the cavalryman says, and he holds out his hand to take the *shar* and examine it more closely, but the executioner shakes his head and steps back. "Careful, now! You wouldn't like to get cut."

"Are you implying I am one of *Them*?" the cavalryman asks, the sections of his face not covered by a mask going red with outrage. "First the nonsense at the door and now this? How dare you suggest—"

"Oh, my dear man, I only meant that a magical knife is still a knife and is still quite sharp!"

Yardley lets out a soft *tsk* and shakes his head as Mickelson hands the *shar* over to the cavalryman, who examines it with a kind of bored curiosity.

"He's got no tact—that's his problem! Ah!" We both turn to see three servants walking into the ballroom with trays in their hands. As they near the dais, I see each tray has been prepared with four knives, fashioned in the style of the *shar*. Yardley waves them up to the dais and motions to another servant to open a round oculus set high into the domed ceiling overhead, revealing the cold light of a full moon.

"It's almost time," he says, rubbing his hands together, and I smile back at him, even though my heartbeat picks up. How am I supposed to steal the blasted thing *now*? I've got smoke powder in my pocket, and I could throw it on the floor and use the cloud as a cover. Or I could knock over one of the servants with the trays, and in the confusion switch out the real knife for one of the replicas. But a second later I realize it's too late: Mickelson climbs the dais and announces the ceremony will begin.

Immediately, servants with long silver poles extinguish the many candles until only the light of the moon above illuminates the ballroom. Yardley joins Mickelson on the dais and puts out his hand for the *shar*, and, reluctantly, the head of the Luciferidies reaches into the sheath and pulls out—

I blink.

It's not the *shar*.

Instead, Mickelson holds a short wooden sword, roughly carved like a child's toy. I wait for someone to say something, for Mickelson or Yardley to shout out in surprise, to ask where the true *shar* is, but no one seems to notice and gently, gingerly, Mickelson hands the wooden knife to Yardley. As it passes under the light of the moon, something bright lodged in the handle winks back a reflection, and I bite back a gasp: It's pyrite, fool's gold, a metal used in glamour charms. Someone's switched out the *shar* for this toy and glamoured it so that everyone in this ballroom sees it as the *shar*—everyone except me, the blank, on whom glamours won't work.

I twist around and search the crowd, trying to figure out who might have the real *shar*, when I see the cavalryman and his mother disappearing down the dark hallway the servants led the cut Others through only minutes earlier. A scowl climbs onto my face, and I reach into my robes, feel for my gun, and follow.

They pick up speed, speaking in a language I can't understand but in voices that sound less like a man and his mother than two men, and I race after them, tightening the grip on my gun.

The mask slips over my eyes, obscuring my vision, and I

yank it from my face and drop it to the floor as I follow the men. The hallway ends in a short set of stairs that leads to a door, and the two of them burst through it, revealing the darkness of an alley. I'm far enough behind them that the door slams shut before I reach it, and for half a moment I worry that maybe it's locked, maybe they're waiting for me on the other side, but I don't have any time to think, just move, and I put my hand on the knob and throw open the door and nearly fall into the alley.

Gasps greet me—the Others, cut and discarded and huddled together, touching their slashed-open cheeks, whimpering in their foreign tongues—but I ignore them, focus instead on the two men, who are ripping off their robes, their masks, when they turn and see me—and laugh.

"You!" I say, and the Ersland brothers grin at me. "How did you get in here? Where did you get your totem?"

"Totem?" Nils Ersland laughs again. "You mean this?" He reaches into a pocket and pulls out a little wooden cylinder fitted with another lump of pyrite. Carefully, he wrenches the pyrite from the base of the cylinder, and I know I'm supposed to react, that to anyone else, it looks like one of the Luciferidies' totems has instantly transformed into a piece of plain wood. I narrow my eyes and Nils tosses the pyrite and the wooden piece to the ground.

"Where's the *shar*?" I ask, and he glances at his brother, who reaches into the voluminous black robes and pulls it out with all the flourish of a stage performer.

"Come and get it," Jorah says, smiling. "Yes," Nils says. "You want it, don't you? And we would be so happy to give it to you."

There's a cry behind me, and I glance back to see the youngest of the Others brought up to the dais, a child who could turn invisible and flickered like candlelight when Mickelson brought the knife up to her face. She's got her hands on her face now, and she's staring at them like they belong to someone else when she looks up, past me, and lets out a gasp.

I turn just in time to see Jorah leap forward, the *shar* slicing through the air. I stumble back, thumb the hammer of my gun, but it's Boone's advice all over again, a gun's no good in a knife fight. I'm too slow, too slow with the *shar* arcing toward me, whistling as it cuts the air, the Others shouting, crying, wailing. I know I have no magic to be stolen by the *shar*, but I do have skin that can be cut and blood that can be spilled, and just when I lift my gun, intending to blow a hole right into Jorah Ersland's chest, he slices one way, and I jump to avoid the knife, and in that second of distraction he reaches out and presses a hand to my cheek.

I jerk my head away, but it's too late: I see his eyes go wide, his mouth muttering something, a single word, and it sounds like a man's name at first, *tom, tom, tom*, and then he gets louder, shouting it. Nils gasps, stares at me, his whole face lit up with something like greed. The word slips out of him with a breath and explodes like a bomb: *"Blank!"*

The woman coiled on the ground lets out a small yelp of

fear, the Others all rearing back at me like I'm poison, and the *shar*, the Luciferidies, the danger all around them disappears in light of the monster in their midst. They scatter, running into one another, into the Erslands, into me, their voices rising in half a dozen mixed languages that all somehow sound the same when pitched with fear, and through the din I hear Nils call out, "Take him! Take him!" But Jorah doesn't move, the *shar* limp in his hand, a dazed expression on his face, and only when I make a grab for it does he come alive, spitting and angry and swearing at me in Norwegian.

The door behind me, the door to the headquarters, bursts open, and there's Mickelson, there's Yardley, there's the crowd of onlookers all staring at the mother of the Turkish cavalryman and the friendly sailor boy squaring off with the *shar* between them. I hear Jorah shout something to Nils, turn to see him lift the *shar*, and the thought just goes through my head—*What was the last power the* shar *stole?*—when Nils tosses his brother a lighter and Jorah strikes out a flame, which glows like a star in his hand before blossoming into a comet of fire that explodes right in the Luciferidies' faces.

Fire manipulation, I think, and then I throw myself to the side, landing hard on my shoulder. The crowd screams, and when I twist onto my back, I see flames rise from Yardley's voluminous robes, see him flap the fabric and whip it into wings of fire that send him howling, knocking into the walls of the alley.

"Water!" Mickelson shouts. *"Water!"*

But I don't know to whom he's calling, because the crowd of onlookers has fallen into chaos, all of them running, screaming, trying to avoid the flames that Jorah streaks into the sky. A woman more fire than person shrieks and darts back inside the building, and a moment later a column of smoke pours out from the still-open door, turning the air oily and thick. I pull the sleeve of my robe over my face, my eyes streaming tears, and I try to crawl to Jorah. My blankness won't protect me from this; magical fire can't burn me, but this isn't magical fire—it's *real* fire, controlled by the *shar* but created by the lighter, and it's going to kill me if I'm not careful.

I scramble to my feet, avoiding another column of fire, and I throw myself at Jorah, knocking him off balance just enough to send the *shar* flying from his hand. We roll together, sky and ground spinning around us, but when we stop, he's on top, his knee in my chest, his face contorted with rage.

He's shouting something at me, shouting, and there's that word again, "*Tom! Tom!*" I watch his hand rise up in a fist and I brace myself for the hit, but instead he grabs the front of my shirt, drags me to my feet, and shouts something at Nils, who holds the *shar* and shouts back, "Let him go! Later! Later! We'll get him later!"

In his moment of confusion, I yank myself free from Jorah's grasp and lurch toward Nils, but another wall of fire rears up at me, sending a pile of burning debris across my path. Coughing, I throw an arm across my face, the heat of the fire so intense that it's almost solid, pressing against me, pushing me back toward the burning building. Through the smoke and the flames, I hear Jorah and Nils shouting to each other, see them turn and run, the bright blade of the *shar* glinting gold in the firelight.

"Get back here!" I shout, but the roar of the flames eats up my words, and as the burning debris in front of me spits out sparks, I let out a swear and back away. I blink furiously as I look for some way through the fire and after the Erslands. No longer controlled by the *shar*, the flames seem as though they might be dying down, and I'm just about to chance jumping over the still-burning pile of wood in front of me when a hand reaches up, grabs my shoulder from behind, and pulls, and I turn to see one of the Luciferidies growling at me, his face a mess of charred meat and blood.

I spin free and, without thinking, leap over the flames, and when I land, a heat so sudden against my legs forces out a cry of pain. I glance behind me to see that my huge, embroidered robe has caught fire, the fabric burning and blackening so fast it's as though it's been dipped in ink. The monster inside me goes hysterical, yanking the robe from my shoulders so hard that I feel my bones jerk in their sockets, and when I still see smoke rising from my pants, I smack my palms against my legs, shrieking, the smell of burned hair and skin filling my nose.

A crash behind me shakes me back to the present, and I look up at the Luciferidies' beautiful headquarters consumed with fire, the windows letting out columns of smoke and screams. Someone—I can't even tell if it's a man or a woman—tries to batter a way through the flames, only to fall to the ground. I back away, turn, and run, run blindly, wildly, thinking of nothing but *Get away get away*, get away from the screaming, the fire, the building behind me going up in smoke and flames, and the devil-loving Luciferidies falling into hell, and the *shar*, the *shar* that I know is still in Nils Ersland's hand and not mine, not ever.

I run through the streets, my whole body buzzing, my legs so unsteady that I'm crashing into narrow alley walls and tripping over loose pavement stones. I'm not sure where I am, I'm not sure I can ever find my way to the docks, but I'm a sailor still, and I can follow the smell of salt water, the sound of ropes and creaking decks and snapping sails, and finally, finally, there it is, there *he* is: Boone, waiting for me, staring up at the thick plumes of smoke rising over the city. I have just enough time to tell him we have to go, now, quickly, and it's to his credit that he gets on the boat, that he waits until we're out on the sea to hear my story, that after it sinks in he hits me only once, a solid punch right into my cheek, before climbing belowdecks and tearing apart every bit of furniture in his cabin.

Twenty-Four

OCEAN

I LOST THE *SHAR*.

I lost it. I let the Erslands have it and, what's worse, they know what I am. They'll be gone from Constantinople now, disappeared to who knows where, with the *shar* and my secret in their possession.

I try speaking to Boone, curling up for hours outside his cabin, tapping at the door, talking to him, apologizing, explaining, but he's silent for so long that I finally go away, and when I do see him, he's unshaven and thin and looks right past me with bloodshot eyes.

We take a steamer to Athens and then glide through the Mediterranean, my least favorite body of water because it doesn't look real. It's too blue, too clear, too warm and sunny and inviting and false, because every sailor knows you can dress up the ocean in pretty colors and soft smiles but it will always be hard and dangerous and cold.

When we arrive in Lisbon, Boone disappears into the city for so long that I wonder if he's up and abandoned me at last, and I sit, as faithful as a dog, at the docks with our luggage for one, two, three, five, eight hours, watching the sun cross the sky and jiggling my empty pockets.

But he comes back, and his eyes are still dead and his expression is still dull and he still doesn't look me in the eye, but he comes back, and that's enough for me to let out the breath I'd been holding all day.

"I had to send a wire," he says, his voice flat, and I nod.

"That's all right," I say, because I don't want him to think he owes me an explanation.

"We're still going to New York."

"All right."

"Get the bags."

And that's all he says to me for the next three days.

Because this ship is smaller—a real working merchant ship, taking us on as "flotsam," as paid passengers—we have to share a cabin again, and I can't bear the weight of silence between us in that cramped little room, so I leave Boone there with his notes and his plans and his steadily emptying bottles of liquor and spend my hours on the deck and beg the other sailors to give me watch up the masthead. *"Please,"* I tell them, "*please*," and when they finally say yes, I climb to the top of the ship and settle into that spot between sky and ship and sea and stare out at the water and try not to think about all the things I think about.

I try not to think about my secret, what the Erslands can do with it.

I try not to think about Boone's plans, destroyed.

I try not to think about Essie, about revenge, about losing my chance to look her in the eye and pay her back for what she did to me.

But every time I try to empty my head of thoughts, I see faces: the Others from Constantinople, the juggler and the water-freezing boy and the floating angel and the little invisible girl, there and not there, winking out like a ghost, shivering, solid, gone and back again and then back forever with a crimson slash down her cheek.

At least the *shar* is out of the hands of the Luciferidies. I don't know what will happen to them now, if they even still exist anymore. I saw their headquarters, their leaders, and a good portion of their membership go up in flames, and the only way anyone could live through a fire like that is with magical intervention. But I doubt there are any Others in Constantinople skilled enough to save a man burned so severely, and even if there were, I wouldn't blame Them for not wanting to waste magic on the Luciferidies. If I had to guess, the magical world is, at least, safe from them.

But what will the Erslands do with the *shar*?

I wonder about it, and then I close my eyes.

"There's nothing you can do about it anymore," I say, and I say it over and over until it finally feels true.

A week into our journey, and I can't sleep again, lying on my bunk and staring up at the ceiling of the cabin, wishing I could see right through the wood and the nails and the rigging, straight up to the stars.

I turn and look out the porthole window, muzzy with salt spray because our cabin sits low on the ship, close enough to the water that I can see its surface, black and smooth like oil. It's a dark night, cloudy, the sea distinguishable from the sky only by tiny rims of silver that outline the waves, thanks to the sea lanterns hanging from the decks above. I rest my hand against the wall of the cabin, letting the ship rock into my bones, and that's how I feel the first bump.

Nothing more than a nudge from somewhere out there, somewhere in the water, and at first I think I imagine it, and then I feel it again: *thump.* Low. Deep.

My sailor's heart starts pounding, my hand going hot and sweaty where it touches the wall. I pull it away, grab my shirt from below my bunk and throw it over my shoulders as I race from the cabin, through the gangway, and up to the deck, because we've hit something. The ship's hit something, a reef, maybe, or a sunken ship or something else, something small like a split mast or island shoal, but a sign of a bigger, hidden danger lurking ahead. If the crew hasn't heard it or felt it— and most likely they haven't; most likely only I felt it, lucky enough to have my hand on the ribs of the ship at just the right moment—they could be sailing us right into trouble.

I burst up onto the deck with my lungs already churning air and my eyes wide with fear, and the first thing I see is half a dozen sailors leaning over the edge of the bulwarks, look- ing down into the ocean at a spot in the water right where my cabin would be.

They know, I think, and I'm relieved for half a second before I realize that they know because whatever it was is big enough for them to feel it, which could mean it's big enough to tear this ship apart. My blank blood starts pumping, fear and excitement and visions of shipwrecks, falling into the water, swimming in blackness with no charm to catch me or magic to keep me safe, and I'm ready to dive into the ocean with a hammer between my teeth and a bundle of lumber under my arm and repair the hole in the ship that will surely emerge any minute now, any second.

"What is it? What did we hit?" I ask, my voice fast, and one of the crew turns, puts a finger to his lips, beckons me over with an expression on his face that's so strange—so *happy*— that I am sure it must be a trick of the light until I cross the deck and put my hands on top of the bulwarks and look down to where he's pointing and see *them*.

Whales.

A dozen, maybe, although it's hard to tell, their muscular bodies dipping in and out of the waves, but there are enough of various sizes that I can see it's a group, a family, mamas and babies and a few giants that must be the males, the fathers, swimming great, lazy circles around the others.

"We didn't hit them," the crew member says, so quiet, so hushed, like we're not on the deck of a ship but standing inside a church. "They hit us."

I watch them swim for a moment, my hands gripping the railing so hard that my knuckles pop from my skin, because I'm waiting for the call, the shout, the action—whale, ho!—that will send me running for sharp lances and a whaleboat. But there's nothing except silence, nothing except the slap of their bodies below and the even breathing of the men around me, and I realize, of course: This is a merchant ship, not a whaler. I'm not here to hunt.

"We see them sometimes in these parts," the man says. "They get close and ride the wake of the ship. Look—see? Those big'uns are females. The littles are their calves."

Females and their calves. On whalers, we'd look out especially for them, because the calves are smaller, easier to catch. They're not as good for oil, but you can catch a baby and hold it in a net and let it cry, and whales are just like people in that they can't abide a baby's cries. A calf calling out for its mother, for its aunties and uncles and papa, will bring a dozen whales to you, and then it's just a matter of picking off the ones you want. After it's done, after the water goes red and there are one, two, maybe even three great dead whales floating in the ocean around the ship, we'd let the calf go—let it go so it could grow up and get nice and fat and full of oil—and sometimes, sometimes it would see its dead mama in the waters, swim up to her and nuzzle her big body, cry and circle and cry and circle and we'd have to throw things at it—not harpoons but bits of wood, twisted iron we had no use for, shoes that had lost their partners—we'd have to throw things at it to drive it off, and sometimes it would take a long while.

"Stupid beast," a sailor said to me once, after watching a calf circle our whaler for the two days it took to strip apart its mother. "Doesn't it even realize that whale's dead?"

And it did, it did, of course it did.

This is what I'm thinking about when I look into the water at these whales, playing, bobbing, touching noses and heads and tails to one another's bodies, bumping up against us like we're nothing but another whale. I'm confused, because I've seen whales run when they notice ships approaching, seen them whisper to their babies and gather them up like they remember the bites of harpoon, the chases.

"Why aren't they afraid of us?" I ask, and the crew shrugs.

"Blasted if I know. They can tell we're not after their oil. Maybe they can recognize different kinds of ships. I don't know. But I've seen it before, and they can see we mean them no harm."

He pats my shoulder and drifts back to his duties, and the rest of the crew follows. I'm alone at the bulwarks, watching the dark shapes curve and curl into the water. I drop my chin onto my hands, feeling the spray of the waves on my cheeks, my eyes half-closed but my heart pounding, because it's been years since I've been this close to a whale I hadn't been expected to kill. I feel the hunter instincts, the monster instincts, rear up inside me, calculating speed and strength and distance as easily as I breathe, but then I let my hands relax on the railing. I'm not going to kill them. I'm just going to watch them.

I watch them, swimming and singing, and it's impossible to look at whales and not think of Prince Island, of Essie and the Roe witch. Whales never swam anywhere near the docks—they were far too smart for that—but the witch would call to them sometimes. Sometimes, maybe only once or twice a year, I would see them swimming in the water just off the rocky hook where the Roes built their cottage.

"They come for Mama," Essie told me once. We stood in the water, the waves at our ankles, our toes buried in the sand, watching the whales swim and circle and rise up to the surface in great, bobbing arcs. "Someday, they're going to come for me."

It was just sunrise, the sky before us dark, the sea lit up with pinks and reds, the whales dark shapes, and together we stood in the water and Essie's face glowed.

"It's magic," she whispered, and she slipped her hand into

mine and squeezed it tight. "It's magic, Mal," and I knew she meant natural magic, not the work her mother or grandmother did with their charms and their promises but something purer, deeper, something that tied her to the whales and the island and told her what she was, where she was.

I reach down and pick up a lantern from where it rests against the bulwarks and throw it down, into the water, watch it fall and splash and the whales slide away to avoid it, and then I reach down again, this time to grab a thick knot of rope and throw it at the whales, and when they still don't swim away, I turn and find a heavy hook, a tin can, my boot, and I throw it all into the water at the whales, because there is nothing in the world that reminds me so much of the girl who destroyed my life than a whale.

At the first splash, I hear a shout of alarm, but I ignore it, focused on driving away the whales, and it's not until I'm standing in my socks, panting over the railing, tears like acid in my eyes and the whales still there, still swimming, that I realize I've drawn a crowd.

"All right?" A voice, uncertain. "That was our gear you just tossed into the water."

"I'm sorry," I say, still breathing hard. "I'll pay for it."

"You will," the man says, an edge to his words, but they leave me alone.

I turn back to the water, and still those blasted whales are swimming, as if they knew all along that I couldn't hurt them, as safe in the water as Essie Roe is on her island. I wish I had a harpoon. I wish I had the *shar*. I wish I were eight years old in the water, with Essie's hand in mine. I wish I could understand, ever, what it was like to feel magic, the magic of Others and spells and charms and the magic that Essie held close, the magic of having a home.

I drop my head into my hand and rub my forehead, and with my eyes closed and the smell of salt in my nose and my free hand hanging by my side, I can almost pretend I'm back there, on the island on that morning, with the whales rising in the water and the sun rising in the sky, and I almost expect to feel her hand slip into mine again, those fingers small and warm and squeezing tight. I *can* feel it. I feel my skin tingling, feel my hand reaching out to her, even though in time and distance and every other way of measuring anything she is so far away.

"What are you doing, boy?"

The spell breaks, my hand clenches into a fist, and I turn around so fast that it's almost a spin. Wide-eyed, I see Boone standing watching me with that empty look of his, one of the crew members, looking worried, just behind him.

"Nothing," I say, and he stares at me so long, stares at me like a stranger.

"I . . . Boone, I'm sorry," I say. I realize, as soon as the words leave my lips, that despite everything that has happened, I haven't told him I'm sorry. From the way his expression changes, goes darker, harder, I know it's too late for apologies, too late for any of that, but I can't help saying more. "I'm sorry, and I never meant for any of this to happen. I didn't think the Erslands could make it into the party—"

"Why not?" Boone asks, his voice flat. "You told them where it would be."

"That—it was an accident, you know that."

"And it was an accident when you let them touch you?" Boone takes a step toward me. "It was an accident when you let them run off with the *shar*? It was an accident, Mal?"

I don't realize I'm moving backward, moving away from him, until I feel my back bump up against the bulwarks.

"I'm sorry," I say again.

"Sorry." He hisses out the word like it's poison. "Sorry for what? For being foolish? Weak? For walking about in a daze? What is it, Mal? It seems there's plenty for you to apologize for."

The monster inside me growls, and I have to clench my jaw to stay calm.

"I'm not foolish," I say, and I speak slowly to keep my voice from trembling.

"No? Tossing hooks and lanterns into the ocean?" he asks, and my eyes dart for an instant to the crew member, still watching us. "Where are your boots?"

Another growl from the monster, pacing and pushing from within, and I let out a desperate laugh. "I like the feel of salt air between my toes," I say, and when Boone gives me a strange look, I grin, I laugh again, a wild laugh because I am so exhausted, so tired, and I feel myself losing control.

"Stop it," Boone says, and when I just laugh harder, he lunges for me, grabs my shirtfront, shakes me hard. *"Stop laughing!"*

He reaches back and slaps me across the face, one hard slap that knocks the breath from my lungs and the smile from my lips and the monster from its cage. It's like when I fought Jorah Ersland back in Paris, the thing inside me off its leash and furious with freedom, and I don't feel any pain, I don't feel the cold of the wind, I don't hear or see or know anything except that Boone is in front of me and I have two fists and a burning, *searing* urge to kill him.

But he's so strong, he's so fast, he throws me off him, and when I come at him again, he sidesteps and lands a punch in my gut that travels all the way up my spine to rock my skull. He's shouting something at me, shouting that he trusted me, that I betrayed him, that I'm worse than a snake, a wolf, a rat, and he did everything for me and I did nothing for him and he hates me, he hates me, he hates me.

Hands I don't feel pull me away from him, wrench us apart so fast that one second I'm rocking my fists into his body, bloody and stupid and wild, and the next I'm on my feet on the other side of the deck, watching him bow under the pressure of another half dozen men, all of them shouting at us, shouting to stop, shouting for answers, shouting, *"Stop screaming! Stop it, boy!*" And then there's a slap across my face, a ringing in my ears, and I blink through streaming tears and matted hair and blood and see the captain staring at me, horror and confusion on his face.

"What is this?" he asks, looking from me to Boone and back again. "What in the name of the seas has happened?"

Boone heaves for air, his face a mess of blood and bruising.

"Don't trust him," he says, breathing hard. "Don't trust him!"

"Why? What's happened?" The captain sounds utterly bewildered, staring at Boone, and in that moment, a wild panic builds inside me, a whirlwind of shock and pain and fear because *he's going to tell them. He's going to tell them what I am.*

"Let me go!" I say, and I twist against the hands that lock me in place, and Boone's lips curl into a snarl, and my mouth drops open in a prayer for mercy, because if the crew finds out I am a blank, they will throw me into the ocean and I will die.

"Please," I whisper, but he's too far away to hear it, and anyway I can still see my fist marks on his face. *"Please don't."*

Boone's eyes narrow to slits. He looks at the crew holding him, shakes his head, and they let him go, so he can stand up to his full height, so he can walk across the deck and stare down at me and hold my chin in his hand and look me in the eye when he says it, when he exposes me.

"He's a…"

"Boone."

The hand on my face trembles, drops, and he turns away.

"He's...a foolish, stupid boy," Boone says. "Too dreamy and dazed to be relied on. Put him in the brig until we reach New York."

And I know the captain must have nodded, the mate must have been waiting with manacles, the crew must have known to drag me away, but I can look only at Boone, his eyes closed, his face tipped up to the sky, weak and shaking like he's just lost his only child.

Twenty-Five

NEW YORK

HE LEAVES ME IN A ROOM IN NEW YORK. I hear him lock the door behind him, and the sound of the key in the handle seems to vibrate long after he's gone.

He went to visit the markets, the auction houses, his old hunter contacts, and I know he's still searching for the *shar*, and I know it's useless, but I don't say anything. He wouldn't listen to me anyway.

At least he took the manacles off my wrists as we neared New York, crossing down into the brig with a lantern and a bowl of warm water and soap and a razor and a mirror.

"You should clean yourself up," he said, and that was all he said. He put the lantern down on the floor and glanced at me, once, and I couldn't tell if he winced because of how I looked—pale, probably, and dirty and bloody and bruised—or because he put me there. But I didn't ask, and he climbed up the ladder from the brig and that was the last I saw of him until we docked in New York City.

"I'll get you a room," he told me. "You can stay there until…well…you can stay there. You can have a bit of money, too, to get you started."

"All right," I said, and I was surprised at how easily the words slipped from my lips, as though I hadn't just agreed to end our partnership and go out on my own. He nodded and asked me to carry my bag, and I followed him again, from the docks through narrow streets to another tiny upstairs room that didn't belong to us, as I'd done countless times over the past four years and as I'd never do again.

It's dark, this apartment: two cramped rooms, only one with windows. A sink in the corner drips brass-colored water, and it's a luxury, a sink in the apartment and not out in the hall, but the dripping drives me mad until I finally wedge a spare shirt up the faucet. When it's quiet again, I sit in the window with the pane pushed up in spite of the biting late November wind and breathe in the scent of this city, horse and mud and the sharp, burning smell of hot chestnuts. I sit and stare out the window at the children playing below and the mothers on the stoop and the drifting, snowy balls of lint that come from the clothing mills down the street and leave the air dry and sharp. I think about where I can go and what I can do, and the answer that comes back is: nothing.

I can't hunt anymore, not with Boone and not with anyone, because no doubt the Erslands will spread the word about me, and the community is small enough that word will travel. I'll have to avoid the bars soon, the markets, and the familiar routes of travel. Maybe I'll have to change my name, although my name isn't the problem—it's my blasted green eyes, the kind of detail bright enough to stick in someone's mind, and my dark hair and my narrow face and...and me, myself.

Who do I think I'm fooling? I'm a blank. I'm a monster. If the nonsense on the ship proved anything, it's that I'm losing the fight against the curse in my blood. I'm a danger to everyone, even my only friend. Even myself.

How am I supposed to hide *that*?

The world outside goes gauzy, tipsy, and I close my eyes and press my forehead against the chilled, grimy glass of the window. There's that panic again, flooding through my body, and before I know what I'm doing, I'm wrenching the window all the way open, throwing my legs over the sill, climbing down the gutter pipe to land on the front stoop. I can't be trapped in that apartment anymore, and with no destination in my mind except "forward," I walk.

This city makes me feel small in the same way the ocean makes me feel small, like I can disappear between the buildings, inside the crowds. The narrow streets choke with horses, trolleys, carts, strangers, and I relax and fall in line, letting them carry me forward like a river. The sounds—shouting, footsteps, wheels and hooves and bells—fill my ears like a kind of white noise, and I can almost feel myself shrinking, my muscles relaxing. I let this city soak into me, and I walk, first west to one river and then south to the harbor, and by the time I find a park bench that looks out onto the water at the southern tip of the city, I am the kind of good exhausted that finally rocks the monster to sleep.

And then, I see it.

It's fluttering along the sidewalk, pages flapping like an injured bird: a newspaper. But I know this paper like I know the color and texture of my own skin. It's the *Island Gazette*, Prince Island's own newspaper, printed on the island and full of the latest news on whalers, oil prices, sailing outfitters. And, of course, the dealings of the Roes.

Ignore it, I tell myself, and I watch it roll and float in the stiff breeze, heading for the harbor and the water. I watch it with my hands in my pockets and every muscle as tense as a spring, and when it looks like it might blow away for good, I jump up and race after it and snatch it, wet and stained and torn, from the street.

For a moment, I can only hold it. I have no doubt the paper came from one of the dozens of sailors milling about the harbor—some of these boats are whalers, and although I don't see any that I recognize as Prince Island ships, no doubt a good number of them stopped at the island before continuing on to New York. When I finally open it, my hands are shaking so badly that I have to sit and rest them on my thighs to keep the paper steady.

The *Island Gazette*. This week's edition.

I skip over the first pages, long columns that list the ships that came through Prince Island's docks, along with information on their size, owners, and amount of whale oil in their holds. The next pages are full of advertisements for better duck-canvas raincoats and stronger harpoons, and the last page is devoted to job listings, but just before that is a single page headlined ISLAND DOINGS.

My skin tingles. I smooth the crumpled pages against my legs and read.

Society news, the church bazaar, listings of marriages and births and deaths—I ignore them and focus on the inch-long articles about the islanders. My eyes scan for any mention of Essie or the Roe witch so fast that my head spins and I have to take a breath, read more slowly.

"Nothing," I whisper, and I let out a tight breath and unclench my hands.

I start to crumple the paper into a ball when I see it: *Roe*, the word jumping out at me not from the articles but from the notices at the top of the page. The deaths.

Something jerks inside me, *Essie Roe dead, dead, dead*, and then my eyes focus, and I manage to read it properly: "George Corwin Howell, twenty-two years old, son of Curtis Howell, owner of the *Bayard*, *Ceres*, and *Dove*, sailed alone from the island in a storm on Nov. 25, body and vessel found Nov. 27.

Howell was earlier seen at the Roe cottage and it is believed that he undertook his final risky sail in an effort to win the affection of Essie Roe."

To win the affection of Essie Roe.

The affection of Essie Roe.

Essie Roe.

Heat blooms up inside me, and this time I really do crumple up the paper, crush her name between my fingers, and toss it into the wind. She's still torturing people with her magic and now a boy is dead. I can see it: Essie, beautiful and haughty and drunk on her magic, pushing and pulling and manipulating just because she can. The tracker I met in Boston and that sailor from Prince Island, the one at the bar in Paris, both of them said the same thing: She's tearing apart marriages, families, all because she couldn't be bothered to control her magic. And now a boy is dead.

Does she even care? Does she even realize what she's doing? And, seas—this is only the beginning of her power. What kind of tyrant will she be with the full power of the Roes behind her?

I would give anything to have the *shar* and to be able to confront her, at last, after all these years. Someone needs to stop her, but who could? With her magic, she could make even her worst enemy fall in love with her.

Another breeze rips toward me from across the water, and I wrap my jacket more tightly around myself and pull the collar up over my neck. In front of me, the masts and sails and lines of the ships docked in the harbor are as thick as a forest, reminding me of nothing so much as the docks of Prince Island.

And that's when it hits me.

I'm a blank. I'm alone. I have nothing now—no home, no friends, no job—and so I have nothing anyone can take away from me. Kill me? The monster will do that eventually. There are only a handful of people Essie Roe can't control, and I'm one of them.

It's decided.

I'm going to finally tell her what she did to me.

I'm going back to the island.

Twenty-Six

MY FEET PICK UP SPEED UNTIL I'M RUNNING down the streets, pushing between the crowds of people that, only a few minutes ago, I was happy to drift through, anonymous and forgotten. I'm going back. I'm going to talk to her. I feel small and scared at the thought of making my way through the streets of New Bishop, seeing the people who drove me away, and I feel wild and thrilled at the thought that, finally, I will confront her. Finally, she will come face-to-face with someone who cannot be forced to love her.

I'm going to show her she's weak and I'm going to tell her she's a monster. Maybe she'll just laugh in my face and tell all her lovesick sailors to toss me into the ocean but it'll be worth it, just to show her there's something she can't touch.

I practically fly up the gutter pipe of the building we're

staying in, reaching the windowsill in one leap and hauling myself back into the room. I never unpacked my things, but looking at what belongs to me—the ropes, the knives, the bullets, the gun—I tear my bags apart, paring down everything I own to a few spare pieces of clothing. I don't have any money, not after our whirlwind tour around the world, and my eyes linger on Boone's iron chest, the spot where he keeps his purse. I could take a little. Leave a note, promise to pay him back. He was going to give me money anyway, and maybe this will be a relief to him, my leaving. He doesn't even need to say good-bye.

Good-bye.

A huge fist reaches into my chest and squeezes, because if I leave right now, I don't know if I'll ever see Boone again.

I don't know what to do, standing with my bag in my hands and my eyes on the chest—stay or go, stay or go?—but then the decision is made for me; a key jingles in the lock, the door opens, and he's back.

"Mal?"

He sees the bag in my hand, my weapons strewn across the bed; he knows what's happening. My hands shake as I turn and gather my cap from the nightstand.

"I'm going to go," I say, still not looking at him. "You don't have to . . . I'm going to go."

Silence, and I squeeze my eyes tight for a moment, take a breath, and tell myself: *Just face him. Shake his hand and then leave.*

When I finally turn to look at him, he's watching me, a

strained expression on his face, and he carefully, slowly, reaches into his vest, pulls out a small piece of paper, and holds it out to me. I take it.

It's a ferry ticket to Prince Island.

"What...what is this?" I ask, staring up at him, because how could he know? How could he know me so well?

"It's another chance," he says.

I blink at him, confused, before I realize he hadn't guessed that I meant to go back to the island for Essie. He's talking about something else.

"A chance...for what?"

He hesitates a moment and then swings his small leather bag from his back, opens it, and pulls out a narrow, wrapped bundle. He takes his time opening it, but I know what it is, I know it, I can *feel* it, and when it's finally exposed and lying in his hands, I don't even flinch.

The *shar.*

"Where did you get it?" I ask, my voice strangled and raw, and Boone gazes down at it, blinking like he can't believe he's actually holding it.

"I found them.... I found the Erslands. They were going to sell it after all, take the profit and build a confederation, but I found them first. I m-made—" His voice breaks so suddenly that he looks startled, glancing up at me and then quickly back down at the *shar.* "I made a deal with them. They promised to give me the *shar,* to split the profits with them, so long as I gave them..."

He trails off and then looks at me, his eyes clear, that uncertain look back in his face, that look that seems to be asking if he's making a mistake right now.

"I told them I could deliver to them the magic of the Roe witch." He lets the words hang in the air for a moment, swallows. "They agreed. A share of the profits for the magic of the witch. It'll be enough. Not as much as it could be, but enough. Mal"—he tilts his head at me—"I can't ever get close to her like you can. No one could. I need you for this."

It takes me a moment to realize he's asking me a question, really, and in that moment I don't breathe, don't think, don't see anything but the *shar* or hear anything but rushing wind in my ears.

"The Erslands know what I am," I finally say, and he winces.

"They promised to keep your secret. It was—it was part of the deal." He takes a breath. "We can start again. We'll have the money, we can do it. Together." His voice has gone very soft. "Do you understand what I'm saying? Partners."

He holds the *shar* out to me like a peace offering, and I stare at it, confused. The monster screams to take it, now, take it and cut open Essie's soul and have my revenge, but my hunter instincts tell me to think this over.

The Erslands gave Boone the *shar*? They offered to keep my secret?

Something about it doesn't feel right, and when Boone sees me hesitate, his mouth jerks into a smile.

"This is what you want, isn't it?" He tilts his head at me again, studying me. "You can say no. It's all right. I'll understand. It's your decision."

"Really?" The word slips out from me before I realize how young it makes me sound, like a little boy offered a toy or a piece of candy. *Really? For me?*

Boone's smile broadens, and he nods. "Of course. Of course it's your decision. That's how it always should have been, and if you join with me again, that's how it'll be. Partners. Real partners. We decide together."

I can't help it. I smile. I put out my hand to shake—real partners, equals—and he looks at me, surprised. In that second, I wonder if I was wrong. Boone doesn't like touching me, and I've never reached out to him like this. But just as I doubt him, he returns my smile and slides his hand into mine, and we shake.

Partners again.

Twenty-Seven

PRINCE ISLAND

IT'S BEEN FIVE YEARS SINCE I'VE SET FOOT on this island, but I can feel every piece of it in my bones.

The ferry drifts closer to the harbor, and I lean over the railing to get my first glimpse. It looks exactly the same as the day I left it: the low-ceilinged buildings that line the docks, busy with blacksmiths and carpenters and sailmakers and coopers; the taller buildings of brick and stone just beyond; the factories at the south of town, huge, square, gray, puffing rancid-smelling smoke into the air; and to the north, far from the noise and stink and hurry, the stately homes of the richest folk on the island, the ship owners and bankers and lawyers and captains with their front yards choked with the skeletons of summer roses and their houses like sleeping white bridecakes.

Will they remember me?

My heartbeat quickens as the ferry navigates its path to the dock, and a hand creeps up, touches my cheek, my nose, my hair. How much do I still look like the little orphan boy who slipped into their home and disrupted their lives?

"Ready?" Boone asks, coming up behind me, and I turn and nod. The ferry bumps and shudders as it coasts to a stop against the docks, and Boone smiles faintly.

"Welcome home."

When we arrive at the docks, Boone slips a dime to one of the many small boys waiting at the gangway to get our bags safely to our room, and then he pulls my cap low over my eyes, yanks my collar up to my cheeks, and leads me through my hometown.

My pulse picks up as I step across the docks, feeling in the air the low, dim growl of the factories that make up the south side of the town. It's a thrum as familiar to me as the stink of burning whale oil, rising in thick plumes of black smoke that sting my eyes and wrinkle my nose.

The vibrations work their way through my bones, or maybe that's just me, shaking to be back here again.

Boone and I fall into the crowd—and it is a crowd, made

up of dozens of anonymous sailors here for a visit or looking for work. It's a cold day, the feel of winter always coming
quicker to an island than the mainland, and so there are plenty
of people bundled up the way that I am. The eyes of the islanders pass right over our faces, ignoring us the way they're used to
strangers in their streets, but I can't shake the tightness in my
chest. Someone's going to recognize me. Someone's going to
figure out who I am.

"Where to?" Boone mutters to me, and I nod in the direction of the western part of town, where the boardinghouses sit.
It was his idea: Take me straight to one of the boardinghouses,
and then he'll head back into town and use his Silvertongue
to find out all he can about Essie Roe.

"Remember," he'd said, back on the boat, "your girl isn't a
real witch yet."

"Don't call her my girl," I said. "And of course she's a
witch."

"Love magic." Boone rolled his eyes. "I promised the Erslands the magic of the Roe witch. Ocean magic. Not romance.
When you cut Essie Roe, she'll need to have the power of
the Roes."

I rubbed my forehead, thinking. "Essie's mother is the
witch now. I don't know how the magic passes from her to her
daughter."

"Then you cut the mother."

But I was already shaking my head. "I'm only going back
to the island to use the *shar* on one person. It's Essie Roe who

deserves to be cut. Not her mother. If you want to take the *shar* to her, you can do it yourself, but I wouldn't trust your Silver-tongue against her magic."

Boone frowned. "Fine. Essie it is. But don't forget: Until we figure out how she becomes the Roe witch and until she has that power, you can't cut her. Understand? She's useless to us until then."

I'd nodded and agreed, but now, back here again, I realize it could be weeks before Boone manages to fig-ure out how Essie gets her powers, and meanwhile I'm here, trapped, waiting. A girl brushes past me, a girl I recognize as Charlotte Brighton, a married lady now but a child in pig-tails when I last saw her. She was a tiny thing who used to bring me sweets at the priory, and seeing her makes my heart strangle with panic and fear, and I have to fight the urge to wrestle the *shar* out of Boone's bag, race down to the Roe cottage, and cut Essie to ribbons just so I can get off this island.

Every brick, every window, every storefront is like a little kick in the chest, a little memory coming back to me: Here is where I used to get my breakfast, and here is where I bought groceries for the priory, and here is where the children would gather every afternoon to play their games and turn their backs on me and Essie.

"There," I say to Boone, pointing at the boardinghouse, and he nods. The main room of the boardinghouse is full of people, sitting at the huge fireplace and talking over long tables, but they're sailors, foreigners, no one who would recognize me, and besides, Boone walks just ahead of me, ready to deflect any suspicious questions with a single word.

He rents the room, we climb the stairs, and then he leaves me.

"Sit tight," he says, and unlike in New York, when I craved movement and freedom and light and air, today I pull the curtains, blow out the lamplight, and collapse on the bed with my eyes closed.

After a few minutes, I can't take it anymore, and I spring from the bed and attack our bags, ripping them to pieces and emptying them out several times before I realize Boone doesn't trust me half as much as he says he does.

He took the *shar* with him.

"No one on this island will talk about you."

That's the first thing Boone says to me when he makes it back that afternoon, balancing two bowls of clam chowder, a pair of mugs, and a lantern.

"What?" I sit up, blinking at the light, and he sets down the bowls, mugs, and lantern and pulls out a chair.

"It's like you're a ghost," Boone says, and he drops into the chair and huddles over his chowder. I blink at him for a moment and then join him, the curling scent of the soup so richly warm and familiar that I have to shake off a wave of childhood memories.

"I asked around about you—"

"You did? Why?"

Boone shrugs. "Don't you wonder what they think about you?" he asks, and even though I don't say anything, I know he knows my answer. "Well, your name is taboo around here. Asked if anyone remembered a little orphan boy raised on this island, and it was like asking after the devil. I had to use magic to get anyone to admit they knew who you were, and even then, no one would admit *what* you were. One thing's for certain: They'd never expose you."

"Why's that?" I ask, and Boone takes his time, licking his spoon clean before answering.

"I think they're embarrassed. Place like this, magic's a way of life, and they didn't even realize the threat they had right under their noses. How would it look to all those sailors arriving here to buy their charms if word was to get out the people of Prince Island harbored a blank for thirteen years?" Boone grins at me, his teeth white in the lamplight. "They're as desperate to keep you a secret as you are."

I frown and shove a spoonful of soup into my mouth to hide my disappointment from Boone. I know he thinks it's a good thing, the islanders wanting to forget me, but there's something about hearing I'm the secret shame of the island that makes my stomach twist.

"And what about Essie?" I ask, and Boone's expression twitches, just for a second, like he's caught off guard and not sure what to say. But a moment later the smooth smile reappears, and I wonder if it was just a trick of the light.

"I went down to the cottage to see her," he says, and I sputter on my mouthful of chowder.

"You *saw* her?"

"And the mother," Boone says.

"How is she? What's she like?"

"Still selling her charms to soppy sailors and lovelorn lasses. Still without the power of the Roes."

"That wasn't what I meant," I say, but Boone just shrugs. "Did you find out what she needs to do to get the power?"

"No," Boone says, and he smiles. "But it's only a matter of time." He drains his mug and pushes back his chair while I watch him with narrowed eyes. If I'd been anyone else in the world, I would have believed him, but I've lived with him for four years now and heard him lie dozens, hundreds of times, and I know: He's lying to me now. There's something he's not telling me, something about the Roes. And Essie.

"How much time?" I ask, and Boone shrugs again, effortless and unconcerned.

"Not long."

When I frown, he knocks his knuckles on the table. "Listen. It's not anything you have to worry about, all right? I'll let you know when it needs to be done and until then, just stay here."

"But for how long, Boone? When can we move? When will Essie be ready?"

"Relax," he says, and he says it with a sharpness that stirs up memories of our fights. I feel myself tense, my hands twitching into fists, and when Boone sees the change in me, he leans back in his chair, his expression soft but cautious. "You need to trust me. Can't you trust me?"

I don't know. Can I? Because only a few days ago he had me in chains and then we ended our partnership and now he's taken me back to the one place I've tried to avoid my whole life, and he's lying to me about Essie. He *knows* how she gets her magic and he's not telling me. I want to ask him outright, but when I open my mouth to speak, the easy smile slams onto his face like a mask, like armor, and the monster hisses, *He will always lie to you.*

"Of course I trust you."

And he's still smiling, like always, but there's a wariness in his expression, even as he lets out an exaggerated sigh of relief.

"Good! That's that, then," he says, and he finishes his bowl of chowder and drops his spoon on the table. "This little island has some good food, doesn't it!"

Such ease, like we're old pals again, and I smile back at him as though I don't want to take my mug and slam it onto the table and grab him by the collar and shake him until he tells me what he's not telling me.

The monster flexes its claws.

"It has some good drink, too," I say, and I pause for a moment before I add slyly, "and good ladies."

"Mal!" Boone laughs, and there's that wariness again, but I can see I've got his attention. "What would you know about that? Didn't you leave the island at thirteen?"

"I've heard rumors, then. Come on. When have we landed in port and not gone out on the town?"

"Traditions change when one of us is despised by the local community," Boone says, wagging his spoon at me.

"Then we'll visit a part of the community that only cares about how much money we've got in our pockets," I say, standing up from the table.

"You mean *my* pockets," Boone says, but he joins me, rising to his feet with a smile. "All right, boy. You've convinced me. Where to?"

The monster lets out a frenzied cry of triumph, of anticipation, and I spread out my arms, warm and friendly and inviting.

"Boone, let me introduce you to the fine ladies of the Codfish."

It's nearly too easy. The Codfish, the island's grubbiest—and most entertaining—bar, sits way out at the edge of town, the clipping piano music calling to us as we make our way through the streets. Boone's eyes light up at the sound of the music, the scent of perfume and liquor, and within fifteen minutes he's lost in the crowd, singing, swaying, one arm throwing back drinks and the other slung around the waist of one of the 'Fish women. Boone's wrong that I haven't got money: I slip five dollars to a pretty red-haired girl who, a moment later, winds her arms around Boone, peeling off his jacket and whispering something in his ear that makes his eyes light up. When she leads him away, she makes sure to pass by my table just long enough to drop something into my lap, and as Boone follows the girl up the stairs, I look down at the dusty little scabbard and bright hilt and smile.

The Codfish opens up right to the fields, and after I slip the *shar*'s sheath onto my belt and head outside, I stop for a moment and stare out at the grass.

It's just past sundown, and the light is still golden, hitting the grass so that the field looks made up of thousands of glowing tails. After the noise of the bar, the quiet of the grass settles me. My feet want to pound across the fields and rediscover the paths of my childhood, the foxes' dens and plover nests and small nooks perfect for sleeping, dreaming. I stretch out a hand and let the grass tickle my palm, twitch across my skin, and then I close my hand into a fist and let it drop by my side.

Those grasslands belonged to us, but she took them away from me.

I don't care anymore about what Boone told me, that the *shar* won't be worth it with just her love magic, that we have to wait. I don't think about any of that; I just turn south, along the beach, and walk a path well trod by hundreds, thousands, of sailors searching for magic and safety and promises from the Roe witch.

The sky goes dark as I walk, the blaze of colors above my head deepening with every step. In my childhood, I used to go with Essie to watch the sunsets on the western shore of the island—we kept north, near the marshy pond known as the Great Gray Slough, even though the best place to watch the sunset was the Roe cottage itself, which jutted out practically into the ocean and was the island's southern- and westernmost point. We'd sit and watch, and Essie would talk about the colors, and the older she got, the flowerier her language: "Like the pearly opalescence of a moonstone," she'd say, and I knew she had to have gotten that out of some book she read, she had to have been repeating it from somewhere else. Even though sometimes it was boring, watching those sunsets, I liked going with her. It made me laugh, those things she'd say—"a purer orange than a tiger lily's petals," "golden as a Roman goddess," "the crimson of a lover's lips." I'd laugh at how silly they sounded until she frowned at me and said to stop making fun.

There's a good sunset tonight, and even though it's prettier over the ocean on the western side of the island, it's still plenty pretty now, stretching over the fields and shooting up the sky with threads of gold, of orange, of pink-purple-blue melting together and turning the whole island rosy warm with color.

I pause to watch the patterns of clouds shift and blend, and when the sky goes purple like a bruise, I keep walking.

When I finally see the Roe cottage in the distance, I tense, and even though I'm still a mile away, I pull the *shar* from its sheath and squeeze the hilt. I have to stop myself from running the rest of the way. With every step, I go over what I'll say to her: *Do you recognize me? My eyes? My hair? Do you remember what you did to me? Do you realize what you took away from me? And now I'm going to take something from you.*

The words run around and around in my head, blending and overlapping like music. I feel the little monster waking up, growling and pacing and getting stronger with every step. I should try to control myself a little better, but I'm here with the *shar* and with Essie, and I can't put a leash on the blasted thing any longer. The *shar* might be worthless without the power of the Roes, but I don't care. I don't even care what this means for me and Boone, that if I cut Essie now, before she's ready, I'm ending our partnership forever. All I think about is Essie, her magic, the *shar*, losing the island and meeting Boone and falling into the hunter world, all my travels and adventures bringing me back here again.

All along, I've wondered what it is I'm supposed to do, who I'm supposed to be.

Maybe this is it.

Maybe I was never supposed to find a home or free myself from my blankness.

I've always been a monster. And monsters destroy things. Things like magic and friendships and futures.

I can't even think about what will happen next, after I cut her, after I lose Boone. My future ends at the doorway to the Roe cottage. Maybe *I* end there, too. Maybe this is the last thing I do as myself, as Mal, the good-natured orphan, the sailor with a smile. Maybe when I cut Essie, I'm going to hand myself over to the monster for good.

But I don't think about that, either. I near the cottage and my hand goes slick with sweat around the hilt of the *shar*. I'm close enough to see figures behind the glass of the windows. There's a lit lantern on the table and people walking inside: two heads, one silver, one dark.

It's her, I think, and the monster paws the ground.

I walk—no, *stalk*—closer to the cottage, and my breath goes ragged. My head feels light, but I know what I have to do. I know it with more certainty than I've ever felt before.

Do you recognize me? My eyes? My hair? Do you remember what you did to me? Do you realize what you took away from me? And now I'm going to take something from you.

A hundred feet from the cottage. Fifty. Twenty.

I am going to open the door. I am going to open the door, and I can already see her surprised expression. Maybe her mother will notice the knife in my hand, maybe she'll try to stop me with a spell, and maybe when it doesn't work, she'll realize who I am, that I'm back.

Do you recognize me?

I'm going to take something from you.

I feel it building inside me, all the anger and frustration and fear and loss, and I reach my hand to the door handle and before I can touch it, it springs open, a girl rushes out, the door closes quickly behind her, and I blink in the darkness because *there she is.*

Essie Roe.

Black hair and white skin and pink cheeks and blue eyes, and in the second I take her in, I realize she's softer than the girl in my mind. She's smaller. She's more beautiful. Her mouth falls open in surprise, surprise to nearly run into someone, and then she steps aside.

"My mother is in," she says, gesturing at the door, and in my head I hear *Do you recognize me?* but I can't say anything. "You can go inside."

"Wait," I say, because she's started to move away, and at the sound of my voice, strangled and raspy, she glances back at me, frowning.

"Do you recognize me?" I whisper. "My eyes? My hair?"

Her own eyes go wide.

"Do you remember what you did to me?"

Her breath stops.

"Do you realize what you took away from me?"

My hand tightens on the *shar.*

"And now—"

"*Mal.*" She says my name and then she closes her eyes and then she rushes forward, comes toward me, almost falls against me, wraps her arms around my waist and presses her cheek to my chest and holds me, hugs me, like I haven't been touched in years.

"You're back," she whispers, and it sounds like an answer to a prayer. "You're back, *you're back!*"

Twenty-Eight

I CAN'T MOVE.

For a moment, I can only stand there, my arms hanging limp at my sides, the smell of her hair filling my lungs, her cheek so warm and soft pressed against my chest. She holds me so tightly, like I'm about to disappear, and I can't remember someone holding me like this—ever. She knows what I am, she knows how dangerous it is for a magical person to touch a blank, but she must not care, and that thought more than anything is what freezes me solid.

"Mal." She whispers my name, and the spell breaks: I shove her away.

"Don't touch me," I say, squeezing the knife, and now I see her eyes trip down to my hand and go wide at the *shar*.

"But...but you came *back*," she says, all disbelief. "I

thought…you came back because…Didn't you get my messages?"

I blink at her. "What?"

Her expression goes hard. "All these years…" She glances at the cottage. "Wait. Just wait a moment."

Before I can say anything else, she disappears inside. I can hear murmured voices, her mother asking her a question and Essie responding in calm, quiet tones.

When she comes back, the monster whispers, *cut her before she can say anything else. Before she can distract you again.*

And I tense and flex my fingers around the hilt of the *shar*, but when she slips back out a moment later, a bundle in her arms, I still can't move.

What are you doing? the voice asks, but I don't have an answer.

"Follow me," she says, and she reaches out and takes my hand again before leading me away. There's that feeling again, skin on skin, and it's like a shock of lightning. I can't even help it; when she squeezes my hand, I squeeze back, and I let her lead me away, north from the cottage. The rocky ground under our feet slowly grows weedy with sea grass as Essie pulls me deeper into the heart of the island, pausing just long enough to scoop up a lantern that glows at her touch—bewitched, I'm sure, by her mother.

I realize a moment too late where she's taking me: the grassy fields, our old hideaway, and when I pull back, she whispers to me, "Please! It's important. It's a secret, Mal."

It's a secret. The words set off a vibration of feeling inside me. I want to cut her and leave and I want to forget everything that's happened and pretend I'm Mal the little boy again. I don't know what to do anymore, and all I can do is follow her, letting the grass tickle my arms and legs, inhaling the familiar smells of dirt and sea breeze and wild, growing things.

It's better like this, the voice says. *Get her alone, away from her mother.*

"Here."

She comes to a stop in a little clearing piled with white stones: hundreds, maybe thousands of white stones. I see cut lengths of rope, a heap of rusted metal fishing hooks, grass twisted into bracelets and knots. It's her private place, just like when we were children. It's a place no one else on the island knows about.

I could cut her now, and even if she screamed, no one would stop me.

She sets the lantern on the ground but holds the bundle in her arms.

"I wrote to you," she says, and then she holds out the bundle so I can see a notebook. "I thought...I hoped you got the messages. But..."

"How?" I ask, and she touches a symbol drawn on the cover. I recognize it. Sailors often have books like these. They come in pairs: The sailor keeps one, gives the other to his wife or sweetheart, and whatever is written in one appears in the pages of the other. Lovers' letters, they're called. Long-distance diaries.

"I gave you the twin months before you left. Remember?"

I frown. Not only do I remember, but I have it in my pocket, and when I pull it out her eyes go wide.

"Then you *did* get my messages."

"I didn't get anything."

"But—"

"See for yourself." I open the notebook to show her my scribbles. Slowly, she reaches out to take it, and I hand it over to her.

"But Mal—*look*." She lifts up the notebook, and first I just see my scrawls, but then, blooming over the page, a second set of writing appears. My eyes widen. "I've been writing to you for years. I didn't realize—"

"That lovers' letters don't work for blanks?" I say, my expression hard again. "You understand that blanks destroy magic, right?"

A look of annoyance crosses her face for a moment. "I thought, at least, you'd see..." She shakes her head and hands me her own journal. "Here."

When I don't take it, she opens the book to the first page and holds it up for me to see. The pages are covered, top to bottom, in her tight, neat handwriting, spelling out the same six words over and over.

I am sorry. Please come back.

Cold prickles sweep through me.

"I missed you, Mal," she says softly. "I shouldn't ever have...I told your secret, and I am so sorry. I've regretted it for years, and it's all—I wrote about it all here." She pushes the book out to me again, but still I don't take it. "I thought your coming back...I thought you had forgiven me at last."

"*Forgiven* you?" I let out a laugh and Essie flinches. "Forgiven you for what, exactly? Did you think I've forgiven you for betraying me? Or for telling my secret? Or for forcing me out of my home? Or do you think I've forgiven you for what you've become?"

"What I've become?"

"I've sailed the world but I still hear stories about you," I say. "Essie Roe, the sorceress. She finds a way into your mind and into your heart. Lures away husbands. Tears apart friendships. What did you promise to that boy if he sailed his boat into a storm?"

"You don't know," she says, sounding—unbelievably—angry. "You don't know what it was like to stay here without you."

"Torture, I bet."

"It *was*. I was alone, Mal. None of them wanted anything to do with me, and then one day I woke up and I could control them. And what's more—they *wanted* to be controlled. I could feel what they were thinking when they looked at me." She holds up a hand to her pretty face. "They wanted me and they wanted to give themselves to me and I was foolish and wild and liked it and let them." Her hand drops back to her side and she lets out a sigh.

"I'm trying to control it. It's difficult. It's like I've got this force at my fingertips and it's begging to come out....I don't know. I don't know how to describe it. Do you know what I mean?"

Do I know what it's like to feel like there's something within you that you can't control?

"The boy and his boat—"

"That was a mistake," she says quickly. "I never meant for him to—that was a mistake."

I stare at her, her bowed head, the eyelashes dark on her cheeks. Essie Roe, the girl with the ice-cold heart, except she doesn't look cold now but beaten, scared.

She still deserves to be cut, the monster says. *She still betrayed you! You'll never get your home back. You'll never get back the years of wandering.*

And maybe she does still deserve it. I hold up the *shar.*

"Do you know what this is?" I ask, and she looks at it and shivers. "It's a tool meant to take away your magic—forever. I came to this island to cut you with this knife. That's what I came back here for. I never forgave you for anything. I came here to punish you."

Her eyes dart between my face and the knife, and for a moment, she tenses: hands drawn up, shoulders hunched, lips pressed together into a thin line. And then, she lets out a breath and her arms fall to her sides. She looks into my face, and she gives a little laugh.

"What's funny?" I ask. I don't like how her laughter sends a flutter of pleasure through my stomach.

"You, coming back here to take away my magic, when I always thought..." She shakes her head. "Maybe it's for the best. I'm a wretched witch, Mal, and I don't even have my full magic yet. I thought I was ready, but... I'm exhausted. You want to take it all away? Then do it."

She holds out a hand, palm up, and she looks into my eyes, steady and trusting and ready, and it's like looking into a memory: me, right here in this field, putting out my hand for her, my whole life about to change with the slash of a knife.

Carefully, I slip the *shar* into its sheath.

"I don't forgive you," I say, "but I'm not going to cut you. At least, not today."

I turn to leave when I feel her hand on my arm, and when I glance back, she's pressing something into my chest: her journal.

"Take it," she says. "Please just take it."

She slips it into my pocket, and before I can give it back to her, she's disappeared through the grass, the lantern a bobbing glowing bird beside her.

Twenty-Nine

I AM SORRY. PLEASE COME BACK.

Twenty pages, filled, front to back, the handwriting changing from neat and tight to loose, sprawling, but the message always the same. Back in the boardinghouse, the *shar* in its place beside a snoring Boone, I touch a fingertip to the words, pressed so hard that they almost carve into the paper and leave ghosts on the other side. She wrote this to me. She sent me messages.

Dear Mal, I miss you.

That's the first real letter.

Dear Mal, I miss you. Come back.

They're all like that to start with. Over and over, she misses me, she's sorry, she wants me to come back to the island. And then: She's lonely, she's worried about me. Am I getting her letters? Do I ever think about her? Do I hate her?

Come back, Mal. Be my friend again. I don't want anyone but you.

I rub a hand against my forehead and I read her words, and as I read, I watch her grow up.

She's twelve and going to the docks every day, not for attention from the boys but to look for me, my ship, because surely I'm coming back, surely I wouldn't leave her.

She's thirteen, and the pages are splattered in mud because she was just pushed into the slough by a group of island girls, jealous of the smiles she lured from the boys.

She's fourteen and fighting with her mother, the witch, who won't stop asking her if she feels anything, her gift coming out, and when Essie says no, her mother doesn't even look angry or frustrated anymore, just sad.

"Pitying," Essie writes. "Like I'm missing a limb."

She's fifteen, waking one morning with her gift, and she uses it on her mother and gives herself one perfect day: Her mother makes her breakfast and braids her hair and cups her cheeks in her hands and calls her lovely. Then she lifts the spell, and her mother's smile falls away so fast that it leaves Essie cold.

"I'm never going to use my magic to make someone love me," she writes. "Not ever again."

But it's not so easy, because there are all those cruel islanders with their wide-open hearts, and Essie's sixteen and beautiful and she can't help it, she writes, she can't help but pay them back for all the pain they've caused her, and when married men run away from their wives to be with her and best friends beat each other bloody over her favor and boys die to win her heart, she likes it. She doesn't want to, but she likes it.

I'm losing myself, Mal, she writes. *I've been alone so many years that I feel like I'm losing my mind. My magic's changing me.*

I reach the last few pages, and the words are so faint that it's almost like they're not really there.

I'm done, she writes.

My magic's gotten too easy for me, and I nearly can't help myself anymore from using it to hurt people. My mother says I need responsibility. She says the only thing that will keep me sane now will be to take on the mantle of the witch. Maybe she's right. I've resisted it for so long because I know it will tie me to this place forever, but now, I'm ready.

I'm sorry, Mal, for so many things, but I hope that what I'm doing now is right. I hope that it means I still have a chance at happiness. Do you see any of these letters? I don't know. I picture you far away somewhere, sailing. I picture you high up a masthead, looking out at the sea. I picture you with whales, not hunting them but watching them. I wish I could see my future and know for certain that you're there, somewhere. Even if that day should be many years away, it would be enough, knowing that someday I'll see you again. I miss you, my friend. There is so much I wish I could tell you, but I'd settle for just seeing your face one more time.

I close the journal. I blow out the lantern and sit for a long time in the dark, watching the stars circle over our island.

She's a traitor, the monster tells me. *She's a monster. She took everything from you.*

She did. But she was also once my friend. I can't forget that, either.

The sun's high in the sky when Boone finally wakes up, clutching his head and moaning about the ladies of the Codfish.

"They slipped me some kind of black magic," he says, running a hand over his face.

"It's called liquor," I say. "And you took it all yourself."

"No, there was something else. Call it years of experience, boy, but I'm sure of it. I bet I know where they got it, too. I thought your girl would have gotten out of the love business now she's found a man, but it seems I'm not so lucky."

"What's that?" I ask, turning sharply to him. Boone gives me a careful smile.

"Oh, that's right—she's not your girl."

"No. What's that about finding a man?"

"Didn't I mention it yesterday?" Boone lifts an eyebrow, all innocence. "The Roe girl's engaged."

"*Engaged?* To who?"

"Some salt who came to the island weeks ago. Man named...oh...Frank—no—Franklin Lindsay." Boone rises from his bed and stretches, yawning so long and so lazy that I know, I *know*, he's waiting for me to ask more questions.

Fine. I will.

"What else do you know about him?" I ask, and Boone's mouth twitches into the smallest satisfied smile.

"'Jealous brute' seems to be the way most people describe him. A fellow he sails with told me he found out a lady he'd been courting had spent time with another man and he went after both of them. Almost killed them."

"Essie's engaged to *him*? That doesn't make any sense. Roes don't marry."

Boone gives me a sidelong glance. "This one will."

Engaged. *Engaged.*

All day, I run it over in my head. Roe women don't marry. They live alone in their cottages, first with their mothers and then with their daughters. Always two, always a pair, and no men.

"I'm going to be different," Essie used to tell me when we were very little. "I'm going to have a handsome husband and a big family."

But the older we got, the less she talked about love and marriage, husbands and fathers.

While Boone heads back out into town, I sit in the room, reading the journal over and over. She doesn't mention falling in love, even when she was using her magic to tangle up the people of the island in a messy web of affairs and romances. Even the pages from a few weeks ago, when she must have met Franklin Lindsay and agreed to marry him, have no mention of him.

Boone, when he left, promised to find out more about him, but by late afternoon I'm jumping out of my skin, and I can't wait anymore. I throw a scarf around my neck, wrapping it high over my mouth, pull on my coat, pull down my cap, and leave.

These streets, again.

I'm lucky my face stays hidden, because I keep nearly running into familiar faces or walking past familiar places and I must look like a ghost walking around his own funeral. That tight kick of recognition deep in my belly happens so many times that I feel sick. I don't know what I'm thinking, walking around like this. At first, I head toward Main Street, the shops and people there, but it's so thick with memories—the butcher and the scent of blood, blue-gray smoke wafting from the tobacco shop, the tiny apothecary covered ceiling to floor in hundreds of playing card–sized dark drawers—my head spins, and I have to lean against a brick wall, yank the scarf from my face, and breathe.

"All right?" someone asks me, and I turn and jump and duck my chin back into my coat collar.

"Fine," I say, and the boy—he's about my age, and he's got a beard and a pair of scratched half-moon glasses, but I recognize him—gives me an odd look.

"Do I know you?" he asks.

His name is Michael Dalton. He's twenty years old. His father captained the *Angel*. When he was seven, he was in an accident that left him half a pinkie short, and when he was fifteen, he made a game of tossing my cap into the harbor every chance he got.

"Unlikely. This is my first time on the island," I say, looking away from him. "Excuse me."

But Michael doesn't move out of the way, and when I glance up at him, his expression hardens. My blasted green eyes.

"I'm meeting someone," I say, "so I'll have to head out."

For a moment, Michael doesn't move, and then he slowly turns aside to let me pass. "Yes," he says, still giving me a strange look. "You'd better get going."

"Cheers," I say, touching my cap to him, and I walk quickly away, feeling his eyes on my back as I go.

I should head straight for the safety of my room, but I still want to get a glimpse of Franklin Lindsay, and so instead I walk down to the docks, which are thick with islanders but at least also have enough visiting sailors that no one gives me a second glance.

I ask around for him, and first I say I'm a whaling agent

who's heard good things about him and I'm looking to hire him, but when I get odd looks, I switch my story, say I'm a friend hoping to catch up with him. That only gets me stranger looks, and so finally I just say I need to speak with him.

"I saw him at the counting house not ten minutes ago," a sailor tells me. "Complaining about his pay."

I thank the sailor and walk down the length of the dock toward the gray-shingled building that handles the paperwork and contracts for the ships that come through the harbor. It's a tiny building that looks out over the docks. Windows line the wall facing the water, and as I near it, I slow my pace long enough to get a good look inside.

Two men stand near one of the accounting desks, arguing. One I recognize: William Bliss, who had just taken over as dockmaster from his father when I left the island. The other— tall, broad, with a face like a brick—towers over him, arms swinging in the air as he shouts something.

Franklin Lindsay.

I watch them for a moment, and William Bliss looks like he's holding his own, shaking his head as Lindsay seems to ask him something over and over. Lindsay looks ready to throw a punch when Bliss points to a pair of handcuffs hanging on the wall— threatening to call the police on him, I bet—and Lindsay responds by sweeping a pile of papers off a desk onto the floor and shoving past Bliss to get to the door. I turn away just as he walks back onto the dock, but when I glance back, he's glaring at me with narrowed eyes. Great seas—what a stupid-looking brute.

When he opens his mouth to say something, I quickly smile, push my hands into my pockets, and stride down the docks, whistling.

That's Essie's future husband?

It doesn't make sense, and I want answers.

I won't get them out of Boone, and so I don't go back to boardinghouse row, even though it's late in the day and Boone will likely be back any moment, wondering where I've gotten off to. Instead, I walk quickly through town, and when I reach the grasslands in the center of the island, I wade into them. If Essie wants to talk to me again, this is where she'll go. I walk until I reach the edge of the Great Gray Slough, alive with the buzzing of insects and the raindrop-like noise of dozens of small fish leaping out of the water as they're chased up the shore by bigger fish, birds.

I sit and I wait and I watch the sun slide across the sky and into the sea. I watch the clouds above go dark. I watch the moon ripple across the surface of the slough and one moment I'm alone in the mud and the grass and the next, there she is.

"Mal."

She sounds uncertain, although when I look up at her, her face in the lantern light is happy, hopeful. I pat the dry spot beside me, and she drops gracefully to my side. We sit with our shoulders, hips, knees touching, just like we did as children.

"You didn't bring your knife," she says.

"How can you tell?"

"If you had it with you, you would have taken it out," she says. "You would have wanted me to see it."

I give her a look. She's right.

"Did you read my journal?"

I slide it out of my pocket and hold it out to her, but she shakes her head.

"It's yours. I wrote those letters to you."

Frowning, I put the journal back in my pocket.

"Did you come to ask me about it?" she says, and I shake my head.

"Why him?" I ask. Her eyes widen for a moment, and then she lets out a long breath.

"You heard, then?"

"You didn't write anything about it in your journal."

"No."

"Well?" I give her a long, even look. I don't even know why I care to hear what she has to say, except that for years I thought I had her all figured out, but these past two days have flipped everything around.

"It's . . . I can't even begin to explain it."

"Do you love him?"

Her face screws up with uncertainty. "I . . . I don't know how to answer that," she says finally.

"Well, clearly you've got peculiar taste in beaus. He's a brute. I could tell just by looking at him. You can't love him."

She lets out a long, shaky breath. "I know what I'm doing."

"Is this all to become the witch? He's involved in it

somehow." I mean it as a question, but from the way it comes out, the way she looks at me, I know I'm right.

"I've got to," she says. "I've got to take over for my mother."

"Why?" I shake my head. "For what? I read your journal. Scared of the magic inside you? If that's true, I'll cut you and take it away and you can be free."

For a moment, something like hope lights up her face, and then she shakes her head. "You don't understand. My mother . . . this island . . . they expect me to become the witch."

"You've spent your life not living up to your mother's expectations," I say. "And if you can name a single person on this island you count as a friend, I'll jump into the slough."

She lets out a soft snort of laughter. "All right. Fine. You know well and good I only ever had one friend here."

"Then speaking as your once-and-only friend," I say, "get out of here."

Another laugh, but this one is hollow.

"I mean it. You've always wanted to see the world. Then do it."

She looks away. "I can't."

"Why not? Really? You don't want to be the witch? You want to go? Then go."

"Where?"

I shrug. "Does it matter? Pick a boat and sail away. I've been all around the world, Essie. There's plenty to see in any direction and nothing keeping you here."

But she shakes her head. "It's not that easy."

"It is," I say, and I'm fired up. I'm angry, but it's not the wild blank anger. It's something more hopeful. I turn and look at her, look her right in her pretty face. "It is exactly that easy."

She looks like she's going to make another protest, and if she does, I realize I'm going to have to leave. I can't sit here and argue with her about why she shouldn't stay on this little island, why she shouldn't take on all the burden of her family's magic. I'm offering her . . . friendly advice, I suppose. She doesn't need to take it, but I'm not going to waste my breath trying to make her understand.

So when she opens her mouth, I tense, I get ready to walk away, but then she smiles.

"What was your favorite thing that you saw?" she asks, and it's so surprising that I startle. She watches me, waiting for an answer.

"It's a secret," I say finally, and then I don't say anything else. She doesn't deserve to be trusted with my secrets, and from the way her face falls, I know she's thinking about that day.

"Mal—"

"No," I say, because I know she's going to apologize, and I've just realized that I don't want to hear it. I don't *need* to hear it, not anymore.

"I was young," she says.

"I know."

"I was angry."

"Essie, I know."

"Please," she says. "Let me explain. I was so foolish. You

said you were going to leave, and it got me so scared. I just wanted to scare you back. I didn't even think about how they would react. I thought they would be angry, of course, but I didn't think they would be so scared."

"Why not?" I ask. "I'm a blank. I'm dangerous. I've got a monster living inside me."

She gives me a strange look. "Is that what you think?"

"It's what I know," I say, and I feel a shiver work down my spine. "There's a curse in my blood. There's something in me I can't control, and someday, it's going to swallow me whole."

Her mouth twists into a frown and she looks away, looks down at her own small, pale hands. "I feel that way sometimes. I have magic within me, Mal, and it wants to come out. It's begging to come out, and I know I have to let it. And part of me wants it to happen and part of me is...so scared. I don't know if I'm strong enough."

She lifts her chin and I watch her in profile, her eyes steady and staring straight ahead, her mouth set, determined, and she looks like a lily, but a lily made of steel.

"Of course you are," I say. "Do you really think anything can change you? You think anything—even magic—can make you do something you don't want?"

She glances at me, surprised, and then she laughs, and it's a sound so beautiful that I have to laugh along with her, even though I ask her what's the joke.

"That was just exactly what I was going to say to you," she says, looking into my face. "It's what I've always thought.

There's nothing wrong with being a blank, Mal. You have a Talent just like any magical person in the world."

"I *destroy* magic."

"So what? You grew up with me, and you haven't destroyed my magic."

"It's going to change me. Don't try to convince me otherwise. It's changing me already."

"No, it's not." She sounds annoyed. "I am a witch, Mal. I can sense magic, and I can sense changes in magic, and you feel exactly the same as when you were a little boy. If anything was changing you, especially anything magic, I would have been able to tell."

I stare at her, surprised, and then I shake my head. "All those stories about blanks turning evil—"

"It's all just superstition and ignorance. You're not a monster. You're Mal. Nothing will ever take that away. Do you hear me? You're not powerless. You decide for yourself who you truly are. It's your choice. You can choose something better."

She says it like it's the truth, so plain, so easy, and then she takes one of her hands and slides it over mine.

"It's dangerous to touch a blank," I say, glancing at her, and she shakes her head.

"No more dangerous than touching a witch."

I wait for the monster inside me to say something, to urge me to punish her or yank away my hand or remind me of how much she hurt me, but the voice is quiet, and I wonder: *What if there never was a voice?*

I wait for her to say something else, but she's silent, her hand soft and warm around mine. And I feel...still. Calm. I can't remember when I ever felt like that. It might have been the last time I sat with her in the grass, listening to her stories, worried about nothing because I had everything I wanted right there. I had my friend.

And she's not a monster, either. She's still my friend.

Who else could look at me and see what she does?

We sit together in the darkness and hold each other's hands and I hear her breath and smell her skin and it's like my whole body wakes up, comes alive and then relaxes all at once, and I know.

It's as easy as that.

I might not belong on this island or in any of the cities I've seen in my travels or any place in the entire world, but I belong with my hand in hers. That's the home I've been looking for. Not a place, but a person.

"Essie," I say, my eyes still on the water in front of us, "you're going to leave this island with me."

"What?"

I glance at her, the surprise on her face. "You don't want to stay trapped here? Then set yourself free."

Again, she looks like she's going to argue with me, but then her fingers squeeze tight and fast around mine, and she smiles.

"It's that easy, is it? All right." She laughs. "Where are we going to go?"

I laugh back, a real laugh this time, and I'm about to respond with a joke when the sharp snap of sails causes us both to look up, over the slough, out to the water. A fishing boat tacks into the wind, heading for the little village just south of here, and Essie frowns.

"Is it that late?" She lets out a tight breath. "I have to get back to the cottage. My mother will expect my help."

She takes her hand away and stands up.

"Pack your things and meet me at the docks in the morning. Do you have any money?"

"You think I need money to convince a ship to take me on as a passenger?" she says, laughing. "I'll give them more charms than they can carry, and they'll take us anywhere in the world."

"Good," I say, and I stand up, too, and hand her the lantern. "Don't be late."

She pauses and gives me a wry smile. "After wasting the last five years?" she says softly. "I don't want to miss another minute."

Another smile—and she's gone.

Thirty

FOR THE FIRST TIME IN AS LONG AS I CAN remember, I feel light. It's a sensation so strange that it takes me almost my whole walk back to town to put a name to it.

Hope.

I feel hope.

Hope for the future. And it's all because of Essie. I shake my head, hardly able to believe it. I was wrong about her. All those years, I was wrong about her just as much as I was wrong about myself. Maybe I'm not ready to believe in it entirely, that Essie was always my friend, that she's truly sorry for hurting me, that I'm not going to change into something terrible, and that the home I was always looking for was never a place at all, but her. Maybe I can't believe all that, yet, but I think I can someday. For now, that's enough.

I'm going to tell Boone that our partnership is over, this time for good. He can do what he wants with the *shar*, with the Erslands—I don't care. The brothers can tell every hunter in the world what I am, but the thought doesn't terrify me, not anymore. I'm done with the hunting. It doesn't matter that I don't have any other plan for my future. Just knowing that I can *have* a future is enough.

I've nearly made it back to the boardinghouse when I see them: Illuminated in a circle of light from the whale-oil streetlamp, Boone stands talking, whispering with Franklin Lindsay. They're too far away to hear, but whatever he's saying, it makes Lindsay shake his head, curl his hands into fists.

"No," he says, the word cutting across the street to reach me, and Boone leans forward, his lips moving fast, his expression calm but insistent.

I watch them for a moment, my stomach tightening, and just when I decide to go over and interrupt, they break apart and Lindsay strides off down the street while Boone stands in the light, watching him with a faint smile on his face. He pushes his hands into his pockets and, whistling, walks toward the boardinghouse, but when he sees me, he pauses.

"What were you doing?" I ask, and he tilts his head at me.

"What was I doing when?"

"Right now. Talking with that man."

"Franklin Lindsay, you mean." Boone pulls his hands from his pockets. "The man Essie Roe has promised to marry."

"There's no reason for you to be talking to him."

"Don't be silly. There's plenty of reason. I'm here for the Roe witch, and it only makes sense to find out all I can about her." There's an edge to his voice, and heat flares up in my chest.

"What does that mean?" I ask, and Boone shrugs.

"Do you know how the Roes get their magic? Do you know what changes them?"

"No," I say. "Do you?"

Boone laughs. "Maybe I do."

"How?"

"Maybe I just needed to ask the right questions."

"Did you charm her?" I ask, and I feel cold, hot, sick, all at once. "Did you Silvertongue Essie Roe?"

"Mal! Those slippery morals of yours are reappearing! What do you care if I charmed her? You're here to cut her, aren't you?" Boone says. "Your last chance. *Remember?*"

"What did you do to her?" My voice rises, breaks, and I take a step toward him but he backs away, light as a cat.

"I didn't do anything. I just asked the right questions and told her there was no need to remember we ever spoke. She wants to be a witch, Mal. She's ready for it. She knows something needs to happen to her. She needs someone to . . . knock it into her."

"What? What does that mean?"

He doesn't smile. He doesn't move. He stares at me and says, his voice as soft as a whisper, "Did you know the girl is going to have a child?"

His words pull all the air out of my lungs and leave me gasping, gaping.

"Franklin Lindsay certainly didn't know," he says, eyes glittering.

"You *told* him?"

"Where is this outrage coming from, Mal? You're all too happy to go along with the jobs when they're easy, but the moment it gets difficult, you leave it up to me. *I* charmed Ruth when she wouldn't give us information. *I* fought that man in Paris who surprised us. *I* saw Tagore for what he truly was: a threat. And *I* took care of him."

"Tagore?" I stare at him in surprise before I remember: minutes after leaving Tagore's office and Boone running up to a guard, whispering something in his ear. "You told the guard to kill him?"

"I took care of him. Like you never could. Like you *still* can't. The girl needs to change to become the witch. I wasn't going to wait around forever for it to happen."

"What did you do, Boone?" I'm shaking now, shivering and shaking. "What did you tell Lindsay?"

"I told him that the girl's child is not his."

For a moment I can only stare at him in shock, and then a scream of rage flies through my throat. I leap at him but he's ready for me, a knife in his hand, his eyes glittering and his teeth bared. I don't care. I swing at him, my body a coil of energy, of rage, and I shout, "He's going to go after her, Boone! He's going to hurt her! What did you do!"

"I'm doing what you can't!" he says, breathing hard, and all I want is to wrap my hands around his throat but he's too fast, sidestepping me, dancing out of my way, landing blows to my face and ribs and temples that leave my head ringing. I should have realized. He taught me how to fight, and I've never beaten him yet. We grapple together, and I let out a howl of frustration and rage that only makes him laugh.

"Look at how angry you are!" he says, and he steps back, the light falling across his face, and I see, for the first time, the loathing in his expression. "Look at how angry you are when all along it's *you* who betrayed *me*."

Dazed, I stare at him, the taste of blood in my mouth.

"I offered you so much, Mal! I took you in, I took care of you, I gave you one chance after another only to have you reject me and turn away from me. I *do not understand you*."

"You never did," I say, and until the words fall from my mouth, I haven't realized how true it is: He never understood me, not in the way Essie does. He always saw me as a monster, a problem to be dealt with, a wolf pup who would someday grow fangs and claws and rip out his throat, and how did I not see all that?

"Do you think this is easy for me?" Boone asks, shaking his head. "I thought you were my brother. My *son*. I near raised you. And you're ready to kill me now for—what? A girl who destroyed your life! You are so reckless, Mal. So stupidly, terribly reckless. I tried to believe for a long time that the rumors about blanks were simply rumors and you would never betray me, but I was wrong."

His hands curl into fists that shake, and I can hear the tremor in his voice as he speaks, the catch in his breath.

"You truly are a monster," he says, tightening his grip on the knife. "But you are also very, very valuable."

"Valuable?"

"The deal I made with the Erslands?" Boone takes a step toward me, then another, another, and instinctually I move away. "I wasn't lying. They're giving me the *shar*, and I'm giving them the power of the Roe witch. We're going to split the money, Mal, but they wanted so much more, too much, and I thought I wouldn't be able to deal with them and then they asked for something else. They asked for you.

"Did you know there's a market for blanks? One in a million, truly, and the Erslands have been looking for someone like you for a very long time. They had their suspicions about what you were ages ago, from the first moment they saw you, and they think they can control you. They think you can make them a lot of money, and they offered me ten thousand dollars to take you away."

"I saved your life. In Baltimore, all those years ago. You owe me. *I saved you*," I whisper, forcing the words out. It's the only thing I can think to say that might rescue me now, and Boone pauses, considers, and for a moment, he looks so sad, so weary, and then he smiles.

"You did," he says. "I've been in your debt for many years. And all those weeks ago, I paid you back by trading your life for two satchels of kraken meat."

My eyes go wide as he reaches into the leather bag around his shoulder and pulls out a length of rope.

"Make it easy on yourself, boy," Boone says, and he grits his teeth as he speaks. "I'm not going to hurt you, you know that."

"Stay away!" I back up, back up, my feet scrabbling for balance, my hands for weapons, and Boone steadily nearing, one hand, the hand with the rope, out like he's trying to calm down a skittish horse.

"It'll be all right," he murmurs. "It's over. It's all over."

And he jumps.

I dive right, not thinking, just reacting, and look back in time to see Boone skid to a stop, his boots kicking up dust. Scrambling to my feet, I reach for the hilt of my knife, but the moment I pull it out, Boone grabs my ankle and sends me crashing down again, where I land on my elbows and knees, my bones shaking inside me, the knife spinning away into the darkness.

Frantic, I try to kick him off, but Boone grits his teeth and holds on and growls at me, "You forget, I taught you how to fight!" and yanks me, hard, toward him, toward his rope and his knife and his face like an animal's, all bloodlust and bared teeth. As I slide along the dirt, I feel my heart pump hot blood through my veins, the old fire within me waking up, throwing sparks, stretching through me, and when Boone tries to get his hands on me, I look up at him and all the fear and confusion and betrayal crystallizes into black, cold fury.

"Do you know how many times I've had to hold myself back from attacking you?" I say, breathing hard, and then I explode. Heat flows through me, tightens my hands into fists, and when Boone tries to jerk away, I'm ready for him. I leap forward. His knife swings out, singing through the air, and I duck, I bob, I reach under his arm and grab his shirt collar and try to throw my weight on top of him, but he's quicker than that. He knows me and he rocks back, rocks me off balance and scrambles to his feet, the knife still out between us.

"Come here," he says, and he's panting for air. He puts out a hand and beckons me forward. "Come fight like a blank."

He's goading me, angering me so that I'll make a mistake, and it's working. I'm furious—I scream and launch myself at him again, duck the knife again, but this time he swings it at a different angle and catches me down my arm in a line of fire that makes me gasp and howl.

"You're no good to me dead," he says as I put my hand to my arm. Blood slips through my fingers, but it's a shallow cut, and now that the stinging shock has passed, I ignore it, ignore him. This time when I go at him I duck early enough to grab a loose brick from the sidewalk and swing right at his knees.

The knife falls to the ground as Boone bellows out a yell, drops to the dirt. When he puts down a hand to steady himself, I run forward and stomp on his fingers, feeling at least a few bones crunch under my boot. He yells again, yells at me to stop, but I'm too hot right now, I'm wild and he's weak, and now I can't help myself. I grab him by the shirt collar and pull him to his feet, pull back my arm and hit him in the jaw, again and again and again. I'm glad we've rolled out of the light of the streetlamp, I'm glad I can't see what I'm doing to him, even though I can feel my knuckles split open on bone and blood slicks my fingers. Boone gasps with pain, with confusion, stumbling back, me right on top of him, and I'm going to kill him. I'm going to choke the life from his throat because Essie is in danger and I have to help her and I can't do that with Boone attacking me and so he has to be stopped. I press my hands against his throat and he's choking, he's sputtering for air, he's trying to fight back, and then he's laughing.

Surprised, I loosen my hands just enough for him to speak, whispering and hoarse, and he says one word, over and over again: *"Monster... monster... monster..."*

And I realize, he always expected this to happen. He always knew that someday I would turn on him and that someday he would get rid of me, because at the end, I was always only just a blank, just a wolf pup. I was never Mal.

I loosen my grip but keep my hands at his throat and I ask him, my words squeezed through clenched teeth, "When did you decide? When did you decide to sell me?"

He heaves for air, eyes roving wildly, lips pried open into a gasping smile.

"The Ersland brothers—"

"No!" I press my elbow against his chest and look into his eyes. "When was the *first* time?"

The smile slips from his face and he swallows. "Baltimore harbor. The poker game. I gave them my marker. I put your life up for a bet."

It's like he's burned me, and, stumbling, I fall back, limp as wet rope, my head swimming.

"If I hadn't saved your life..." I say, and, slowly, he pushes himself up from the dirt, one hand reaching up to massage his throat.

"I would have lost you in a poker game for two hundred dollars," he finishes. "And I would have saved myself years of trouble." He stumbles a little, breathing hard. "You know... for years I thought I was such a fool, nearly giving away a good lad like that, because of course, if I had, you would never have saved my life." He leans heavily against the bulwarks, still panting for air. "I thought I was lucky that night, and then time passed and I realized, no: I was cursed. I had you like a millstone about my neck, and I knew you were a danger. I knew you were going to end my life someday if I did nothing. But you had saved me and I owed you and so I did nothing."

The wind picks up around us, pressing into my cheeks, blowing my hair across my forehead, stinging my eyes raw.

"And now," he says, "either I can fix that mistake I made all those years ago, or I'll die for it." He glances up at me, a sly smile spreading across his face, his eyes narrowed. "Well?"

We're still, so still, and then he moves first, leaping across the dirt for his knife, and without thinking I dive forward, arms stretched out, and he's first but I'm faster, I'm younger, and I snatch the knife up and away and leave him clawing nothing but air.

He gasps, scrambles back, looks over at me and the knife and laughs, a high, mirthless laugh.

"That's it, then," he says, sounding weary. "Go and kill me. Isn't that what you want? Go ahead. I raised you and kept you safe, but you're just a monster. Just a blank. You want to kill me, don't you? Do it."

And I want to. I want to. He's the closest thing I'll ever know to a brother, to a father, to a best friend, and I want nothing more than to pick up the knife and kill him like he's a whale, cut his lungs to ribbons and watch him drown on blood. I'm shaking, I'm burning, the hole inside me wrenched open again and deeper than ever, black and sucking, and there's a demon inside and it wants to come out, wants me to let it loose, whispers to me that this is my nature, this is what I am, I am a killer, a monster, a blank. And then, like a spell, I hear Essie's voice in my ears, hear her and see her and feel her. *"There's nothing wrong with you, Mal. Do you hear me? You're not powerless. You decide for yourself who you truly are. It's your choice. You can choose something better."*

My skin goes slick on the handle. The knife trembles in the air, trembles and falls, and I kick it over to him.

"*You* do it," I say, and my voice shakes but I stand tall. "I know what I am."

He eyes the knife, breathing hard, his hand twitching, but before he can move, the sky rips open with noise, light, heat, a lightning bolt unlike anything I've ever seen or felt or experienced, so unreal that I can't even breathe. I just stare up at the sky, shaken and confused.

And then the screaming starts, a howl so loud, so sharp that it might as well be solid, and Boone and I clap our hands over our ears and wince and I squint up at the sky, which has gone purple-blue and boils like tar suspended over our heads.

"What is this?" Boone asks, his voice high with panic. "What's happening?"

Another flash of light in the distance, this time smaller, blue, sustained like a ball of fire, and it rises into the air just above the spot where the Roe cottage sits. And I know. I know what this is.

"Essie," I breathe, and then I run.

Thirty-One

I'M HALFWAY TO THE COTTAGE, MY LUNGS
and muscles burning, when the first explosion hits. The ground
underneath me trembles, and I nearly lose my balance. When
I look up, I see the ball of purple-blue flame spin and sputter
in the air high above the cottage, throwing out lightning bolts,
and I don't know what's happening except that it must involve
Essie, Lindsay, Boone, and whatever he's done to unlock her
magic.

I keep running, and as I run, rain bursts from the sky, as
thick and heavy as paint. It falls for a few minutes, streaming into my eyes and soaking my clothes, and then it stops.
On again, off again, like a child playing with a watering can.
I've heard stories about the power the Roe witch has over the
elements, over the skies and winds and waters, but I've never

seen anything like this, this wild, uncontrollable magic ripping through the sky.

When I'm close enough to see the cottage, lit up from above by the ball of blue light, I gasp and stop. Inside the light is a *person*, frail, slight, arms outstretched and hair lifted, twisting, black: Essie.

I call her name and the wind pulls it from my lips, whips it into the air, and it's gone and I'm chasing after it, running at the cottage, shouting for her. It's so loud, the wind and the lightning and thunder and rain drowning out everything. I can barely see anything, but I just make out a figure crouched on the ground, staring up at Essie, still spinning and trapped in the ball of light. It's Jennie Roe, Essie's mother, the real witch of the island. When I reach her, I grab her shoulder, look into her face, and shout at her, "Stop this! Why don't you stop this!"

But she's white and shaking, and even though I've only ever seen her as the powerful Roe witch, she says in a voice that's part mew, part plea, "I can't. No one can!"

The rain stops and the air turns hot, hot, dry and hot like I've only experienced in deserts, where the sun bleaches all the wetness out of a place and leaves it brittle and bare. My clothes begin steaming, the very air around us going smoky and dense, and I wince and shake off my jacket.

"What happened?" I ask, turning to Jennie, and she stares up at her daughter.

"That man! He came for her! He—" Her words break

off as the ball of light drops, lowers, throwing up even more wind and heat, and now I can finally see Essie's face—or what's left of it.

"What did he do to her?" I ask, more to myself than Jennie, because her face, that perfect face, has been split in two, cut and mangled from her right eyebrow to the left corner of her lip. Blood streams down her front, staining her dress, making her skin look even more unnaturally pale.

"He turned her into a witch," Jennie says, her voice soft with wonder and...something else, something almost like triumph.

"This is what it means to be a witch?" I ask, pointing up at Essie's ruined face, the heat and turmoil spinning off her. "This is what you wanted for her?"

Jennie gives me a hard look. "It wasn't easy for any of us," she says. "This is what must happen."

"How is this right?" I ask, and when she doesn't answer, I start shaking so hard that I want to slap her. "You never understood her! You never listened to her! She wanted something else in her life!"

Jennie's eyes drift upward, taking in her daughter's floating, furious form. "This was always going to be her life. She belongs to the island."

The ground shakes again, the heat rises, and far off out on the grass, a streak of lightning touches down, licks the grass, and explodes into fire.

"There isn't going to be any island left if we don't stop

her!" I say, and I run forward until I'm just underneath her and tip my face up to the blue light. "Essie! *Essie!*"

Something in the light flickers. I catch a wrinkle of emotion skittering across her vacant face, but then she spins away, the heat rises, the wind picks up. I twist my head and watch the fire in the grass expand, roar, eat through the fields like a beast, sending up a wall of heat so fierce that I have to throw my arm in front of my face to shield it.

"Essie!"

"Mal!" My name, but the voice comes from behind me, not above, and I turn and see Boone, running across the path that leads to town. "She's gone mad!"

"Because of you!" I lift a hand and point at her. "Look at her! Look at what you've done to her!"

Another bolt of lightning sizzles across the sky, raising the hairs on the back of my neck, and Boone gasps.

"She's found the magic," he says, his eyes wide with wonder.

"It's going to kill her!" I spin and look back up into the sky. "Essie!"

I wave my arms above my head, shouting her name, and, bathed in purplish-blue light, her figure shivers, her head sways, her eyes—closed until now—open, and her gaze drifts toward me. I see her lips move, and I wince as the cut across her face stretches and pulls.

"Essie," I whisper, lifting a hand to her, and the wind begins to die down, the sky overhead to calm. She's floating now, drifting downward as gently as a feather, her eyes unfocused and glazed but trained on my face.

"That's right," I say, my voice soft. "Come back."

Softly, slowly, she falls through the air, coming to rest on the sand. I want to rush over to her, hold her, but the light still flickers blue-bright around her, and now that she's so close, I can feel the heat coming off her as though she's on fire. Below her feet, little wisps of grass smoke and wither, and I watch as sand sputters, pops, melts into twisted gold drops.

"Essie," I say, reaching out my hand to her, but she looks right through me. When I try to come closer, her mouth opens in a scream, and a shock of lightning explodes upward into the sky, throwing off a wave of energy that knocks me backward and sends Jennie Roe crashing to the ground with a cry of pain.

"She's out of control!" Boone shouts. "You have to stop her!"

And he's right, I know he's right—Essie's magic is too wild, too unstable. If we don't do something, she's going to tear this island apart, starting with us.

"You need to do it," Boone says, and I feel him slip something hard into my hand. "*She* needs you to do it."

I look down but of course I know what it is: The *shar*, shining and quiet, and all I need to do is cut her and all this will be over. She'll be back, she'll be safe, she'll no longer be a witch.

We were going to escape, her and me. We were going to be free.

I turn and look at her, the *shar* hanging from my hand,

and she's so beautiful, even split open, even covered in blood. I don't want to lose her. The ground trembles, and I can feel her slipping away, giving herself over to the wild creature inside her, and it would be so easy to cut it away.

"Do it, Mal," Boone whispers. *"Do it."*

And I do.

I reach out into the air with the *shar*—and cut.

Boone's eyes widen. He looks down at the hairline mark across his chest, so thin that the blood that beads along it doesn't even flow but hangs, suspended, just across his skin. It's so small. But it's enough.

"What did you do?" Boone touches his chest, looks at the red on his fingers. *"What did you do?"*

"She's not a monster," I say, and I throw the *shar* on the ground. "Neither am I."

"Mal."

"You can't lie anymore. Not to anyone."

"Mal!"

"Do you hear me?" I'm shouting now, my hands balled into fists. *"No more lies."*

I expect him to leap at me, teeth bared, but he cringes, he crumples, tears well in his eyes and before I can say anything else, before I can even feel a stab of pity for what I've done to him, he turns and runs.

"Wait!" I say, but there's another shiver in the air, and I turn back to Essie. She's shaking, whispering something I can't hear.

"It's all right," I say, putting out a hand to her. "I know you can hear me. Essie? You're in there, I know it."

Her eyes snap open and she hisses like a cat, writhing under the blue light, and now the heat is so bad that I can feel my skin blistering as though I just fell into an oven.

"This isn't you! You can control this! Do you hear me?"

Another scream that cuts off almost as soon as it begins, Essie's eyes going black for one second, and then bright, startling blue. She focuses on me and gasps.

"Mal!" she says, her voice weak, desperate, and the heat— just barely—abates.

"That's it," I say. "Fight it! Come back."

She's shivering so hard I don't know how she can stand, and I can see the magic coursing through her like a flood.

"I c-can't!" she says, sweat beading along her ruined face. The heat rises again, and I let out a gasp of pain, my skin so scorched I'm amazed it doesn't burst into flames.

"You can!" I say, and I force myself to take a step toward her, into the fire.

The pain's so bright, brighter even than the light in front of me. I can see spots swim before my vision, feel my body scream in protest, but I have to help her. She needs me and I need her, and I reach forward and whisper her name, and with my last burst of strength I break through the wall of heat surrounding her and take her hand.

She throws her head back, buckling, but I don't let her go. I grab her, pull her closer, let her scream and throw off lightning and fire and wind, but I'm not going to let her go, not now, not ever, and as I wrap my arms around her and feel my skin burn and blister, she vibrates against me, crying out in pain.

"Come back, Essie," I whisper, but I'm not sure she can hear me. "Come back. *Come back to me.*"

She gasps, and the world lights up in a blaze so fierce that for a second it's as though she's called the sun back into the sky. As soon as it appears, it disappears. It all disappears—heat and wind and fire and light—and she crumples to the ground, my Essie again.

She's beaten and bloody but real, alive. I hold her in my arms and touch her ruined face, her forehead, her cheek, the corner of her lip that isn't mangled and destroyed. Her eyelids flutter open, her eyes find my face in the darkness, and I know she must be feeling so much pain right now, pain from her injuries and pain, too, from the man who caused them, but all I can do is touch her, hold her, whisper her name over and over.

She's here.

She's alive.

There are still some things to be grateful for.

Thirty-Two

"I KNEW WHAT HE WAS GOING TO DO THE moment I saw him."

"Shh..."

"I could have stopped him. I have that power. I could have stopped him but I thought... I thought he might have stopped himself. I didn't think he'd ever..."

"It's all right. You don't have to talk about it."

"He found out about the baby. I don't know how. He was so angry. He always thought he couldn't have children. *I* thought he couldn't have children. That's why I picked him, Mal. I don't know how it happened. Magic, I suppose..."

I'm quiet as I wring out the bloody rag, watching the water swirl pinkish in the white basin.

"He's gone now. He said he would leave the island, and I

know if he had stayed...he would have found me. He swears he's going to come back, Mal. He swears he's going to come for her."

She lifts a hand and places it on the small round lump under her dress, just below her ribs, the lump that I can't believe I didn't notice before and now I can't stop seeing.

"I'm the witch now, truly." Her voice is so soft, full of wonder.

"He did it? That's what it took—him hurting you like that?"

But she looks away. She never talks about that part.

"I can't leave. I'm the witch now. I can't leave."

"Don't speak." I lift the gauze, and she closes her eyes as I wrap it around her face. It must hurt, but she sits as still as a statue, barely even breathing until I tie the bandage in place. She opens her eyes and looks around the little room we're in. She couldn't go back to the cottage afterward, and so I found her a small apartment, an upstairs room with windows far from the eyes of the islanders. They know, of course, what's happened. They saw Franklin Lindsay gallop on his horse to the cottage; they saw the sky light up; they saw Lindsay catch the last ferry off the island; they saw Essie stumble, bloody, into town, her hand a fist over the bump under her dress. They saw me.

"There's something I have to tell you," she whispers, but I know what it is she's going to say and I'm not ready for it.

"Sleep now. You need to sleep."

She glances at the bed.

"Will you stay with me?" she asks, her voice so small, and I tell her I will.

She's asleep in seconds, her face turned to the wall, her body small and curled up on her narrow bed, and for a long time I watch her, watch the covers rise as she breathes, watch her fingers twitch. She holds her head, her face, so carefully, even as she dreams.

I can hear her nightmares when they start, and when she begins shaking, crying out, I go to her side and smooth her hair and whisper to her until she stills. After one particularly bad spell, she turns, sees me with hazy, half-closed eyes, takes my hand and pulls me up onto the narrow bed with her before wrapping my arm around her, pushing her back against my chest, and falling asleep again.

We stay like that for hours, and although I'm exhausted, I can't sleep. I feel her heartbeat under my hand and breathe in the smell of her hair mixed with the sickly sweetness of the medicine. The windows rattle from the wind and snow and rain outside, but I pull up the blankets and I hold on to her to keep us both from flying apart.

I stay with her for a day, then a week, leaving her side only to visit the corner general store and grocer and the apothecary on the north side of town. As I walk the streets, I notice the people of Prince Island skirting out of my way, clutching their children, averting their eyes and then turning to stare at me. It didn't take long for the whispers to spread: Mal the blank, back again.

They don't want me here. They think I had something to do with the fight with Lindsay, with the child. They know Essie stays in town, far away from the cottage and the Roe witch, and they're waiting for me to leave so that she'll go back, take up the role she was born for.

But I don't tell Essie this, when I come in from the streets, my cheeks red from the wind, my arms full of little packages. A week later and she still shakes in her sleep, still sleeps far too much, still can't talk to me except in broken sentences that make no sense and only at night, when it's dark and all that exists is her weight beside me and our voices in the air.

"I keep having dreams," she says softly one night, and I hold her a little tighter and press my lips into her hair.

"It's all right. They're just dreams."

"No. They're... They show me things. Things... things that will happen."

I'm quiet, thinking about what she might mean.

"Is this your Roe magic?" I say, but we both know that even though her veins flow with power, she hasn't made a single spell. "What is it, then? You can interpret dreams now?"

"Not me," she says, and she threads her fingers through mine and places our hands on her growing stomach.

"She's not even born yet."

"I know."

"What does that mean?"

She says nothing for a long time, squeezing my fingers, and then: "She belongs here."

My stomach tightens and my pulse quickens. "We don't have to talk about that now."

I'm sitting at the table downstairs when I hear a knock at the door. Just one. A single rap that makes the whole room shiver. There aren't any windows beside the door, but I know before I open it and look outside who it is.

There's Joseph Garrity the butcher, Henry Appleton the rope-maker. There's Amos Lawrence and his brother Abbot, and John Warren standing next to William Shaw. I see the faces of boys I grew up with in the dozen men standing before me, and underneath their grimaces and frowns, I can remember them laughing, teasing, taunting, trading marbles with me or dunking my head under the waves.

"What can I help you with?" I ask, and I keep one hand on the door and the other resting on the hilt of my knife.

Garrity stares me down for a moment. When he was fourteen, he pressed me into a puddle of mud because his mother had given me his favorite pair of shoes.

"It's time for you to be moving along."

I lean against the doorframe, crossing my arms over my chest. "And here I thought I kept my own schedule."

They stare at me, unsmiling. Two of them carry lanterns. The rest ball their fists at their sides and let them hang there like clubs.

"I've got business here," I say. "I'll leave when I'm good and ready."

"You'll leave *now*," Abbot says, and he's still thin and reedy, still missing a chin. Garrity glances at him before looking at me.

"We don't know why it is you chose to come back," he says, his voice deep and slow, "but you've been causing trouble since you got here."

"And what trouble is that?" I ask. Garrity jerks his head toward the building, and I know he means Essie, her scar and her storm and her taking up a room in town, when no Roe witch in the history of the island ever lived anywhere but the cottage.

"It's all your doing," he says, and the way he says it in that heavy voice of his makes it sound like the truth.

"I'm helping her."

"Send her back to her mother," Garrity says. "That's where she belongs."

"She's not well. She needs time to rest."

"And what're we supposed to do while the witch sits up in bed?" a man asks, and it takes me a moment to be sure, but I finally recognize him as Nathan Lorring, one of the boys who was there that day on the docks when Essie told them all my secret. He used to give her flowers and candies and call to her when we walked by. "Sweet on the witch girl," his friends would tease him, and now he stares at me with hate and fear in his eyes and says, "She has a job to do."

"What's that?" I ask, trying to stay calm, because the way he says it, like he *owns* her, sets me on edge. They think it's all *my* fault she's like this, but it's not. It's their fault, this blasted island and their demands, their expectations, all of them thinking she's their wish-granting pet, their pretty broken bird who needs to sing.

"Take a step back," Garrity says, and it's only then that I realize I've walked outside to face them, the wind biting into me, my knuckles white on the handle of my knife.

"She doesn't owe any of you *anything*," I say, and the men tense. "She's not your witch. She doesn't belong to you. If she wants to stay here for the rest of her life or leave the island—"

Garrity's hand snaps up and closes around my throat, cutting off my words and pushing me back against the wall of the building.

"Now, you listen here, blank," he says, his voice very quiet. "We'll hear none of that. We've got ships to sail and whales to hunt, and we can't do that without magic. The witch needs to get on back to the cottage and take her place. She doesn't need to hear any more from you about leaving the island." He lets up just enough that I can gasp for air, and then he leans in, his face no more than a hand's breadth away.

"You're a rat. A monster. You're poisoning her," he whispers. "You're filling her head with lies. And we're not any of us going to stand for it. *You don't belong here.* One way or another, we're going to see you gone."

His hand slips from around my neck, and I lean against the building, breathing hard, glaring at them with narrowed eyes.

"You don't scare me," I say, my voice raspy and raw. "And I'm no monster."

Garrity just shakes his head.

"I don't care what you think you are," he says, and he nods to the other men, who reach into pockets and pull out knives, ropes, sharp awls, and hooks, staring at me and surrounding me like a wall.

"If you stay here another day," Garrity says softly, "we're gonna put you in a grave."

The next day, I'm with her when she takes off the bandages.

"It was a belt," she says, watching my eyes trip along down her face. "The buckle. He hit me with the buckle."

She'll wear a scar for life, a diagonal slash right across her face, eyebrow to lip. Right now, it's angry, red, the edges of the scar jagged and ragged like badly mended canvas.

"I'll have to get some hats with veils," she says, trying to smile. "Or maybe you can find me whatever those ladies wear at their masquerade balls. I could pretend to be a French lady every day!"

I smile back at her, but it tears at me to think of her forever spending her days hiding what she looks like, pretending. It's not her fault that this happened to her. Why can't she have sunlight on her cheeks?

Slowly, carefully, she rewraps her bandages, and I watch her hands, checking to see if they shake or fumble, but she's doing well, remarkably well. She's always been stronger than she looks. When she's done, she runs her hands through her hair, twisting it over one shoulder, and then she stands, crosses to the nightstand, and pulls out an envelope, her hands shaking now.

"I...I want you to have this." She sits back at the table with me before handing me something small, something that I at first think is a lady's calling card, the kind neatly drawn up by calligraphers and decorated with flying angels and left on marble-topped, delicate little tables, but then I pull it from its onionskin envelope and see it's something much rarer and more precious: a photograph. A calotype to be precise, printed on soft paper with soft colors, and it's Essie, the old Essie now, the beauty.

"He asked me to make it for him," she says, her voice soft. "I could tell it was important to him. He wanted to own me. Or some part of me, at least. But after I saw the photograph, I couldn't give it to him. I kept it for myself. And now I want you to have it."

I turn the photograph over and see her name written there in her own hand, because it's easier, less painful to look at those letters than to look at her face, whole and untouched and perfect. But she's giving it to me and I have to look at it. I set it on the table between us and look into her pretty face, the curve of her jaw, her arms: one hand tight in a fist at her side, the other resting lightly on the soft roundness of her belly.

It is not strictly proper for a young lady to call attention to her delicate condition, but in the photo Essie stands proud, defiant, chin lifted and eyes set. She is so beautiful and I can't look at it anymore and I can't look at her now, her head swathed in yellow-tinted bandages, her stomach just a bit bigger now, rounder with that creature's child.

"Why?" I ask. "Why do you think I want this?"

She's quiet for so long that I can hear her breathing, still slightly labored, shallow.

"I want you to have something to take with you," she says, her eyes resting on my face.

"Take with me?"

"Mal." She puts out a hand and covers mine. "I'm not leaving the island."

"What?" I look up at her, and even though I should have

been expecting this, even though I'd been preparing myself to hear this for days, it still jars me like a hit from an iron bar, and I can't fight the shock that ripples through me. "Why not? Why would you ever want to stay here? Essie! Are you mad? You can't stay here! He's going to come back—he's going to come after you!"

She watches me with her clear blue eyes. "I know. Mal, I know."

"But *why*?" I lean forward. "Essie, you don't owe anyone anything. You can leave. Just come with me."

"I can't." She sounds so sad. "I belong here. My magic—"

"I'm not listening to this again. It's easy, remember? We just get onto a ship and sail away. You told me I have a choice. Well, so do you. You don't have to stay here, Essie."

"I do. I have to."

"For who?" I shake my head. "For your mother? For the island?"

She frowns and then touches her stomach. "For her." She shakes her head. "I thought I could just leave, but ever since I felt my magic, Mal—I feel *her*. This is her home. I can't take her away." Her hand lifts from her stomach back to the photo, which she slides along the table toward me. "Take it with you. You can't stay here."

"Why not?"

"You know why not. The islanders will kill you. Any day now, they're going to come after you."

"Lucky, then, that I'm such good friends with a witch."

She takes my hand. "I'm not going to let you stay and put yourself in danger."

"Amazing," I say. "That's just exactly what I was going to say to you."

"Mal—"

"Why are you so set on sending me away?" I ask, shaking my head. "Why don't you want me here?"

She takes a breath, lets it out slowly. "Do you remember that day in the grass?" she says, her voice soft. "When we found out what you were?"

"You think I could ever forget?"

"You never asked me, ever, what spell I was trying out on you. I tied a cord around your hand and the spell didn't work, but you never asked me what the spell was supposed to do."

I blink at her, stunned, but she's right. I never did ask.

"It's just a little spell, Mal," she says. "Tie a rope around a friend's hand. So long as you hold the rope, he can move, but the moment you let the rope go, he's stuck, rooted to one spot. I made that spell up. You see: Even then, I wanted you to never leave me. I wanted you never to go anywhere without me. You're my best friend. I'd rather know you're alive than keep you here with me."

She gives me a pained look, and I think back to the day when she came to watch me sail away.

"Remember that day in the grass, Mal?" she had said. "Remember that rope glove? You know, if you weren't a blank—"

"If you weren't a blank"—what? *If you weren't a blank, I'd tie a rope around your hand and make you stay.*

"You want me to leave?" I ask, my voice shaking. "Fine. I'll make you a deal." I reach into my satchel and pull out a piece of paper and a stubby pencil. "I'll leave today, right now, for Boston. This is where I'll be staying." I slide the paper over to her. "I'm going to give you two weeks to get yourself ready and meet me there. All right? Two weeks. And then I'm going to go to New York and sell that blasted *shar*. Then I'll have enough money to take you anywhere in the world."

"A deal . . . What's the catch?"

"You agree not to make a single spell for those idiots. You don't belong to them, Essie. You don't owe them anything."

Slowly, I rise from my chair. She doesn't stop me.

"Think about it, Essie," I say. "Don't decide just yet. Think about it."

I reach up and touch her face, the bandages, my fingers light and searching on her skin.

"You're not their witch. Remember that. You're Essie. My friend," I say, my voice soft, and she closes her eyes and presses my hand to her cheek. There's that feeling again, that feeling of belonging that I get when I touch her. I've just found this, and I'm supposed to give it up? I'm supposed to let go and trust that it'll all be all right?

Yeah.

And I can, now, because if she's taught me anything, it's how to hope.

So I do the hardest thing I can possibly imagine: I pull my hand away. I pick up my satchel. I tell her I'll wait for her, two weeks. And then I leave.

That very night, I get on a ferry. I'm sick of this island, sick of the stares and the history and the whispers following me around like bad ghosts.

I listen to the whistle of the ferry, shrill in the darkness, and my hands grip the wooden bulwarks and I'm making a mistake. I should jump overboard right now. I should go back to her. I should—I don't know. I can't stay on the island and she can't leave and it isn't fair, none of it. Home's just a place to build a future, and I thought she was it: my home and my future all wrapped up. I think I might have just let it all slip away.

But still, I wait. I wait for her, even though I know she won't come. I go down to that stupid ferry dock at Boston Harbor and I sit and I watch, every day, for hours, watch the face of every person who walks off and wish one of them were hers.

She doesn't come.

Of course not.

Instead, she sends a letter, and I know what it says even before I read it because the first thing I see is her beautiful face, the photograph, her good-bye.

My love, it begins, and my chest tightens.

I love you. I wanted to write that to you so many times over the years, but I was never brave enough to put it on paper and believe it. I was never even brave enough to say it out loud. So I'll write it now. I love you. I love you. A hundred times over.

I love you, and I am sorry. I can't leave. I have to do what's right for her, and she deserves a chance to know her home, Mal. I can't take that away from her.

But I made you a deal, and you're right. I can't become the next witch. My mother is furious, but I don't care. I want a better life, Mal, for me and for her. I want to be free. You've shown me the bars of this cage, Mal, and that's a gift I won't ever forget. I know who I am, and I want you to know, too: You are so much more than your blood. You are so much more than your blankness. You are Mal, and you deserve to be free.

I love you. I'll write to you. We will see each other again.

Yours, always and forever,
Essie

Thirty-Three

NEW YORK

I REACH OUT TO WHAT FEW CONTACTS I remember, but it's not hard to find a buyer for the *shar*, an auction house that promises the bidding will make my name famous among hunters the world over. But I tell them I don't want to be famous. I don't even want a share of the bidding. I set a price, twenty thousand dollars to take the *shar*, and they agree, they agree with sighs of relief and smiles and after I shake the auctioneer's hand, he says, "Thank goodness the *shar* was found! I thought Howard LeCouer had finally succeeded in destroying it!"

I blink at the man. "Destroy it?"

"Well, that's what he was working on, all those years. He meant to destroy the *shar*'s magic, and I, for one, am very glad he did not succeed."

But I don't care, not anymore, and I don't have anything else to say.

The buyer brings me into his study, and as he turns the dial on a combination safe, I wander past the shelves of items, carefully catalogued for the next auction. When I see a large leather-bound journal, open to a page crisscrossed with notes and a detailed sketch of the *shar*, I pause.

"What's this?"

The man looks up. "Oh! LeCouer's journal, of course. We bought it after word broke about the *shar*—thought there might be some information about its whereabouts, but it's all just notes on experiments. Go on, take a look if you'd like."

I pick it up, and the moment my hand touches the page, the diagram melts away, the image replaced with lines of careful writing. I'm so surprised that I glance at the buyer, wondering if he's seen anything, but he still has his head in the safe, busy counting out my money.

Quickly, I flip to the front of the book, and inside there's a note:

Beginning this journal on April 22, 1824. After several attempts, I've successfully enchanted the pages to hide what is truly written here. The only people capable of reading these words are myself and my assistant, Romesh Tagore,

*on whom, owing to his peculiar ability, the enchantment
does not work.*

Peculiar ability. His blankness?

I thumb through the pages, reading about LeCouer's
research into the knife's history and its magic. It's clear he
wanted to destroy it—most of the pages detail his many
experiments—and so I skip to the end of the journal,
wondering if he'd figured it out. And there it is, on the very
last page:

*I must wait until Tagore has returned from his visit
abroad to put this theory to the test, but I am confident
that I have discovered the key to destroying the* shar's
*power forever. It is so simple! The knife works by draw-
ing in the quality of the individual it cuts. Therefore, to
render it a magic-less knife once again, one must simply cut a magic-less individual. To eliminate the* shar's
power, I must cut a blank.

I stare at the words, my head dizzy.
Cut a blank.

I pull aside the *shar*'s wrapper and stare at the blade, shim-
mering with the power of Boone's Silvertongue magic. The
knife feels so heavy in my hand, heavy with magic and history
and the thousands of lives it's destroyed. If I sell it, I'm going to
be a part of that.

What was it Tagore told me? "There's power in being a blank."

I stare at the knife.

Slowly, I take the blade and rake it across my palm, right across the nine-year-old scar that Essie gave me, the one that changed my life forever.

A shiver of ice runs through me, the world going blurry, and for a moment, hope leaps inside me, a soaring feeling that I'm changed, I'm different, *it fixed me*, but then the moment fades and I know...I'm still just Mal. Still just a blank.

But the *shar*...It vibrates in my hand, hissing, and I'm so surprised I almost drop it, unsure of what's happening until it goes still, and...I didn't change, but the *shar* did. In fact—I swing it through the air for a moment, testing it, but I'm certain: The *shar* isn't magic anymore. It touched my blankness and it wasn't strong enough to take it away, but it still absorbed it, and now it's just a knife, as harmless as any other. The *shar* is dead.

I stare at it in surprise, not sure what to do, and then I slide it back into its hilt, take its wrapper and bandage my palm, hand it over to the auctioneer, and sell it for twenty thousand dollars.

"Quite a bit of money for a young man!" the auctioneer says. "What will you buy with it?"

I squeeze my cut hand and smile.

"Freedom."

Thirty-Four

OCEAN

SHIPS ARE LIVING CREATURES. THEY HAVE veins running through them, the rigging that stretches from mast to sail, and they have muscles and they have bones. They speak in creaks, in cracks, in moans. In high storms, the wind blows through the space between the mast and the sail and makes a kind of noise like an organ, a low bellow deep and loud and long that trembles and shivers.

A ship at sea can be a monster or she can be a mother or she can be a cradle or she can be a coffin, and now, I'm learning that she can be a home, too.

I'm lucky. I take my money down to the docks and take my time talking to ship owners and ship builders and captains looking to sell off their old rigs and sailors looking for partners, and then I find her. She needs new paint and repairs and a good crew but she's small, she's fast, she's light, a two-masted schooner only eight years old. And she's mine.

I take on a skeleton crew at first, a mix of green hands and old-timers who don't mind that their captain hasn't seen twenty years, and I don't ask them to sign contracts. At the sailors' bars up and down the New England coast, I hear over and over how foolish this is, how dangerous.

"You're mad," they say. "You'll lose half to desertion and the other half to laziness."

"Any man with a brain," they say, "won't be daft enough to take on without a paper protecting them."

But I don't want to work with any man who feels like he must sign his name to a piece of paper, who feels he can't be free, and despite the warnings and the head-shakings, I find my crew. I shake their hands and look them in the eye and explain to them: There are no contracts here, nothing but their word. They share in the profits if they stay and they'll be tossed off in the nearest port if they're lazy lag-abouts, and I have to shake a lot of hands but I find them and they take on with me like they've been waiting for me.

And I tell them one more rule: no magic. No sea charms or spells. I tell them their captain is a blank and that it's not a knotted rope or a shell on a chain that keeps them safe but their own wits and muscles and instincts and one another. I see the fear in their eyes, and I tell them to trust me. That takes time, too, but finally I see my crew relax and even take pride in our little magic-free ship. Folks say we're mad about that, too, that the ship will see a bad end soon, but I've never needed magic to sail and I'm still alive, aren't I?

We start out small, transporting goods for hunters, transporting the kinds of things that can't go on merchant ships, and it takes time, sorting out the crew and learning about my girl, my new ship, but she's sweet and she's strong and she keeps me safe, and that's all I can ask of her.

And I feel it, the first month out at sea, my crew humming at their work, and land far away. I tell my mate, a boy only three years older than myself, that I'm going to climb the mainmast, and he starts to give me an odd look, the kind of look that I got in bars and pubs on the mainland, the kind that says, *You're mad*, because what captain risks his life climbing a mast? But then I watch his face relax and watch as he nods at me and I know already he's going to be a good mate, he's going to understand that this isn't a ship like any other: She's my ship and it's my rules and my world.

I climb the mast, one hand over the other, and as I climb, I feel that same heady lightness as when I climbed the tree in Burma, as when I plunged headfirst into fights and danger and death, grinning and on fire. My heart pulses and I blink and sweat beads on my temples, my neck, my arms, and I pull myself onto the spar and hug an arm around the mast and look out at the ocean.

And I feel...

Nothing. But it's not the nothing of numbness, not the nothing of darkness and death. It's the nothing of sitting at the top of the world with the ocean stretched out below my feet and the sky stretched out above my head and me caught like a slip between them. The nothing of air in my lungs and sunlight on my skin and a strong deck underneath me and a crew relying on me. It's a pause. It's a breath. I climb the mast and sit on the spar and look out at the world and feel stilled.

I reach a hand to the hole in my chest, but I can't feel it anymore, and I wonder whether it's sealed up or scabbed over or whether it never really existed at all.

Or maybe it's not any of those things. Maybe it's just full, full not of Essie or the island or Boone or any one person, but a new purpose. To sail my ship and give my crew a family and find myself a home that never stops moving, that floats, that flies.

I stay up the mast a long time, long enough to feel the sun beat red against my cheeks, and then I climb down. I get back to work.

Two months after I leave port with my new ship and my new crew, I see him. We had stopped for the week in London and I told the crew to enjoy themselves and then I wandered the streets for hours, breathing in the stink of the city. On our second night, I'm only a mile from the docks when I feel a hand on my elbow and I turn around and there he is.

He has the kind of yellow skin you see on a freshly plucked chicken, and it's slack and thin where it's not scabbed over and raw. His eyes drift in his head, dazed, and I don't need the reek of poppies to tell me that he had found whatever solace he was looking for in a pipe.

"I know you," he says, his voice low and throaty. "You're my...my son."

"I'm not," I say, and the hand on my elbow tightens.

"Tell me your name."

Maybe it's a mistake, but I feel like I owe him that much.

"Mal," I say, and the glazed eyes widen.

"Mal..." A smile limps to his lips. "I know you."

"Are you all right?" I ask, but he just shakes his head.

"Do you want to take care of me?" He sounds amazed. "But I take care of you. I protect you. Two men came to me and wanted to find you and I killed them. I killed them both for you."

A shiver runs down my arms. "The Erslands?"

"I owed you," Boone says, and I don't think he can even hear me. "You spared my life. You could have killed me but you didn't and...I owed you. But now we're even. I saved your life and now we're even."

"Come on," I say, my stomach tightening. "You must be hungry."

But he pulls away from me. "I saved your life," he says, drifting away. "We're even."

"Boone." I watch him stumble through the alley, and when I try to follow him, he waves me away.

"We're even," he says, his voice soft, certain. "We're even."

I don't see Boone again, but the next day I go to the market and find Ruth. I give her a kiss and an envelope full of money and instructions to find Boone, to make sure he has someplace warm to sleep and food in his stomach. Every month, I drop another envelope in the mail, and when Ruth writes back to tell me he's better now, he thinks she's a queen for taking such good care of him and should she tell him who's really behind all this, I write back no, and I keep sending the envelopes and I wonder if he'll ever try to find me. I wonder what he has to say.

Ruth isn't the only person I write to. Now, when I've decided on my sailing route, I write it down, I put it in an envelope, I mail it out to a smudgy little island that's more rocks and hopes than land. It's slow, mail at sea, but it's enough that when I stop at ports now, I have letters waiting for me. It's enough to know that she's thinking of me, that I can tell her I'm thinking of her, that we can stretch a line around the world that begins with me and ends with her.

In one letter she asks me if she should stop, if it's too painful, and I write back, no, keep writing to me, write to me forever because of course it is painful, of course, but I'm through measuring my life in terms of pain.

So she sends me more letters, and she fills them with her hopes and her fears and her dreams and her secrets, always her secrets. But she's not guarded with them anymore—they flow out of her like water, and I know she tells them to me because she knows they fill me up, make me whole. They give me hope.

At night, before I fall asleep, I read the letters and blow out the candles and think about them, let them run over and through and around me, let them sink into my skin like rain, let Essie's words drift through my mind and calm me:

Remember when...

I thought of you again today...

I'm still dreaming, Mal, but the dreams are so beautiful....

Those dreams, always the dreams, and they're the last thing I think about so that when I go to sleep, I can see what she sees, what her daughter sends her. Maybe they're just fantasies, maybe they're just something Essie's mind concocts to put her at ease, but I prefer to think of them the way she sees them, as glimpses of the future, as promises.

I close my eyes, and they come to me: Essie's daughter, tall and black-haired, wearing the kind of dress only a rich man could buy her. Essie and her mother shouting at each other, screaming at each other, a baby crying in the corner. A wedding, a husband, a house...and that same house, split neatly in two as though by a giant fist.

She tells me she dreams of me laughing, but I'm not the Mal of the past, not a boy but a man, face lined by sun and wind, and I tell her I found my own life at sea, I belong to no one and no one belongs to me. She dreams that she leaves the cottage and the whales leave the ocean and her daughter leaves her and she is alone and broken. She dreams and I dream of her girl, the gift she gives her: strength to finally leave the island. And together we dream that we see each other again, that I reach out my hand for her to help her aboard a ship, my ship, my home, and when she asks me where we are sailing to, my hand tightens around hers and I tell her:

"Everywhere, my love."

ACKNOWLEDGMENTS

This book was written during a whirlwind that included many moving boxes and one small person (more on her later). It is without an ounce of exaggeration that I say if not for these wonderful people, there would be no *Drift and Dagger*. Here they are:

There really would be no *Drift and Dagger* if my amazing editor, Bethany Strout, hadn't asked me how I felt about companion novels. Bethany, thank you so much for always believing in me and this book. I am so grateful for your bravery, guidance, thoughtful criticism, and enthusiasm.

To my agent, Sara Crowe, your support means so much to me. I still can't believe how lucky I am to have such a ferociously talented agent (with amazing taste in baby clothes).

Thank you to the fabulous teams at Little, Brown Books for Young Readers and Orchard Books! It is an absolute delight working with all you funny, fun, whip-smart people. And a special thank-you to my tireless publicist, Lisa Moraleda, for giving *Salt & Storm* a fabulous debut and for answering my many (many, many) e-mails with patience and warmth.

Big, BIG hugs to my crit partner, Natasha Sinel-Cohen, for advice both book- and baby-related.

Merci, again, to Juliette Caminade for help with the French and for not batting an eye when I explained the weird little world I've created.

My year as a debut was a little less rocky and a lot more fun thanks to the Fall Fourteeners, who were always there with wisdom, enthusiasm, and open in-boxes. Let's get that reunion going, all right?

To all the Boston kid lit writers I've met so far and to all the authors I met on tour, at conferences, and online: You guys continue to confirm that the kids publishing community has some of the kindest, most welcoming, smartest, and funniest people in, like, the world. I am so glad I found you guys.

Thank you to the Writers' Room of Boston for giving me a much-needed home away from home as I neared the final stretch.

Thank you to my wonderful friends for supporting me and *Salt & Storm*—the Villa girls, the Chicago folks, the Boston crew, the '07ers (plus WAGs and babies), and everyone else who tweeted, Facebooked, e-mailed, and demanded that their local bookstores stock my book. You rock.

Speaking of bookstores, I am so grateful to all the bookstores that championed *Salt & Storm* and put it into the hands of readers. Indie bookstores have had a special place in my heart since I was checking out board books, and it means so much to me to have my books on your shelves.

To my amazing family: How can I put into words how

special you all are? If I piled on top of one another all the notes of congratulations, support, and encouragement, all the flowers and thoughtful gifts, they would reach the moon.

Thank you to my second parents, Mark and Anne Toniatti, for your love and unflagging enthusiasm and for hand-selling my book to every person you meet. (I know I owe all my State College fans to you guys.)

My parents, Keith and Denise Kulper, have supported me at every step in this crazy journey, and I am so grateful to them both. In a very real way, I don't think I could have written this book without my mom. When I had both a newborn and an unfinished draft, she took the baby for walks, tackled mountains of laundry, fed us dinner, and did it all with a smile. Love you, Mom.

This book is dedicated to my brother, Sloan, who has opened up my world since I've opened my eyes. Thank you (and my beautiful new sister-in-law, Gahyee) for giving me the best excuse to fly across the globe.

Finally, to all the mammals who share my home: You guys are the love and joy that keep me going. Abby, you are a wonderful snuggle buddy and running partner (good girl!). Dave, you are the love of my life and the greatest partner I could ask for. I love you. And my little Iris, you have turned my whole world upside down in the most wonderful way possible. I will always remember finishing this book with you, only a few days old, in my arms and thinking I was the luckiest person in the world to have the things I love most sitting right in my lap.